MUST LOVE OTTERS

MUST LOVE OTTERS

ELIZA GORDON

Just say NO ... to
SRIRACHA ☺

Happy reading,

♡

Eliza Gordon

Jenni SY)

Published by West 26th Street Press, 21 W. 26th Street, New York, NY 10010

ISBN-13: 9781494362324

CHAPTER ONE
BATMAN JERRY

"911, what is your emergency?"

"My husband … he's not breathing. He's blue. His lips are blue. Jerry, wake up! Wake up!"

"Ma'am, did he choke on something? Tell me what's happened so I can help you."

"I think it's his heart. He has a bad heart. He didn't take his pills today. Or maybe he did, I don't know. This doesn't matter! Help me, goddammit!"

"I'm trying to help you. Where is your husband right now?"

"On the bed. He's on the bed," the caller says.

I look at the clock. Sixty seconds since the call started. Nineteen minutes until my shift is over.

"Okay, an ambulance is on its way. What's your name?"

"Linda."

"Okay, Linda, I'm Hollie. Before the ambulance gets there, we need to do a few things. Can you listen to his chest or feel if his heart is beating?"

"I can't. Oh, his lips are so blue."

"Why can't you listen to his chest, Linda?"

"Because … he has a chest plate on."

"A chest plate?"

"He's dressed up. It's Batman night." Excellent. Oh, Batman. Your timing is impeccable. I'll have to do yet another karmic inventory to see where I screwed up. I hear my father's voice: *It's not all about you, Hollie.* Guilt squirts into my gray matter.

"Listen to me, Linda. Check his neck. Two fingers alongside his neck."

"His chest plate goes up his neck."

"We gotta get the chest plate off so you can check for a pulse and maybe start compressions."

"Hang on … I gotta put the phone down." *Shuffle, shuffle, grunt, curse.* "I can't get it off."

This is bad. If we can't get to his chest, dude's gonna die. If he's not already floating to the bat cave in the sky. "Linda, can you cut through it?"

"He'll kill me if I ruin this costume. He paid a fortune for it."

I want to tell her that he probably won't ever know because at this rate, his brain is guano. "Linda, listen to me. We need to do CPR. You said he's on the bed?"

"Yes."

"Can you drag him onto the floor?"

"No."

"Why?"

"He weighs 300 lb.! I can't lift him," she shrieks.

I'm supposed to be in control here, but that flash of powerlessness never goes away. Unless you're Les and then nothing bothers you because your soul oozed out of your pores years ago and that mass in your chest formerly known as a heart is now nothing more than an algae-encrusted river rock. With boogers.

"Linda, did he take any drugs tonight? Did he drink anything? Anything I can tell the medics so they'll know how to help?"

"Umm … Viagra. And some scotch. It's Batman night …" Linda starts to cry.

Despite the fact that Batman night is over—abruptly—I feel bad for Linda. "I want you to put the phone down and try to do chest compressions."

"But the chest plate—"

"Work with me, Linda. He'll forgive you for wrecking the costume if you save his life. Okay?"

The rest of the call does not go any better. I do hear later, however, that Batman Jerry (deader than a fruit bat in the vegetable aisle) had a stiffy that would make Zeus jealous. Details I don't need. Note to the world: Viagra + scotch + heart condition = dead with a boner.

That disgusting feeling of *I just listened to somebody die* washes over me. It's gross. Been at this job for two years, eight months, sixteen days, since disappointing my union-loving nurse father—*yes, my dad is a nurse, so get your jokes out of the way now*—and leaving school early secondary to questionable financial management. I am the only person in the family who faints in the presence of blood, an unending source of ribbing at those insipid annual family gatherings. Whatever genetic predisposition to medicine that runs like plague through my family? Yeah. It skipped me. Working 911 was the easiest compromise—I sit in a room and listen to blood, but I never actually have to see it.

But dead people never get easier, especially the ones who are already dead when the call starts. Aneurysms. Heart attacks. Strokes. Embolisms. Mother Nature is a clever, clever girl.

I lean back in my chair and slurp on the remnants of a long-ago melted iced coffee. Les is staring, those beady little eyes fixed on me. I know he's going to do it when I see his hand move to the chest pocket of his ugly brown flannel button-down. The mothballs and Old Spice piggyback a puff of recycled air.

I shake my head *no*.

Don't do it, Les. Don't pull it out.

He does. The Black Book of Death. He's going to put a goddamned checkmark next to my name. Again. To show that I've killed someone else.

It would be funny if he weren't such a raging, infected prick. Little stooge goes into advisory board meetings every two months and pulls out that confounded book to gloat about how many lives he's saved, and how many I've lost. He doesn't mark down Troll Lady's dead people, but I suspect it's because she's playing his skin flute in the unisex bathroom during their lunch break.

I'm not sure what disgusts me more: watching Les pull the greasy black comb out of the back pocket of his Wranglers to straighten the twelve hairs still sticking out of his head, or thinking about Troll Lady's smudged red lips wrapped around his member.

It's a tossup. I feel sick to my stomach.

I'm now twelve minutes into overtime. I will be reprimanded if I reach the thirty-minute mark—"Budgets are tight! Cuts are coming!"—the same war cry from administrators who make six fat, beach-house-owning figures a year. Sorry. Batman died. What was I supposed to do, tell his Catwoman to call Robin for help?

The tiny vacuum starts up. My signal to go home. Troll Lady is aggressively rearranging her collection of frizzy-haired beasts, using the handheld vacuum to suck the dust free and keep their multi-hued coifs at attention. Because she's been here the longest—pretty sure she started with 911 when they were still using pterodactyls as messengers and Flintstone cars for ambulances—she gets away with shit that would never fly for anyone else. I've heard that people have lost their jobs over complaining about her troll collection, the dust it collects, the simple fact that they're horribly ugly, despicable little demon spies for the CIA. She compromises by keeping the troll army small and dusted daily.

"This one, my pride and joy. Elvis. I spent $400, not including shipping. Straight from Graceland! I'll bet Priscilla touched it. Wouldn't that be something?" I try not to listen, but she is loud. Really loud. And my console abuts hers. The troll looks nothing like Elvis. Maybe fat Elvis. Right before he died, drugged out and on the shitter. I wonder what that 911 call sounded like.

I unplug, log out, power down. Grab my logbook. Lock my drawer so the dispatcher due to my console in thirty-nine minutes won't steal the last of my Lucky Charms. I'm the one who painstakingly separated all the boring cereal from the delectable marshmallows, so I'm the one who gets to eat 'em.

Grab the report that confirms Batman Jerry didn't make it through our call.

Sorry, Batman Jerry. Rest in peace.

Chapter Two
Nacho Fun Time

The evening's saving grace: upon opening the apartment door, it smells a little like food. Keith made dinner. I am so grateful.

"Hey," I say, dumping my backpack on the floor. His black jump kit takes up the entire space on the ornately carved foyer bench. The bench I bought to someday grace the grand foyer of my amazing house that I will somehow manage to buy on my pathetic salary. Which is why it's still sitting against the wall in my shitty two-bedroom, rent-controlled apartment.

Why we need a jump kit inside the apartment at all times—"You never know when the Big One might hit, Hol, and people will need my help"—ergo, a 40 lb. bag of gloves, surgical tubing, IV bags, gauze, tape, water purifying salts, and silver emergency blankets sits in my hallway and takes up all the space on my pretty bench.

I sort of hope an earthquake does hit. And when it does, I hope it opens a chasm below this apartment and swallows the jump kit whole. I'll miss my bench, though.

The Yorkies go apeshit. I live here. This is my abode. And every single night, these stupid little ass-licking, ankle-biting shit machines bark like I'm the Creature from the Black Lagoon. Assholes. I hate Yorkies. And by hate, I mean I want to drown them. Or magically turn them into clouds so they will float away on a breeze of my own making.

"Your dad called," Keith says from the kitchen. "Again."

"Mmm-hmm. What's for dinner?"

"Wait! Don't come in here."

"What?" I freeze. The Yorkies are yipping at me. I make my meanest face at them. They bark louder. Why can't we have a cat? Cats are so much cuter than Yorkies. Plus cats look like otters. Otters are the bestest creatures in the whole wild world. Thus, because it is not legal or practical for me to have an otter, we should have a cat. To balance out all the doggish hormones and slobber and ball-licking.

Keith leans around the corner, baggy flannel pants doing nothing for his ass, stethoscope around his neck as per usual. Why he does this, I don't know. I have zero fantasies about humping a doctor. Or an EMT. Because Keith is not a doctor. He's the guy who drives the ambulance and jams the IV in your arm until he can take you to the hospital where a *real* doctor will help you. "I have a surprise for you. Go in the bedroom. Get comfy."

"Oooookay …"

"And by comfy, I mean naked."

He leans close for a kiss but I push him away. He smells like dogs. And Cheetos. Have I mentioned how much I hate Cheetos? Well, I am telling you now: I fucking hate Cheetos. On a dare, I ate an entire bag at Charlotte Smith's ninth birthday slumber party because I wanted the little ceramic rainbow pin she was offering the winner, and I puked orange for four straight hours.

For the record, I won the pin. I still have it. But I don't eat Cheetos anymore.

God, I am a crabby cow tonight. I might need a chocolaty intervention to balance out the meanness.

He wants me naked. Now? "I need a shower. And you need to brush your teeth. You smell like Cheetos," I say.

Keith honks my boob. "Fine, fine. But hurry. You're gonna love this."

I squint at him. Do I hear adventure coming from that boy's mouth? Is this real life? "What's going on?" I ask cautiously. I'm tired of Naughty Nurse. And Doctor and Nurse. And Doctor and Patient. And I Saved You From a Burning Building So You Should Have Sex With Me Even Though You're Unconscious and Could Be Dying from Smoke Inhalation. Shall I continue? All the games either end with me mummified in gauze and anchored to the bed, or with me pushing his stethoscope out of my face while he's pumping away. The romance is overwhelming. I know. Here's a cloth to wipe your fevered brow.

"Go get more comfortable. I mean it—no clothes. Find something to blindfold yourself."

I smile at him. "Really? Is this going to hurt?"

"Hollie …"

"No stethoscope. No medical dramas. I don't want to play *Grey's Anatomy* anymore."

"This is something different."

"Okayyyyy."

"Do you trust me, Hols?"

Does he want a real answer to that? "I'll … get changed." I slide into the bathroom to shave so he doesn't complain about my prickly legs again (if he doesn't like the legs, he certainly won't like my panty tarantula). It's been a while since we did anything that involved being naked. Maybe a good toe-curler is just what I need, even if it involves something battery powered. And a warm shower does sound lovely. Wash the stink of death from my brain and body.

Once the tub tap is turned off, I hear him shuffling in the kitchen on the other side of the wall. Hmmm, maybe he's bought strawberries and whipped cream, or chocolate body glaze, or honey … that would be something we've never tried before.

I throw some lotion on all the newly excoriated body parts and sneak out naked into the bedroom. I catch my reflection in the closet mirror. Turn sideways. Suck it in. I've only got a few years left with this body. I'd better take up yoga. Troll Lady keeps telling me how big my ass is going to get from my job once I turn thirty or pop out a pup, whichever comes first. She's also told me that at forty, white hairs start growing from your chin and the sides of your face, and your body odor becomes unnatural. Which is why there's a huge cupboard of scented baby wipes in the bathroom at work.

These are not sexy thoughts. These are gross thoughts. Must have sexy thoughts.

I pose my sexiest in the mirror. Push out my boobs. Tough because they're a B cup. Okay, A cup. Whatever. The tarantula is under control. It's no Brazilian, but it'll do. I can't imagine having my pubes waxed completely off. First, the screaming. I would definitely scream. Second, doesn't it say something about a guy who wants a totally bare playground? It seems a little … disturbing. Worrisome. Little girls are hairless. Women are not. Third, the ungodly itching. I cannot even imagine how bad that shit would itch when it grows back in—

"Babe, you're not blindfolded."

I throw my arms over my nakedness, embarrassed that I've been caught ogling myself in the mirror.

"Eyes are closed. I swear I'm not looking."

"Okay. Get on the bed. Don't peek," Keith instructs.

"Should I light some candles?"

"Probably not. Fire hazard." The bedroom door clicks closed. We're alone—without Yorkies! Cause for celebration.

I hear him setting up a TV tray. My stomach quivers in anticipation of the coming treats. I've seen porn with this. Food and stuff. Culinary naughtiness. Granted, it involved eating fruit salad out of …

"Lie flat, Hols. And don't move." I do so. He shuffles something around. "Get ready. It's going to be—"

"COLD! Holy shit, Keith, is that ice cream?"

"No," he laughs. "Just hold still. This will take a second."

I try to steady myself, but he's just smeared something, a lot of cold something, all over my stomach. Goosebumps break out on my arms. "Must be cold," he says, flicking my nipple. I smack at him. "Don't move! You'll ruin the surprise."

I'm thinking this must be whipped topping of some sort. It feels like that. Or maybe ice cream because it's really holding the cold. He's layering something else on top of it. I hear a jar opening. And a can. Then something plopping into the mix on my belly. Cherries, maybe? God, it's been forever since I've had a good chemical-infused maraschino cherry.

He opens a plastic bag and I almost open my eyes.

"Tell me those aren't Cheetos."

"Not Cheetos. Almost done. Hold still. This is awesome. I should take a pic—"

"If you so much as finish that sentence, this party is over."

He laughs. "Final touches. You ready?"

"Go."

It's a squirt bottle. Has to be chocolate or caramel sauce. He's drizzled some over my boobs. That will be fun to lick …

Wait a second. Why is it burning?

"Keith …"

"Almost done, babe. This is classic."

"Keith, what did you just squirt on my boobs?"

That's it. I'm opening my eyes.

I do, expecting to be greeted by a belly covered in ice cream, whipped cream, cherries, the works.

"You—you made nachos? On my stomach?"

"Yeah! Isn't it awesome? I saw this the other night on Food Porn."

"Is that a show?"

"It's these two guys who mix food and porn, but the food they make is porn all by itself. They said that this is a fun way to spice things up in the bedroom."

"Keith, my boobs—they're burning."

He leans in for a kiss. "That's so hot, baby …"

"No, I mean like my nipple is on *fire*."

He sits back, reaches over to the TV tray, and grabs the squirt bottle. "Oh. Shit."

"Oh shit *what?*"

"Babe, I'm so sorry …" He can't finish his sentence because he's laughing like a goddamned fool. He hands me the bottle.

"Extra hot Sriracha. Excellent. That's brilliant. My nipples are going to melt off and you're laughing."

"I'm … so … sorry." He stumbles into the bathroom and gets a wet washcloth. When he tries to wipe it off, I smack him again and take the cloth, careful not to spill the entrée onto the bed. Because, of course, we're on *my* side of the bed.

As I'm wiping the sizzling rooster sauce off my tits, Keith sneaks over to the dresser for his iPhone.

"I'm not kidding. You will never get another piece of this ass ever again in your life if you take that photo."

"Come on, Hols. I promise not to get your coochie or any boobage. Just one shot?"

I glare at him, blowing alternately on one nipple, then the next. "I think I need ice. Fuck, I think you blistered me!"

"I did not …"

"LOOK, KEITH."

He flicks on the bedside lamp. "Wow. Shit. I think you're right. Oh, baby, I am so sorry. Let me get some ice. I have WaterGel in the jump kit, but we should maybe eat first, don't you think?"

I don't know if I should cry or scream.

"Here. Just try this." He reaches into the bag of chips and scoops sour cream, guacamole, refried beans, and an olive onto a chip. "Here comes the airplane!"

Instead of opening my mouth, I grab a handful of his culinary masterpiece and smear it all over his face. Ahhhh, that feels better.

"What the—geeze, Hollie, you're going to get this all over the bedding now."

I respond with another handful, this time across both cheeks. Now I'm laughing. He's not sure what to do. I lick my fingers. Mmmm, that guac is good.

"Pass me the chips." He swipes his finger down one cheek and pops it into his mouth. Hands me the bag.

"Damn. Not bad."

The Yorkies·are onto us. They can smell the food. Now they're whining outside the door. Keith, for once, tells them to quiet down. They do. He kneels next to the bed and removes the washcloth from my left nipple. Stares at it closely, then looks back up to me. I think he's asking for permission.

He pops it in his mouth and gives it a little twirl of the tongue. Feels decent enough. Until he suddenly releases and runs to the bathroom. "Still hot. Still hot!"

The bedroom door thrusts open and I'm a goner. Three Yorkies are on the bed like, well, like Yorkies on an open buffet.

"Keith! The DOGS!" As much as I want this to be erotic, it is exactly the opposite. I don't mind a little kink, but bestiality is not on my list.

"Trixie! Pixie! No! Moxie, get down!" he yells, shooing them away. As soon as he drops one dog on the floor, another takes its place.

"Get them out of here, dude! Jesus!"

"I'm *trying*!"

The nachos—what's left of them—are completely inedible. "Hand me a towel, please. Now."

With two dogs under one arm and me holding the third one back from eating through to my navel piercing, Keith tosses me a towel. I scoop and dump the remaining Mexican feast onto it.

"I'm taking a shower."

"So ... are we not going to ..."

"No, Einstein. We're not."

The Yorkies bark at me, pissed that they can't have the rest of the nachos. "Come to Daddy. Mommy's not mad at you, babies, don't you worry. Come here, *mwuah, mwuah, mwuah*." He's kissing them again. Those dogs get more action than I do. Which is disgusting. And pathetic.

I'm sensing a trend here.

"Not their mommy," I mumble, moving in for my second shower in under thirty minutes.

Once cleansed of nachos—nipples still on fire—I dress in clothing decent enough to leave the house. Throw on my coat, grab my keys.

"Where you goin'?"

"I need food, Keith. Unless you have some kibble in the pantry that the Yorkies haven't eaten."

"I don't feed them kibble."

"Leaving now."

"Wait, I'll come with." He dresses and turns the monster TV in the living room to kids' programming.

"I don't think the dogs like *Thomas the Tank Engine*."

"They like the songs on this channel. Keeps them calm." Duh, Hollie.

Keith throws on his ginormous parka with, you guessed it, huge pockets filled with medical supplies. Just in case. He's a caricature of himself.

"Leave the steth, Keith."

"What? No way."

"You look like a tool. Leave it."

He stares at me for a second, that hurt look I'm sure he gave his mother when she told him to stop operating on the neighbor with her kitchen utensils, and pulls the stethoscope from around his neck. He kisses the Yorkies again, three little bastards licking his face and ears, and moves away from the couch.

"If someone dies at the restaurant, it's on you."

"Wouldn't be the first time today."

My phone chimes in my pocket en route to the car. Text from Dad. "Call me. Have a surprise for you." I hate surprises. The last one involved me wearing a ridiculous pink taffeta gown and a cup-cake hat—seriously, a silk and taffeta hat sewn and stuffed into the shape of a cupcake—for my non-sister's wedding to a creepy guy who smells like other women's perfume most of the time.

As we're in the drive-through for Noodle Yu, another buzz from my phone. An email. I should never have introduced my father to technology. I open it to find a registration confirmation from a resort. Dad, what are you up to?

It reads "Revelation Cove, British Columbia, Canada. Gift regis-tration, four days, three nights, Sweethearts' Spa & Stay Package for two. Love, Dad."

"What the hell?"

"What is it?"

"Umm … my dad … you know that resort we were talking about?"

"The one up north?"

"Yeah."

"What about it?" Keith shoves a fortune cookie into his mouth before his debit transaction has finished. He chews with his lips open. The young girl working the drive-through window looks unimpressed.

"He bought us a gift certificate. For four days, three nights."

Keith finishes chewing. "What will we do about the dogs?"

I stare at him. Seriously? The fucking *dogs*? How about, "Thanks, Mr. Porter, for spending a grand on a weekend that will undoubtedly provide many opportunities for me to practice impregnating your daughter."

"Well, uh, I don't think the dogs are invited."

"Does it say when we have to go?"

"*You* don't have to go anywhere, Keith. If you'd rather stay home with your dogs."

He stabs a straw into his soda cup, driving with his knee. "You know what I mean."

"I'm sure you can get your sister to dogsit. It's only four days."

Keith stares at me, as if I've just asked him to donate a kidney to a walrus. "Uh, I don't know if that's possible. I don't trust her to take proper care of them."

"We're not taking them with, if that's what you're getting at."

He pauses too long at a green light. Someone honks behind us and he flips them off. But the vacancy in his eyes confirms that I've clearly just delivered terrible news. "Why not?"

"On a floatplane? And Yorkies on a romantic getaway for *two* is way not romantic and very much not a getaway. We might as well stay home."

"I'm not comfortable leaving them behind, Hollie."

"With your sister?"

"Yes, even with my sister. She kills things. You should see her plants. Nothing but stems and dirt." *So this plan is better than I thought. We leave your three Yorkies with Yvette and come home to no Yorkies. I like this plan. So much. Must resist cackling and witchy wringing of hands.*

"Well, then find a plan B. I don't want to take the dogs with us."

"But I wuvs them … what will they do without their daddy and mommy to tuck them in at night for a four whole days?"

"If you wuvs me, Keify, then you'll stop talking like you've spent your childhood eating lead paint and find a dogsitter." I quickly email my dad back and tell him I'll call tomorrow, and *thank you but you didn't have to do this.* I'm out of the car before Keith has it in park. My appetite has been replaced with annoyance.

Time to give this body some narcotic sleeping aids and put it to bed.

But before that, before I can sneak upstairs and sedate my frustration, I have to get past The Door.

Her door.

A finger against my lips, I motion to Keith to shut up. At all costs, do not speak.

Squeeeeeak, mutters the first step. Shit.

"Hollie? Is that you?" Keith shoves past me and bolts up the stairs. I throw my Chinese takeout box at him, hoping it will explode against his back. It does not. Merely bounces and flies over the railing, splaying open on the grass. Asshole actually laughs at me.

"Yes, Mrs. Hubert. It's Hollie."

A tiny wrinkled body that I think was at some point human shuffles to her screen door. She's wearing the same housecoat as usual—snaps up the front, pockets bulging with spent Kleenex, her lucky, fifty-year-old Avon perfume pin clipped limply over where her left boob should be, if it weren't dangling down around her belly button. Suntan knee-high stockings crumple around bony, knotted anklebones, her feet stuffed in slippers that were pink in their former lives. Behind her, a sickly meow echoes through the kitchen.

"Hollie, I need half-and-half and some frozen peas. And Mr. Boots needs wet food. Go get it."

"Mrs. Hubert, I'm exhausted."

"And I'm a lonely, dying woman who spends her days and nights praying that Jesus will come for her. Have you seen my hands?" She thrusts her hands through the gap in the screen door. Her skin is so translucent, it's easy to trace the bulbous veins snaking up her arms and disappearing under yellowed sleeves. "Hurry up. *Jeopardy* is on soon and I don't want to have to get up again."

I lock eyes with this—this—*creature*, wishing the apocalypse would happen right this second and I would be saved from her terrible wrath. A look up the stairs proves that Keith is nowhere in sight.

Lifting my purse strap back over my shoulder, I do the only thing I know how to do.

I turn around and slither back to my car so I can go to the market to do Mrs. Hubert's relentless bidding, hoping that while I'm gone, Satan will come and claim the prize that's been missing all these years from his wicked collection.

"Take Mr. Boots too," I mumble.

Chapter Three
Cougars Eat Yorkies—Right?

The dream is nice. I'm on a beach. Not a particularly warm one, but it's pleasant. Serene. Subtle breeze. Water laps the shore. Not loud like the ocean—something less fierce, more poetic. And I smell trees. Big ones, whispering to each other about which one will fall next when the wind picks up. *Your turn … no, your turn …* I can't see his face, but his breath next to my ear tickles. My face stretches into a smile. I giggle. He moves his lips to mine. His tongue … it's rough.

Why is his tongue rough? And why does it smell like … I crack one eye open.

"God! Ew! Get off the bed!" Fucking Yorkies. I jump out of the covers and slam the bathroom door. I don't care if I disturb Keith's lazy ass. I have had it with those dogs. I've seen them lick each another's butts—the last thing I want is one of them licking my *mouth.*

I'm more pissed off that they interrupted what had the potential to evolve into an awesome dream. I can't remember the last time someone almost whispered sweet nothings into my ear. Still, I swish for four minutes with mouthwash, until my gums threaten to peel away from bone. I may have burned off another layer of enamel. (My dentist will nag. Again.) I'll need extra Chap Stick today. But at least I won't taste dog ass.

My reflection looks alien. Not like *an* alien—no extra eyes or scaling skin or oozing orifices. Dark circles, though. Probably anemic. I stopped taking the iron supplements because I couldn't poop, not unless I ate, like, a gallon of that Jamie Lee Curtis yogurt, and it was making me gassy. Not great in my line of work. I got tired of panicking every time someone would walk by my console after I'd cut a squeaker. Some things I can't blame on Les or Troll Lady simply due to sheer geography.

The face staring back at me looks ... neglected. My eyebrows need threading. Haven't had them done since the last wedding I went to for some girl who barely spoke to me in high school. Hey, if she wants to invite me to accost her open bar, who am I to deny? Said event was also the last time I saw my former best friend. I would tell you her name, but that's like saying Voldemort out loud instead of calling him "He Who Shall Not Be Named." If we give evil a name, it grows stronger.

My former BFF was evil.

Or that's how I choose to see it. Because anyone who dumps you after you score them weed because you're too weak to say, "No, we're in a foreign country so we should probably not be buying drugs," and then who gets mad at you because you don't have enough cash to bail her ass out when she ends up in a Tijuana jail cell so you call her parents and her uncle lawyer hop-skip-jumps down from San Diego to save her from whatever was lurking in the dark shadows of that damp, dirty, bug-infested cell.

(Wasn't that the right thing for me to do?)

She was the drunk/high one. She was the one who tried to dance on top of that cop car, even though I told her not to. She's just lucky we didn't end up as a missing persons' case on *America's Most Wanted.*

But even if there had been hope for our eleven-year friendship, it got squished when she married a guy who made her stop being friends with anyone who eats meat or lives in unmarried sin or cheers curbside in bustiers at the Pride Parade. (My bustier is gorgeous, for the record. Whale bone, red leather, lace ... HOT.) I guess her man has a ginormous penis. Why else would she break up with fun-loving, ever-watchful me to marry such a wet fart?

Oh my God, is that a gray hair?

A knock at the door. "Hol … phone." I open wide enough for Keith's hand to squeeze through but not wide enough that one of his little shit-munchers can get in here and steal my dirty underwear from the pile of laundry next to the tub.

"Hullo?"

"Hi, Hollie Cat … I wanted to catch you before you left for work."

"Hey, Dad. Thanks for the gift certificate."

"I thought it would be a nice change. Get you out of town for a little while. I know things have been tough at work." Dad's the one I text when someone has croaked on my line. I figure if I can talk to my dad—a man who has seen a lot of death in his line of work—it'll keep me from having to attend those therapy sessions Polyester Patty harps about.

"So, I was wondering if you and Keith could come over this weekend and help me move a few things. I'm not allowed to pick up more than ten pounds."

"Why?"

"Hernia's acting up."

"Dad, you were supposed to get that fixed."

"I am. I will." For a nurse, my father is the worst damn patient. "Anyway, it would be good to see you kids."

"Just me, Dad. Keith has to work."

"The boxes aren't heavy. I feel like an old man asking you, but at least I'll get to see your pretty face."

"You're not old." I hate it when he says that. I don't want to think about my father being old. Old means broken. Old means closer to dead. He lives alone, except for the weekly visits from crazy Aurora who still owns half their house and thus uses it for her primal scream Thursday events. I don't know how he stands her. "I'm not old *yet*, but I'm not getting any younger waiting for grandchildren. When is that boy gonna get down on one knee?"

And then it becomes crystal clear. The gift getaway to Revelation Cove has a purpose: he wants Keith to propose. To me. So I'll get married, and then Dad can stop worrying about his only child, his little girl, floating around in the big bad world all by her lonesome.

Too bad Keith is too worried about his stupid dogs to get the message.

"Tomorrow morning ... ten okay?" I say.

"I'll make pancakes!"

Wow. Now the reflection in the mirror is really depressed. My dad's practically punched Keith in the head with this opportunity, and yet ... A spark glimmers momentarily that perhaps Keith *is* in on it, and he will be proposing. But I know that's not even remotely possible because Keith can't keep a secret to save his life. He almost had a heart attack last Christmas when he ordered me a boxed set of DVDs of some show I'd mentioned in passing. For him to hide an impending engagement, complete with a ring?

Impossible.

And do I really want him to propose? I spend an inordinate amount of time fantasizing about ways to remove the Yorkies from this apartment without getting arrested for animal cruelty. Therein lies my answer. If only I could adopt a brown bear or a cougar—now *that* would be a cool, multipurpose pet. If I could have a bear, I'd name her Bridget. We'd be the best of friends. And any time someone was a douche to me, I'd whisper in Bridget's ear and she would eat the offending party. Or a cougar. Chloe the cougar, and I'd wrap a red bow around her neck and we'd walk down the street together and if anyone looked at me funny, she'd hiss and growl until they soiled themselves and we'd get the best tables at all the sidewalk cafés and I'd never again have to wait in line for my morning hazelnut latte because Chloe would use her long tail to swish all the other caffeine junkies aside. Move aside, bitches. Chloe's in the house.

And when she was a good girl, I could feed her a Yorkie. BAM! Problem solved.

In between saving lives today, I will Google rules about keeping a cougar as a pet.

Or I can just wait another few years and the reflection in this mirror will be all the cougar I need.

Chapter Four
Dance Hall Days

They've replaced the air fresheners in the bathrooms with these fancier models that spit into the toilet bowl every time someone flushes. Make a poopy, instant flowers. Unfortunately, one has already malfunctioned and the entire underground bunker where my section of the dispatch center is located only gets air pumped in through vents. Vents with intake just down the wall from the bathroom. Which means the entire place reeks, compounding the headache already forming behind eyes baggy and tired from two hours of ragged pillow-free sleep on a lumpy, dog-smelling couch.

Les is at his usual spot in the lunchroom, newspapers from local municipalities organized so that one doesn't touch another but all six take up the entire surface of a singular table. I've tried to tell him he can use the Web to get his news, but he shut me down. Something about Big Brother and how the digital era will be the end of humanity, that the reengineered dinosaurs the government has in hiding will roam the planet again soon and then we'll wish we had more things written down on paper or better yet, in stone like the Sumerians did with the stylus and clay tablets. "Those have lasted for six millennium. Your Internet? Ha. Dino food."

I still haven't made the connection between the World Wide Web and dinosaurs, but apparently, it's there. For those of advanced intellect. So, in other words, not me.

He looks over the smudged lenses of his wire-rimmed glasses, pausing as he thumbs through the pages of his Black Book of Death.

"A little light reading, Les?" I ask.

"Postmortem this morning," he sneers. "Expect a memo on your desk before day's end." A memo means retraining in some area where you suck. I've had three memos since I got off probation. Shit, one more memo means I have to sit with a trainer again. Next step is a dock in pay, followed by a union review, and possible termination if the memo results in a finding of negligence on the part of the dispatcher.

Why another memo today?

I stare at the poor excuse for cappuccino sputtering from the spout of the coffee machine, combing through the memory bank for recent folks who died when Operator Hollie was on the job. Probably Batman Jerry. Maybe I wasn't urgent enough with his wife to get his cowl off. Hey, when the Big Man pulls Batman out of circulation, all the chest compressions in the world ain't gonna do shit.

I start to tell Les about the doughnut jelly smeared into his sad excuse for a moustache. I'll leave it. He probably will say it's not from a doughnut but rather brain matter from the alien he ate for breakfast.

Troll Lady slams into the room.

"Who did it? *Who did it?*" she yells. She marches up and thrusts one of her troll dolls into my face—Troll Elvis, his prior black plumed coif now abbreviated and patchy.

I hold up my hands. "I didn't work this weekend. Wasn't me." She squints at me, her mascara-caked eyes narrowing into two blue slits from her CloudlessSkies eyeshadow. Her name badge/keycard clipped to the pocket of her shirt inches closer as she leans her ample breasts into me. I look down, read it. No way.

Her first name isn't Candi—it's *Candida*. I hold in a laugh.

Isn't Candida a yeast found in the … girlie parts?

Candi—Troll Lady—is named after a vaginal infection. How did I not know this?

This day just got a whole lot better.

"Well, *somebody* here is guilty—his hair is all over my console! This is a recent crime! Do you know how much this one doll is worth?" She waggles a chubby finger capped with a pink press-on nail at the four of us in the room. "I should call upstairs. See if I can get an ID tech down here to dust for prints."

She turns on me. "Think if this was the stupid otter statue sitting on your console. How would *you* feel?"

Les is up from his chair. Wraps an arm around her shoulder. Turns to me. "Put your hands out."

"What?"

"Put your hands out in front of you."

Reluctantly, I do, not sure where this is going. Les angles closer, the neck of his button-up stained with too much aftershave, and lifts his glasses to survey my hands. "Turn them over."

This is ridiculous. "I didn't touch Elvis. Go sniff someone else's butt and leave me out of it."

I turn away to retrieve my coffee. He grunts at the back of my head. Troll Lady grabs a paper towel and wipes the schmutz off his moustache.

"We'll get to the bottom of this, Candi," he promises.

"Mommy just gets so attached to her widdle troll babies," she baby-talks. I need to leave before this degrades further.

Two other dispatchers file out of the lunchroom before Les accosts them too.

This morning, I dug through Keith's jump kit in search of the softest gauze he had to tuck in between my nipples and the fabric of my bra, but it's already chafing. No time to whine. Lives must be saved. The Reaper waits for no man, blistered nipples or not.

The morning's calls are routine: someone locked out of their house, three pocket dials, a kitchen fire, one possible broken arm call from an elementary school, four break-and-enters, one with the suspect hog-tied with duct tape in the victim's kitchen. I have to convince her to not use her black-belt training on him—he's already crying from the kick she delivered to his testicles. The usual barking dog calls. One very intoxicated girl who should probably be at school but is instead ripped by noon and is pissed that I won't send the police to her house because she thinks her stepbrother stole the money she had hidden under the mattress even though she was going to use it to take pole-dancing classes because it would piss off her dad and he's a lawyer who makes a "shit ton" of money and how much I suck because I'm not taking her seriously and how her parents pay my salary through their taxes and that I'm a total loser who is probably super fat and has no boyfriend and will never have sex ever again and I probably collect stuffed animals and watch lame reruns and drive a shitty car and I have no boobs and terrible hair and tons of zits and I smell like fish.

Oh, yeah. I love this job.

The worst part? Some of what she said about me is totally true. Wow. That's super depressing.

On second coffee break, I check Facebook because I don't know what else to do. Indeed the memo Les promised showed up while I was in the bathroom. Cowards never wait until I'm at my desk—they leave the mustard-colored warning in plain sight where everyone knows the advisory board is breathing down my neck. I was right. It was Batman Jerry. "Review of procedures and protocol required." Goddammit.

Facebook brings more fantastic news from "friends," i.e., people who don't call or hang out but who would say, "OMG, Hollie, is that *you*? You look exactly the same as you did in eighth grade!" if we were to run into one another at Starbucks, which is totally insulting. Eighth grade was my "transition year," the one my dad spent telling people I was going through that awkward phase we're all prone to. Stellar. Being reminded that I look like a pubescent male child when in fact, I am a female, is not complimentary at all.

The red notification bubble is illuminated with announcements from friends getting married, friends graduating from law/medical/astronaut school, friends having (more) babies, one divorce party, invitations to listening parties for jazz and indie-electro music where vegan Asian fusion and craft beers will be served. I hate that stupid red circle. It is a harbinger of terribleness.

I break free of my dazed and confused stare at the computer screen, pushing aside the fact that cool people are doing cool things while I sit in a basement that smells like a flower truck full of rotting product has slammed into a nursing home.

I lick the first tear off my lip and it tastes terrible. New makeup.

I unhook my headset and move swiftly to the bathroom. The pungent slap of synthetic flowers isn't enough to sober me, despite the fact that I can taste it and my mascara is now trickling down my face in stinging, rose-scented rivulets. I can practically *see* the molecules of air freshener. I don't even care.

Call it PMS, which it probably is, dammit, but I am feeling very sorry for myself. I will indulge this moment because I've learned it's easier to just get it out than hold back the deluge. And I have much to snivel about: an audit memo. Scorched nipples. Friends getting married. Friends having babies. Friends buying houses. Friends getting lives. Friends with mothers and friends with boyfriends who don't make nachos on their bellies.

There is not enough chocolate in the world to make this right.

Troll Lady slams the bathroom door open and fans her face against the noxious perfumery. "Your break is—" She stops when she sees that my emotions have taken a disconcerting detour. "Hollie, are you okay, dear?"

"Yeah, yeah … I'm fine." I suck it in and splash my face. I don't need Troll Lady to pretend she's goddamned Dear Abby and try to offer meaningful life insight. A quick check of my phone reveals that I still have two hours in this shift. I have to pull it together.

"Oh, hey, I'm really sorry about Elvis," I say. "I swear to you, I didn't see a thing. I'd tell you if I did." I squeeze past her squishy self and can't help but wonder what it would feel like if she gave me a hug. Like a mom. Moms hug, right?

One hour, fifty-six minutes to go. I can do this.

"911, what is your emergency?"

"Yes, hello, my husband, he isn't feeling so well, and he sort of fell over in his chair."

Old ladies. These calls scare me almost as much as when little kids are faced with dying or dead parents. "Ma'am, where is he now?"

"He's on the floor. Oh, dear, he might have spit up a little. Herb, Herb, honey, can you hear me? It's Mona …"

"Your name is Mona?"

"Yes."

"Okay, Mona, can you tell me if Herb has any medical conditions?"

"Yes, he has diabetes. And a pacemaker."

"Does he take insulin?"

"Yes. He was just about to take his next shot."

"Okay, stay with me here. I've got an ambulance on its way." I click the right buttons and send the info over to the medics. Answer their return chirps. "Mona, they should be there in just a few minutes. Is there a code to let them into your apartment?"

"No, dear, we're on the ground floor. I will make sure the door is open for them. They can come through the patio." I radio the driver and let him know.

"Mona, is Herb still breathing? Is he conscious?"

"Herb, honey," she says. "Yes, he's a little bit awake."

I pull the protocol flip cards from my shelf to make sure I don't screw this up. I don't want this old geezer dying today. It might be the nudge that sends me over the cliff. "Can you ask him if he's experiencing any chest pain?"

"Herby, does your chest hurt, honey?" She pauses. "No, he's shaking his head no. Oh, he just gave me a thumbs up. Now … now he's pointing to his leg."

"His leg hurts?"

"I don't know. Maybe. Does your leg hurt, Herby?" A muffled voice, deeper than Mona's, rumbles in the background. "I think he wants me to give him his shot."

"Do you know how to give Herb his insulin?"

"Yes, yes, I do. I should do that. Should I hang up, then?"

"No, stay with me, Mona. Just put the phone aside and give Herb his insulin. Then pick up the phone again when you're all done."

She does this, and I hear her grunting, likely trying to get Herb's pants down enough to find skin, cooing to her husband as she talks him through what she's going to do for him.

"Okay, I gave him the shot. Oh, now, there's my sweetie cakes. The color's coming back into his face."

"Mona, let's keep him comfortable until the EMT guys get there, all right? He doesn't need to get up from the floor yet." She tells him this. Small chuckles float through the phone as he tries to tell her he wants to get up. She pooh-poohs him. Yay. Herb is going to make it.

"Mona, do you have family nearby? Anyone who can help you get to the hospital?"

"Oh yes, dear, I can call one of our sons. We have four."

"You have four sons?"

"Yes, we sure do. Such nice boys, all of them. Joseph, Martin, Larry, and Daniel. My little sweeties, although I suppose they're not so little now."

"They're my boys too," Herb says in the background. He's coming around.

"And we have nine grandchildren, don't we, Herby?"

"That sounds wonderful," I say. "How long have you and Herb been married?"

"This year will be our fifty-ninth anniversary. We met when I was a coat check girl at the dance hall, and he would come in with his boys and try to dance with all the pretty girls. I fancied his friend Bert, but he turned out to be a real cad. Drank too much gin. Herb was a real gentleman. But I wouldn't dance with him until he bought a ticket," she laughs.

Dance halls. Coat checks. Gin. Times have changed. Nowadays, if I want to meet a man, I have to flash my boobs on social media or have a sex tape go viral.

"My Herb, he courted me for a few months before we knew that we wanted to be together, but I knew right away—I knew Herby was the one when he spent the whole night talking to me in the stinky coatroom instead of dancing the night away with his friends."

"That is so romantic …"

"My father would only allow him to take me out for an hour at a time, and only to the park to feed the ducks. We still walk by the duck pond, Firwood Lake, over at Laurelhurst Park. Every day. Doctor says we have to exercise, so we moved here next to the park so we could walk and keep an eye on those birds."

Herb mumbles something in the background. "Yes, Herb knows everything about the ducks and geese. We get quite a lot of Canada geese."

"Sounds wonderful," I say.

"Got married right there in that park. Ducks even came to the ceremony. That was a surprise. We had such a beautiful wedding, didn't we, Herb?"

"Expensive," Herb adds. Mona giggles.

"That Spanish lace wasn't cheap. And this was before girls were really out in the work world, so we had to be careful with how we spent our money."

"How long before you had kids?" Herb sounds like he's awake again, and I like Mona. She must be like Everyone Else's Grandmother. I never had one of those. She is a foreign entity—I want to talk to her while we wait for the ambulance, protocol be damned.

"Oh, well, little Joey came around about two years after we were married. Then they were two years apart."

"A lot of diapers," Herb says. He sounds closer to the phone.

"Mona, is he trying to get up?"

"Herby, you lie back and wait. We'll just sit here until the medical people come help. What's your name again, sweetie?"

"I'm Hollie."

"Herby, Hollie says you have to lie still. So, Hollie," she shuffles the phone again, "are you married, dear?"

"No."

"So no kids."

"Nope. No kids."

"Well, you sound young. I'm sure Prince Charming is out there waiting for you ..." I laugh. The Disney regurgitation of Prince Charming never included a man with a weird attachment to medical supplies or pocket-sized terriers. I'll bet Prince Charming never burned Cinderella's nipples with Sriracha sauce.

"Probably. Yes. Someday, I suppose."

"You know, you should meet my Daniel. He's absolutely ador-able. And he's single … He's in real estate. Makes lots of money. Drives a fancy car."

I laugh. Mona is trying to set me up with her son while her hus-band waits for his ride to the hospital. This is a first.

"You know, Hollie, you only get to live this life once. I know that sounds like silly advice from a silly old woman, but don't waste a second, sweetie. If I could go back and do it all over again, I'd still pick my Herby. It would've been nice to have a little girl, but my boys gave me granddaughters. There's no bigger happiness in this world than your family."

"Indeed, Mona. You're so right." That choky feeling surges in the back of my throat, the one that happens right before tears make an appearance. I am losing my bloody mind.

A siren wails in the background. The radio squawks at me that the EMTs have arrived. "Mona, sounds like my guys are there. Herb is a lucky man to have a wife who loves him as much as you do. You really did well here today."

"Thank you for all your help, Hollie. Herby, tell Hollie thank you." He does, his voice a little slow. I hope this is just insulin related and not something more serious.

"You take care, Mona."

"You too, dear. Thank you again." She hangs up, even though I don't want her to. I want to sit here and listen to her talk about dance halls and her son Daniel and her grandbabies and all the silly, romantic things I'm sure Herb did for her, even if he didn't and I'm romanticizing this invisible couple and their perfect, bliss-ful life with lampshades and couches still covered in plastic and Hummel statues and collector's spoons in a glass hutch in the din-ing room.

The screen to my right is black; my reflection stares back at me. I missed some mascara on my cheek, its dark smudge reminding me that I am not whole.

My otter figurine clutches her tiny baby to her chest who in turn clutches her little white clamshell. They smile at me in perpetuity, a constant reminder that they have one another and I have no one. I don't have a clamshell to hold onto for dear life.

"You only get to live this life once." And this is how I'm spending it?

"Hollie?" Patty the supervisor is standing behind me. I turn and find myself eye level with her camel toe. Why this woman wears polyester pants is still a sad mystery I never want to solve but when my chair is lower than it should be and Patty and her sausage-like legs stand next to me … you get the picture.

Oh, but then she leans her butt on the desktop and it groans under her girth. I am fearful for the integrity of the steel structure.

She clicks the redirect button on my console, sending my calls to other dispatchers. Shit. This is going to be about the memo. I know it. Time for my tongue-lashing. And it's going to be so public. I thought she'd at least take me into her office so I could sink down into the very low chair she has placed in front of her desk. Polyester Patty's love for her *Intimidation Strategies for Managers 101* book is biblical. She keeps it between her framed, signed pictures of Donald Trump and Dick Cheney.

"Hollie, I need you to join the party-planning committee." *Oh God no.*

"What?" This isn't the tongue-lashing?

"Candi has been doing it for years, but since you don't have kids and a husband to take care of [*insert knife plunge here*], I know you have some extra time. Especially now that your night classes are over."

I was never taking night classes. I said I was because I didn't want to be forced into helping with the party-planning committee or the annual family picnic committee or the Secret Santa committee or the Sneakers for Shoeless Kids fundraiser. (That's a terrible name for a charity, by the way.)

"You've been here long enough now that you can help with some of the extra responsibilities, right? I mean, we're like a family, and we don't want anyone's birthdays or anniversaries or other special events to go uncelebrated. No one likes to be forgotten."

I do. I like to be forgotten. In fact, I wish you'd get your large, odd-smelling body away from my console and forget all about me. Oh, and take the disciplinary memo with you.

"Hollie?"

"I … uh …"

"We all need to do our part," Patty says. She points at the banner above the main door: *Community Builds Integrity*. Les is staring at me from behind his Black Book of Death. Creepy stalker asshole. I don't know if I want to be a part of his community.

He's so smug. Probably thinks I'm getting an early pre-memo reaming. What he doesn't know is if I have to be on this committee, I'll make sure his birthday is everything it should be.

And more.

But I don't want to do this. I spent enough time on committees and councils and clubs in high school for two lifetimes. I was an easy target—those goody-goody leader types knew Pleaser Hollie would say yes. "I'm, um, really busy when I'm not working, though, Patty."

"Doing what? I know you and Keith usually work opposite shifts because he's on the radio when you're not here."

"My … dad. Yeah, he's been asking me to help out with … stuff. Around his little farm."

"What sort of stuff?"

"Gard-en-ing stuff." The word comes out too slow. She's gonna know I'm lying.

"Well, I'm sure spending two nights a month helping with special events in the office won't damage your green thumb."

"Yeah … I guess."

"Excellent." The desk exhales relief when she stands. "Candi can brief you on upcoming events and give you an idea of what she needs help with."

"Okay."

"Good." She reverses the redirect on my console and picks up the mustard-color memo. "We'll have to talk about this Monday.

I've got meetings in the morning, so come see me after lunch, yes? Good." She leaves no room for my response. Which is fine. Because I have none.

I wait for her to walk away before I zap my console—I need a minute. That crushing feeling, the one where I realize I've just consented to do something else I don't want to do? Its mean, nasty tendrils spiral around my throat.

I could really use some fresh undeodorized air, but I don't dare try to move past Les.

Hypothetically, if I were to try to escape out the side door for just a few moments of real-life outdoor oxygen free of committees and disciplinary memos and calls from sick, dying, and/or angry people, I would be tersely reminded that my shift doesn't end for another hour.

Les regards his watch, pushes his glasses back up his oily nose. Answers a call. The way he positions himself in his chair, stiff and serious, means something big is going down on his line. Good. A reprieve from his icky glaring eyeballs. And, of course, he will do everything right. Mustard-colored memos don't end up on Les's desk. Even if he does screw up, we'll never know because the cliques here protect one another.

"Hollie," Patty's voice echoes across the dispatch center, accompanied by her waving hand. I stand and obey, like a good community-minded servant. "Let's do this now. Monday's going to be a nightmare," she says, waggling the yellow paper in her hand.

And with that, my hope for a better, brighter tomorrow is doused like the last candle in a hurricane. As I unplug and follow her polyester-clad thighs into her office, the friction worrisome in the synthetic fabric wrapped tight around two veritable sausages stuffed full of too many Pizza Fridays and birthday cakes and ham-rich deli trays, I pray that she doesn't catch on fire.

Because I don't think I can muster the energy to grab an extinguisher.

CHAPTER FIVE
END IS THE NEW BEGINNING

Well, that was painful.

I'm on probation. One more memo, and I have to sit with a trainer. As is, I have to redo one of the training modules to "freshen up my skills" and "readjust my attitude to one of calm confidence."

I still don't really know what I did wrong on that call. Batman sucked back a scotch-and-Viagra cocktail. His heart doth protest too much. He died.

Why is that my fault? I didn't force the Glenfiddich down his gullet.

The music's so loud in my crappy car, I think one of the speakers blows out. I only turn it down when a cop pulls me over for a long-ignored busted taillight.

"But I work in dispatch," I say. "Can't I just get by with a warning?"

"I'd ticket my mother if she had a busted taillight. The law's the law."

I have no idea why it comes out of my mouth, but it does. I need someone to pick on. "You should hear what the folks in dispatch call you guys. Especially Polyester Patty," I say as he hands me the ticket. Upon release, I punch the pedal harder than I should, risking further law's-the-law trouble, but it's better than saying anything else to his skeezy little moustache and too-tight motorcycle pants.

Keith's truck is in the lot when I pull in. I don't know if I can do this. I don't even know if I've made up my mind.

Mona's words echo in my head.

Yes. I have made up my mind.

Right?

The Yorkies start their verbal assault before my keys are even in the door. My head resting against the faded paint, atop the apartment's cracked plastic address numbers, I pause. Dueling with three five-pound wads of yappy, biting, bow-wearing fluff makes me want to rent a room elsewhere. At least I'd get some of those free bottles of shampoo and hand lotion. I could rent some chick flicks. Check on Facebook to see if Ty Stone is still single. He was always really good with his hands.

Upon entry, I'm assailed by a cloud of an unfamiliar body spray mixed with beer and farts. Keith has company. The coffee table is a cluttered smorgasbord of medical shit—tubes and tapes and bags and scissors and clampy things. They don't hear me come in because they're too busy arguing about one thingamajig being better than this doodad. Don't know. Don't care.

The giant-screen TV shows a delightfully gruesome reenactment of a partial amputation—the blunted, chewed end of some guy's pretend femur sticking out of his work pants as he screams and fake blood squirts all over the pretend doctors and nurses. I look away. Even though I know it's fake, it's red and squirty and eww.

"Hey, babe," Keith says. "You remember Joe, right? From the picnic last summer?"

I say nothing. Simply stare. Back and forth from one uninspired face to the other. When did Keith put on so much weight? Why are Joe's pants so short? Why are they fighting about medical supplies?

Why are they both wearing stethoscopes?

"So, dude, seriously, we were on this call yesterday, and I totally thought of you. That time when we were training out in east, and we had that skinny little fucker who keeled after that hot-dog-eating contest? Remember him?" Joe nods.

"Yeah, junkie, right?"

"Totally." Keith continues. Oh, the suspense. "So, I've got this new rookie for the next month—whatever his name is—and we had this guy who clearly hasn't been eating anything except heroin hot dogs for the last bazillion years. He was coding out, so we were able to slam in two large-bore IVs, give a couple of fast liters of Ringers. Probably an overdose, but he was blue as my balls and clearly needed an airway, so my partner intubated him but it went into the esophagus—"

"No fuckin' way."

"I know, right? Fuckin' rookies. So I did it myself." Gosh, Keith, such a humble hero. "We couldn't understand why his sats were still in the toilet even with bagging at 100 percent. We had good chest rise and end-tidal CO_2 so we hot-loaded him and ran code 3 to the closest ER."

"And?"

"He died."

"That's it? That's the end of your story?" I say.

"Uhhh, yeah … he was a total tweaker. We shouldn't even have done that much to try and save him. Waste of taxpayer money." Keith and Joe high-five. I stare at them both.

Who are these people?

"Dude, look at *this* one," Joe says, phone aloft. Oh, no. Show-and-tell. Keith and his buddies think it's awesome to try and outdo one another with pictures of the goriest calls. Joe twists his wrist so I can see the screen. The victim is a young man injured in a motorcycle accident. Injured, as in his face has been scraped off and shoved up to his forehead. "Kid got stuck behind the back tire. Peeled it right off." Bone and muscle remain. No evidence that a human face was ever there.

Eyelids close. Cannot unsee this, so don't look.

I say the first thing that pops into my head. Chicken shit Hollie. "Keith, did you PVR that National Geographic special on otters? I set a reminder."

"Oh, babe, I'm so sorry. I didn't have room. New episodes of the trauma show were on Discovery Health overnight."

"Fantastic."

"Aw, now don't be like that, Hol. I'm sorry. I promise I will go online and find you all the otter shows I can so you can watch to your heart's content. My little otter girl …" He pulls back my sweatshirt sleeve and kisses my otter tattoo. Just above the bony protuberance of my wrist. Yes. Otter tattoo. Holding a banner that reads *Enhydra lutris*. Sea otter. Pretty smart tattoo for a drunk seventeen-year-old with fake ID. Except for the location. Mighty hard to hide from Dad when I chose the wrist. But ... I love it.

Staring at Oliver Otter, an overwhelming realization floats upon me, like those parachutes we used in first grade. Flutters down to the ground, the air trying to escape through the single hole at the center of the multicolored nylon circle.

Ruled by mediocrity, I've given up. My get-up-and-go got up and went. It left without me. It didn't even leave me a note.

I agreed to be on the party-planning committee, for God's sake.

This is not the life I want when I see the look on Keith's face. In fact, I can say with the cool confidence Polyester Patty so desperately wants from me: I never want to have sex with this man. Ever. Again.

I do not pass go. I do not collect $200. Instead, I scoop the remote from the end table and bring up the PVR screen. One at a time, I delete the shows. All of the shows. The trauma shows, the surgery shows, the cooking shows, even *Grey's Anatomy*. Gone.

"Hol, what are you doing?" Delete. Delete. Delete. "Babe, don't! Come on!" He drops the pile of packages and crap from his lap, nearly upsetting the beer bottle resting perilously close to the edge of the coffee table. *My* coffee table, covered in *his* shit. "Jesus, Hol, that's like a month's worth of shows!" He wrestles the remote out of my hands, moves back like I've just committed the ghastliest of ghastlies.

Joe is smiling. "And that is why I don't live with a chick," he mumbles.

"Mushroom Cap Joe—that's what they call you, right?" I say. He squints, smile melting. Shifts his head ever so slightly. "Because of the size of your ..." I circle my finger around my crotch. "Were you born like that, or was it some sort of weird industrial accident?"

"You're a crazy bitch."

I stand and tower over him where he sits rigid against the cushions of the remarkably ugly sofa. "I'm not the one with the gnome-sized dick, trying to get into the pants of every new trainee in the city. Everyone knows, Joe. The dispatch center is abuzz with delightful gossip, and your penis comes up more often than not. When we need a good laugh. I'm embarrassed for you, actually. Really, I am."

Oh, damn, that felt *gooooood.*

His face turns even redder and ruddier than it was a moment prior. He guzzles what's left of his beer and grabs his coat. "Fucking glad she's your problem, Keith."

The door slammed closed, Keith turns to me, eyes incredulous. "What the hell is wrong with you?"

"I'm tired. Tired of fucking around, waiting for shit to get better. Because shit doesn't get better—it just stinks and smears and stains everything. I think I might be done with shit." I walk over and turn off the television. "I'm going out. I'll be back in three hours. When I return, I want you and your jump kit and the Yorkies to make like an embolism and dissolve. Gone. Poof. Vanished."

"Come on, Hol, sit down and let's talk about this. You're … did something bad happen today? Did someone die? Is this about your nipples?"

I laugh under my breath. I totally forgot about my blistered nipples. I pick up one of my otter trinkets from the top of my pathetic bookshelf. "You see these two otters? These five-dollar resin animals have more of a life than I do. They have each other. Mona has Herb and they have their sons and the ducks. Shit, even Nurse Bob has his gals at work and his fishing flies and that satanic goat. Everyone has more of a life than I do."

"Is this about getting married? Because we can totally do that if you want."

"No, Keith, this is not about getting married."

"Is it because I didn't record your nature shows? Hol, come on, let's talk about this. You're obviously upset—"

"Yeah. I'm upset. I had a shit day. I'm tired of being bossed around. I'm tired of Les staring at me over his Black Book of Death and of Troll Lady accusing me of touching her trolls and of getting in trouble at work because I'm not doing my job the way they think I should be doing it, and I'm *really* tired of thinking about why my former best friend dumped me and how all the asshats on Facebook get to have sparkly lives while I fester in this shithole—"

"You're just overtired. Let's have a beer and I'll clean up my mess. I can give you a shoulder massage. We can make lists, like the couples' counselor told us to do, figure out what's wrong."

I step away from him. If he touches me—if he looks at me with sad eyes, I'll cave. "I need a break. *We* need a break. I need you to just … go."

"I don't want to go. I want to be here with you."

"I don't want you here."

"Hol, come on."

"I said, I don't want you here. Please. Keith. Take the dogs. You have three hours to figure something out. If you're not gone when I get back, I'll call in every favor I have left with my few remaining cop friends and make sure you're escorted off the premises."

"You're serious."

"As a heart attack."

"But … I thought we loved each other."

"No. We don't."

"Hollie—"

"I'm leaving. I'll be back in three hours. Whatever you can't take today, we can arrange something for your next days off. If you need me to, I can go to my dad's to give you time to unload every-thing of yours from the apartment."

"You can't afford the rent by yourself, Hollie."

"Still not a good-enough reason for us to live together. Goodbye, Keith."

CHAPTER SIX
DROWNING OF SORROWS

"'Nother shot over here," I slur. I should probably stop soon. This is gonna hurt like hell tomorrow, but the place is almost all mine, the music is good, and the bartender is hot.

"Hollie, you want me to call Keith for you, hun?" Ridley the bartender—he is so adorable.

"Rid, why do you have to be gay? I want to get naked with a man who looks like you."

"They all do, sweetheart." He starts to pull my glass away.

"No. I want another one. Pretty please …" I bat my eyelashes at him. Or, try to.

"Maybe something besides schnapps, then?"

"What d'you recommend …"

"Something nonalcoholic."

"That is totally not what I had in mind." I slurp the last drops out of the highball.

Rag in hand, Ridley lifts my phone from the counter, wipes underneath it. It's been chiming at me all night. It does so again.

"You gonna answer that?"

"Why? So Keith can try to guilt me into coming home?"

"Lovers' quarrel?"

"No. That would mean we were lovers. We're nothing but room-mates. And he's a lousy lay. I'd have better luck with—"

"Stop right there. Some secrets are best left unshared." He slides a glass of water with lemon in front of me. I stick my tongue out at him. The phone chimes again.

"Answer that, or I will."

"God, you're so bossy. Why is everyone always bossing me around?" I slide a sticky finger across the phone's face. About twenty text messages from my dad are awaiting response:

What happened?

Keith just called. He's worried about u.

Where r u?

Should I come into town?

Why aren't u answering?

If u don't answer within the next hour, I'm coming into town.

Shit. I text him back. "Dad, I'm fine. Rough day. Will call tmrw. Don't worry. Luv u."

"Keith looking for you?" Ridley says.

"Nope. Dad. He's freaking out. Prolly thinks I'm face-down in a ditch somewhere."

As I scan through my emails, my drunk eyes crossing from the tiny screen, one subject line catches my attention. "Rid, Rid, c'mere. I need you."

He refills another patron's beer and returns to my perch. "Can you read the fine print on this for me?"

"What am I looking at?"

"My dad—he bought me an early birthday present. A weekend at a resort in O Canada."

"Sounds swanky."

"Can …" A slight wave of nausea flits by. I sip water. "Can you see if it says anything about me having to take Keith with me?"

Ridley pulls reading glasses out of his shirt pocket. God, he's like a gay sex god. "It doesn't say much of anything about rules. Is this place really up in Canada?"

"Yup. British Columbia. And I'm goin' there. I gotta get outta town for a while."

"When you going?"

"Dunno. Soon. Gonna get drunk and run away. Just what the doctor ordered."

"Some doctor. Give me his number."

I swallow more water, wondering if I should try to go pee. I really have to pee. "I gotta go somewhere far away from this stupid place. No offense—I don't mean your lovely bar. I just mean ... here."

"I know what you mean, darlin'."

"Yup. I gotta do some soul searching. Find me some otters and whales and maybe a bear and definitely some men because *that* is what I need right now. A real man who doesn't talk about stupid shit and who doesn't wear his stupid stethoscope all the time— seriously, Ridley, would you ever have sex with a guy who wore a stethoscope, even when he wasn't working?"

"Depends on if he's wearing only the stethoscope," Ridley smiles.

"You say that now, but unless he looks like you or Johnny Depp, it's jus' gross. Keith's gut hangs over his pants and he's got this weird hairline thing going down into his boy parts. Like when an Asian tries to grow a beard." The Asian gentleman down the bar gives me a dirty look. "Sorry, man. No, really." I lean closer to Ridley, boobs squished against the wooden bar. Hurts. "And even his penis—seriously, he acts like it's some gift from the gods, but it's nothin' special. He's not circumcised, which is weird."

"TMI, Hol."

"Sorry, man."

"Last call for you," he says, sliding another shot in front of me. I blow him a kiss and try to wink but only one eye cooperates. Not sure which one.

"Yeah, I'm going up north. I gotta take a floatplane to get there. Can you believe this—Keith wanted to take the dogs! Dumb guy just doesn't understand what a woman needs."

"Me, either." Ridley places a bowl of nuts in front of me. Ew. Gross. Nuts. Thank God they're not Cheetos. I hate Cheetos. I hope Keith remembers to take all the Cheetos. "So what's your plan?"

"Dunno. But I ain't goin' with him because, well, I kicked him out. We're done. Finito. He and his stupid little runt dogs."

40

"No more Keith, huh?"

"Nope. No more Keith. Did I tell you that he burned my nipples? He totally did." I clamp my hands over my boobs. They're still sore. "And—I got in trouble at work. Some dude with a heart problem dressed like Batman and had crazy sex with his wife and it killed him. So that's my fault? I didn't spend years shoving cheeseburgers into this guy's arteries. How is that my fault?"

"Don't you sign a confidentiality agreement to work at 911?"

"Yeah ... but you can keep a secret, right?" He smiles. "You know what the worst part is, though?"

"Worse than a guy dying on the phone with you?"

"Mm-hmm. Way worse."

"Hit me."

"I have to join the party-planning committee. With Candida, the yeast infection troll lady."

"That does sound serious."

"You have no idea."

"The whole day sounds pretty awful." He's counting the coins from the tip jar. I watch as the silver discs slide across the smooth bar top under his long, well-manicured fingers.

"Not a total loss. I did talk to this sweet old lady who had this great story about her life with her Herb—her husband is Herb—she made me really think about shit, you know? *Life* shit. Important shit. I started asking myself some serious questions ..."

"Oh, that's never a good thing."

"Isn't it, though?" I swallow the schnapps. The peach tastes too sweet. Maybe I should switch to whisky. Get drunk like a grown-up.

"What are you going to do, then?"

"Dunno."

"World's your oyster, kid. If you hate working at 911, quit. Find something new. You're still young. Everything's still perky and firm."

"So I should be a stripper?"

"Or you could go back to school."

"God, you sound like my dad."

"Should I be insulted?"

"Nah. My old man's good. Just a nag. Thing is, I dunno what I wanna be when I grow up. I can't do the medical thing. Even if my dad thinks that medicine is where it's at and he's a nurse—"

"Your dad's a nurse?" Ridley's smile is so familiar. Everyone smiles like that when they learn about my dad's job. Once the kids at school figured out that, despite his scrubs, he was the one who cleaned up their grandmother's puke, not the one who stitched up her broken hip, the shit got thicker every year. And Dad's last short-lived marriage was to a doctor, but she was a wicked-crazy naturopath who read people's auras and accepted chickens as payment.

"Shut up."

"No, sweetie, that's awesome. But just because he's a nurse doesn't mean you have to follow suit."

"I faint at the sight of blood."

"Then nursing probably won't work out for you."

"But what else *is* there? I don't wanna suck anymore, Ridley."

"You don't suck, sweetheart."

"That's what she said," I giggle at him.

He leans onto the bar, picks up my phone, and looks at the email from Revelation Cove. "You should call them. See when you can go up."

"Ya think?"

"Sure. Why not? What have you got holding you here? Call in sick for a few days. Go clear your head and figure some shit out."

"That's a good idea. You're a really smart guy, Rid."

"Nah. I've just been where you are. I left my old life and came here to get away. Never looked back." He tucks a soft hand against my cheek. "Change of pace will do you some good. Get out of the city for a while." He spins the email around again and looks down at it. "They've got an 800 number. Call 'em."

"What time is it?"

"Just after ten. What have you got to lose?"

"Dammit, damn right. Here I go." I try to get the numbers into the screen but I'm wobbly. Ridley sees me fumbling and dials for me.

"It's ringing …" He passes over the phone.

"I'm gonna give you a huge tip tonight, Rid—hello?" Someone answers. "Yes, um, hello. Hi. My name is Hollie. My dad, he bought me a gift certificate to stay at your establishment, and I'm wondering about your next availability." I hope that word came out of my mouth right.

"What's the name on the gift certificate?" It's a man's voice. Deep. Rugged. He sounds sexy.

"Would it be under my name? Hollie. Hollie Porter. It was supposed to be for me and one other person. I'll need to change that."

"Hang on just a moment, Miss Porter. Let me pull this up." *Tap tap tap* of a keyboard. "Okay, yes, your dad bought you a four-day, three-night stay with floatplane transport for two people, queen bed, Jacuzzi tub. Our Sweethearts' Spa & Stay package."

I start laughing. "No. Dude, seriously. Cancel that. If there's no sweetheart, can I still use the package?"

"You can. It's already paid for, so the room rate is the same whether it's you or you and a guest," Sexy Phone Man says.

"Wait a sec—what's your name?"

"I'm Ryan, the concierge."

"Hi, Ryan. I'm Hollie. Oh. Wait," I laugh. "I totally already told you that, didn't I." I'm trying really hard not to slur. That last sip of schnapps is bouncing behind my eyeballs. "Okay, so I don't want the sweethearts' package because my boyfriend is now my *ex*-boyfriend. He's a total putz who always wears his stethoscope. And he has these reeeediculous dogs."

"Is he a doctor?"

"You know what, Ryan, that's the funniest part. Nope. Not a doctor. Just a dipshit who drives an ambulance. I mean, he's a nice guy, yeah, and maybe someday someone will love him, but not me." I cup my hand over the phone. "Do you know what he *did* last night, Ryan?"

"Do I want to know?"

"I'm totally serious here. He made nachos on my stomach. He thought it would be sexy or some shit. 'Cept he burned my boobs with hot sauce."

Ryan starts laughing. He's laughing at me! It's infectious.

"That sounds … terrible, Hollie."

"You have no idea. Nipples are very sensitive, Ryan. For a girl. I'm not even kidding. I don't know if the girls will ever recover." I pull out the neck of my shirt and look down. Poor girls.

"So, maybe you should come up to the Cove without the stethoscope-and-hot-sauce boyfriend."

"Yeah, that's what Ridley says. He's the bartender. He's totally hot. But he's gay." Ridley winks at me and laughs under his breath. "Ryan—wait—are you gay? Because you sound hot. And you should see Ridley. He looks like The Rock. Not quite that big …" Ridley flexes his tattooed bicep. Kisses it. "Still, smokin' hot. I'd do him. But he doesn't want me because I'm not battin' for the right team."

"Ridley sounds amazing, but sadly, no, I'm straight."

"Do you have a girlfriend?" Ryan doesn't answer. "Because if you do, let me give you a little advice. You should be into the stuff she's into. I mean, I really like otters. They're so fuzzy and cute. But does Keith ever record my nature shows? No! Why? Because he has to record all these dumb medical shows so he can scream at the TV and tell them how lame they are. Like he's a goddamned medical genius or something. Oh—and don't make out with your dogs, because that's totally gross. I hate it when Keith does that. Omigod, so gross."

"Good advice … so, uh, Hollie, when do you think you want to come up to Revelation Cove?"

"Right. Um. Yeah. I don't know. What do you guys have to do up there?"

"Lots of things. Nature hikes, hot springs, boats you can take out into the sound to the little islands nearby. We have a full-service spa on site—"

"Ryan—wait—do you guys have otters?"

"Otters?"

"Yeah, otters. You know, those adorable little babies and their mommies. They eat urchins and clams and they float on their backs … I friggin' love otters."

"I think you will be pleasantly surprised to see the vast array of local wildlife. You name it, they live here."

"That sounds purrrrfect."

"It is," he says, "which just means you need to come up and see it in real life."

"I totally should."

"When would you like to make this happen?"

"Soon. Really soon." Yeah. Soon sounds perfect. The sooner, the better.

"Are you flying or driving?"

"Not driving. My car sucks."

"Where do you live?"

"Portland, Oregon."

"Okay, well, fastest and most economical way is to take the train to Seattle. Then a ferry to Victoria's Inner Harbour."

"That's where the floatplane is?"

"We have flights leaving Victoria every weekday morning. But if you can make it there by six thirty in the evening on a Monday, you can grab the supply flight and I can throw in a perk on this side to make up for the difference."

"So if you were me, what would you do?"

More tapping on a keyboard. "We're slow for the next two weeks—can you come up in the next day or so?"

"Prolly not tomorrow. I gotta figure out the trains."

"How about that Monday supply flight?"

"Shit ..." I don't know if I can do Monday. That's only two days away ... what am I going to do about work? "Umm ..." I look up at Ridley and he's nodding, his thumb in the upright position. "You know what, Ryan, that sounds fabulous. I can do that. Monday's supply flight it is."

"Terrific. Let me get a few extra details from you ... You'll love it here. Guests always say that they don't want to leave when their stay is over."

"Ryan, buddy—we're buddies now, right? Promise me something about Rev—Rev—"

"Revelation Cove."

"Yeah, that. Promise me you don't have Yorkies or Cheetos."

Ryan snickers into the phone. "You're in good hands. No Yorkies here. The coyotes would probably get them."

"You have coyotes?"

"We have a few who live on the island. They keep the rodents under control."

"I feel good about this, Ryan. You're a good man."

"We aim to please."

"And you're sure you're straight?"

"Miss Porter, it's been a pleasure talking to you this evening. We'll look forward to seeing you on Monday evening."

I disconnect and give Ridley a shaky thumbs up. The drunk is starting to morph into that queasy, spinny feeling. He slides a cup of coffee in front of me. "Mmm, that smells nice."

"Brewed it just for you, Hols." He stirs in cream and sugar.

"It's the same color as you now," I say, sipping, sighing loudly. Ridley is so pretty. He's always so clean and he always smells nice and he has gorgeous teeth and his tattoos are tasteful and not too much and he is never mean to anyone and he always listens to me when I'm talking, which I tend to do a lot when I'm here with Keith because my boyfriend—*ex*-boyfriend—always invites his friends so I get bored and Ridley entertains me.

"Ridley, I think I might be in love with you."

"You might not be in the morning, though. How you getting home tonight, sweetness?"

"My very lovely size-eight feet." I attempt to stretch one leg over the bar. Almost fall on my ass.

"Honey, no way those are size eight. I've seen elephants with smaller feet."

"Fine. Size ten. Bully." *Slurp. Slurp slurp.*

"Ballerina, I'm going on break at 11:30." He looks at his watch. "I'll walk you home."

"You don't have to do that." The bobble head on my shoulders feels heavy.

"Yup, I do. Finish your coffee."

"It'll make me have to pee." Ridley raises one eyebrow. "Too much info, I know. But …"

"Finish your coffee. We'll go in a few minutes."

My phone chimes. A text from Kevin. Keith. Whatever his name is. "I'll come back for the TV Sunday."

Good. I never wanted a TV that big. I was fine with the nineteen-year-old Magnavox my dad gave us. I don't care about TVs. I just want one night of sleep in *my* bed without the Yorkies.

Ridley, as promised, walks—supports—me home. That schnapps—sneaky bastard. Rid helps me up to my crappy second-floor apartment and offers a brotherly peck on the cheek, even though I beg him to be straight, if only for a night. "You're so beautiful, Ridley."

"Sorry, Hol, but you don't have the right equipment." He pats my cheek, eyes sparkling under the muted porch light. Why is he a bartender and not a male model … what do his parents look like … what stories are you hiding under those muscles, dear Ridley … does he have a brother. That thought makes it out of the chamber.

"Do you have a brother?"

"Good night, my friend."

"Wait—" I cup one hand around my ear, listening, the other hand clamped onto his meaty bicep.

"What?"

"No Yorkies!" I throw a rubbery arm into the air for a high five. His return is lukewarm. Ooh, my stomach is not happy. I should go inside. "Yeah. Okay, thanks. For everything. I'll just … go to bed now."

"You gonna be okay? In there by yourself?"

"Jesus, now that you put it that way …" I sniff but I don't dare cry. Where did empowered Hollie go? Where did the *I can do any fucking thing I want* run off to?

Oh, right. I drank it.

The apartment door closed behind me, Ridley gone, I realize how very alone I am. Sure, no Yorkies. That's delightful, I ain't gonna lie. And my beautiful foyer bench beams at me. If the wood could talk, she'd tell me she's happy the jump kit is gone. She's free of its suffocating weight. The very ugly coffee table is absent, only dents from its metal legs punched into the stained berber carpet. He took some of the IKEA "art," dirty silhouettes left behind on the apartment-issue eggshell wall. The TV's still here, as he said in his text, but only the dust outline hints that an Xbox once occupied the lower shelf.

The bedroom is cluttered. He clearly packed in a hurry. Some of the drawers are still open. Half the closet is empty. He's forgotten some of his shoes.

But the bed ... he's taken the duvet. Probably for the best. It smelled like dog. But I don't know if I have any other blankets in the apartment.

I'm so tired. I have to lie down before I puke. I will never drink anything peachy again. Put the schnapps up on the shelf with the Cheetos. Only this time, there was no ceramic rainbow pin to win. Just me and the tsunami that is now my life. No rainbows in tsunamis.

I consider taking a hot bath but I'm afraid I'll fall asleep and either drown or die of hypothermia. Then again, if I don't lie down, I'll barf and they'll find me face down in a puddle of my own sick. Wouldn't that just make Les's day? He gets the call reporting my dead, fetid body three weeks after everyone notices I've gone missing. I wonder if he'll write that in his Black Book of Death. "Hollie Porter, demented and pathetic, died in her own vomit because a wire came loose in her brain and she pooped on everything she had going in her life."

I don't have a boyfriend anymore to revive my convulsing, frozen body.

Maybe I'm not drunk enough. Maybe the sobers are making me remember everything that sucks.

Or maybe I'm *too* drunk and the tipsies are reminding me of how much I messed up today.

If I fall asleep soon, I won't start crying. Because if I start crying, I might not be able to stop. I might fill the bathtub with my tears and bathe in my own salty misery instead of emptying the hot water tank we share with the neighbors.

Like any drunk worth her salt, masochism is the next dish on the menu. I plop into the squeaky desk chair in front of my laptop. Click on the folder that holds the letter.

The one from the private investigator. The one that cost me last semester's tuition and yet brought me no closer to knowing anything that would bring about a happy, Hallmark-Channel-daisy-and-rainbow-filled reunion.

My mother. Lucy M. Collins. Last known address, Los Angeles. Divorced twice. One child, not in her custody. Spent time in jail for fraud, money laundering, vandalism over $5000. Associate of activism groups involved in illegal and/or destructive activities. No surviving family on record except for one daughter. Employment history unavailable due to multiple aliases.

Current location: unknown.

I find a checkered tablecloth in the hall cupboard and pull a winter hat on. It's May, so it's not *that* cold, but I'm drunk, and I'm tired, and I'm alone. Hence, cold.

What the hell have I done.

Chapter Seven
Breakfast with Mangala

We're not going to talk about Saturday. Let's just pretend Saturday didn't exist. Even though it did. The pounding in my head, the ferocious slamdance my eyeballs did in their sockets, the vomit I produced while on the phone with my dad because I wasn't going to be able to come out to shuffle his boxes about.

Because he's a nurse, he thinks I'm dying of a brain-eating amoeba, that vomiting and severe headache is likely caused by something awful and terrible and deadly.

"Death by peach schnapps, Dad. That's all this is."

"You've got to get yourself together, Hollie. Union jobs are hard to come by. If you're not going back to school, you can't blow it at 911. Wait until you get your full pension."

"DAD, it's Saturday. I have the day off."

"Right. Still ..."

Then the Inquisition really began. "No, I'm not pregnant. No, I'm not getting married. Yes, Dad, Keith and I broke up. Yes, I'm fine. No, I don't need to come to your house. No, I definitely don't need you to come to my house. No, I'm not seeing anyone else. Yes, Dad, I am really hungover. No, I don't need money. Yet. No, I'm not joining a cult. Yeah, Daddy, I think it might be a premature midlife crisis."

He relented. I slept. By Sunday morning, my humanity returned. When I could stand without wanting to die, I cleaned the shit out of the apartment. Erased all traces of pint-sized pocket pups. Sat, yellow-gloved, skin reeking of Pine-Sol, and second-guessed my choice to leave for Canada so suddenly, which, in hindsight, probably isn't the best course of action with my wimpy bank balance and especially now that the whole rent is going to fall on my shoulders.

When nothing else was left to clean, it was time to face my father. Especially knowing that Keith was due imminently to retrieve the 60-inch.

Dad's house is in the boonies, on the very edge of the city limits. For a smart man, he's really dumb. He sold the 108-year-old house in town, all three bedrooms and two baths with its honeyed hardwoods on a corner lot, the one I probably would've inherited, and instead invested in the boat he and his then-new bride moved into. Briefly. Until they both realized neither were mariners, and the Columbia River doesn't play nice in the winter, no matter how solidly your big dumb boat is moored to the wood thingie along the shore. The boat was not covered by insurance because genius Aurora had my father convinced that the insurance companies are run by the Greys (yes—the aliens with the big black eyes) and so they shouldn't risk it. Thus, when the storm hit, I had to go rushing down to the docks at Hayden Island and watch my inheritance sink to the bottom of the harbor.

Fun times.

They then bought this rundown house, but when the remodel started, the marriage deconstructed with every nail sunk. Aurora's plans for an underground grow op freaked out my law-abiding father. Thank heavens. And yet, they still co-own this house (sans grow op), not out of love but rather because Aurora doesn't trust our nation's legal system, and thus doesn't want to get divorced. Something about Masons controlling the judges and a direct connection to the NSA and the KGB, which is actually not defunct. Don't ask. I have no idea. I stopped listening a long time ago.

But it means Dad won't lose his shirt and have to pay out fifty percent of the house. If he doesn't care, neither do I.

Getting from my car to the front door can be tricky. Mangala might be in the yard. What the hell is a Mangala? The Hindu god of war. A leftover from the days of Aurora.

It's a goat. An evil, blood-sucking vampiric demon of the night.

If I step in his territory and he hears me, he'll give chase until he's able to ram his goddamned pointy devil horns into my ass. The bruises *just* healed from Easter.

Close car door quietly. Phone on silent. Strain ears to listen for Mangala.

Tiptoe, tiptoe.

Front gate creaks. *Shit.* Pause. Distant jingle of a bell.

One step, two steps. I might make it. The porch is only twelve, maybe fifteen steps away. I can do it in half as many if I pretend I'm eight and running on lava.

The bell sounds again. Closer. Just around the overgrown hedge.

Bleeeeeeeeeat. The bell—it hears everything.

RUN!

"Dad, open the door! Mangalaaaaa! Bad goat, *bad goat!*" I alternate feet in front of me, blocking his attempted head-butts. He knocks me off balance, shoves my knee into my gut. Bastard is strong. "Open the goddamned door!" I fall through the front door and look up at my father from the floor, wide-eyed. "Dad! Seriously! Curry!"

Dad laughs, his eyeballs magnified to hilarious proportions from his glasses. Nothing but blue staring back at me, a silver spatula in his right hand. "You say that, but this house hasn't been broken into since that goat showed up." I stand and lock the screen door. Mangala snorts. A line of snot oozes from his snout.

"Can't you lock him up? How the hell do you get your mail?"

"P.O. box. He can sense your fear. Animals know when a human doesn't like 'em." I hate it when he says stuff like that. He sounds like Aurora. And I like all the animals. (Except weird dogs.) I was the kid at the zoo and aquarium with her head squeezed between the bars or face pressed against the glass trying to get the babies to understand that I love them, that I want to be their friend, not like all these other dumb people who yell, "Hey, monkeyyyyy!" at the gorillas (they're apes) or say, "Here fishy fishy fish" to a dolphin (mammal, not fish). *I* am the one who wanted to take care of the otters and the seabirds stuck in fishing nets and ride the back of an orca like that lucky kid in *Free Willy*. Instead, I'm the one who lives with incestuous Yorkies and who has to run from a goat with demon blood coursing through his veins.

Mmmm, curry.

Dad is wearing his fancy fishing vest atop his usual bluish-green scrub pants. "You hitting the river today?" I ask.

"Nah. Just tying flies." The one thing my father hasn't given up—his love of tying flies for fishing. A perfect day for Dad involves throwing the dingy in the lake in pursuit of the perfect trout or standing on the shore cast-cast-casting into the smooth river, his flies attracting the fattest Chinook. Once word got around at work, the orders piled in from coworkers and their husbands.

"You can't lift the boat out of the truck if your hernia is acting up."

"Follow, child. Griddle's on," he says, turning toward the kitchen. "And don't nag me."

"If I don't, who will?"

He pushed his glasses atop his head. "You look skinny."

"Thank you?"

"Are you eating?"

I don't have a mother who worries about my diet—my dad frets enough for two parents. "You taking your cholesterol medication?"

"No changing the subject, Hollie Cat."

In the kitchen, he has a plate of fresh pancakes. "Well, are you?"

"Yes, Dr. Porter. I'm taking it."

I slide onto the dining bench. We've had this dinette set forever. Dad built it when I was five, and no matter how outdated, it still says home to me. He places a stack before me and my mouth waters so viciously, I'm afraid I'll slobber down my front. My dad's pancakes are legendary. In fact, pretty much everything my dad cooks is damn good. Not sure what the hell happened—the cooking gene must've skipped a generation. Which means maybe my possible future children that I probably won't have would've been excellent cooks.

We eat, I deflect questions about what's going on with Keith. Dad tells me about the latest carnage going on with Aurora and her non-daughter Moonstar, how the union elections are coming up again, about a great new wire the guys at the Gresham fly shop sent over.

Inevitably, Revelation Cove comes up. And it's just as I expected. "I was hoping that Keith would get the hint," he says. "I suppose now, that won't be happening."

"Tell me straight—had Keith given you *any* indication that he was going to propose?"

He stares at me. I know my father well enough to know when he's lying. "No indication, Hols. I was just thinking …"

"Just as well. I would've turned him down."

Dad takes his glasses off and looks at me with those searching eyes, the ones that used to see right through me when I came home drunk from a party I wasn't supposed to be at, or noticed when my shirt was misbuttoned after a night out "with the girls" that involved nothing but a boy and sweaty fumblings in the backseat of a sub-compact. It wasn't my idea to give up the V Card in the back seat of a Tercel, but these things happen.

"You can do better. You know that, or you wouldn't have dumped him. I'm sure you could find a nice doctor out there …"

"Like you did, Pops?"

He laughs and pushes his glasses back onto his nose, picking up his fork. "I'm just saying—the gals at work, there are a lot of single sons around your age. Manjit's son is in his residency. He's a little skinny, but a nice boy. Going into cardiology."

"*Dad.*"

"The girls are always asking if you've found a man yet."

"Maybe I don't need a man."

"No ticking biological clock for you?"

"*Your* clock is ticking louder than mine."

"You gotta understand, my darling daughter—I work with a lot of women. The young ones—the nurses your age—they're having or have had their first babies. The ladies my age are bringing in pictures of their new grandbabies. I can't help it." I laugh through a bite of maple and vanilla. Like I said, my dad is two parents wrapped in one. He reaches out and places a soft hand on my forearm. "I'm just saying ... grandchildren would be nice. Someday."

Our eyes meet. I can't bear to tell him that I have zero intention of reproducing. Even someday.

"Thanks for that gift certificate, though. It's very generous."

"I know your birthday's coming up ..."

"In, like, four months." I slide out and collect our sticky plates.

"Still. Can't a father treat his daughter? I figured you could use some time away."

"Your timing is perfect." I kiss the top of his head. His thinning hair smells like the hospital.

"When you thinking about going?"

"Actually ... tomorrow."

"Yeah?" He beams.

"Yeah," I say. An excited giggle escapes as the bubbles froth in the dishwater.

"Wonderful!" Dad smooches my cheek before burying his hands in the suds. He washes; I dry and stack. "Any more thought about going back to school?"

This is the only problem with coming to see my father. The questions. So. Many. Questions. "I'm not going to become a nurse."

"You get over the sight-of-blood thing, Hols."

"No. I won't."

"Listen to me," he says, using the soapy sponge like a magic wand he can use to transform his daughter into something better. "Without a union or an MBA, and now without Keith to help with the rent ... You don't have an endless amount of years to think about this stuff. You could go back, finish your degree. If you get into hospice care, the wages are incredible and our union is strong, great benefits, paid holidays—"

"DAD." The remnants of the hangover headache pop a button in my head.

"Right." He flops the wet towel over the oven handle.

"Show me the boxes."

"Nah, it's all right. I already moved them."

"You're not supposed to be lifting."

"I had the neighbor kid help me. He's saving for a video game player. Was more than happy to take my fifty bucks. Come here, though. I found this."

I follow him into the dining room and he slides a box to me. It's full of my stuff. Soccer trophies, my scrapbooks from the trips we used to take to the Oregon Coast every summer, a dried-out, crumbling Dungeness crab claw, a framed photo under broken glass of me feeding an otter at the Monterey Bay Aquarium infirmary on my tenth birthday, a paper bag of unfocused, fading photos from the year I went to summer camp for children from single-parent homes (thanks, YMCA, for reminding us that more than half will end up pregnant before graduation and the other half will likely become drug dealers or worse, insurance salesmen). A pink hospital-issued *Baby's Book* with only a few entries in it. How much I weighed. The date and time I was born. A single curl trimmed from my goldilocks under aged scotch tape.

Mother Dear left us pretty soon after I was born—as in, bought a Greyhound ticket and left, not *she left us too soon to go to the big all-night kegger in the sky.* As my dad always says, "Some fish just aren't meant to be caught."

The blankness of the lines next to "Baby's Firsts" tell me that Dad was probably too busy learning how to bottle-feed and diaper-change and still hold down a job on three hours' sleep. Man, I never even thought about it, how much of himself he gave just to be there for me. Never missed a game, never missed a school play or awards ceremony, never missed an opportunity to chaperone a school dance just to make sure wandering prepubescent hands didn't find their way onto my ass. Makes the best oatmeal chocolate chip cookies but says he will only share his secret ingredient once I give him his first grandchild. He might die before that happens. Refer to aforementioned conversation.

Wow. My childhood is in this box.

"Thanks, Daddy."

He hugs me. "You will always be my best girl, you know …"

God, I do not want to get emotional right now. *No tears no tears no tears.*

Dad clears his throat and chunks his hand down on my shoulder a few times. We're manly men. No time for blubbering.

I suck back the moisture and excuse myself into the bathroom in search of ibuprofen. Inside the medicine cabinet, I find his cholesterol pills that, of course, I have to count to make sure he has indeed been taking them. Judging by the remaining pills and date on the prescription, he's compliant. Good Dad. I spin the other bottles—there are many. I know these drugs. Tylenol-3. Two depression meds. A muscle relaxant. Some Cialis. (I dropped that bottle immediately.) A bottle of Ativan with three refills.

My dad is depressed? Anxietal? I knew he'd been a little blue after losing the boat and everything with Aurora and then losing the nomination for nursing union president. I wish he'd talk to me. But he won't. Because he's the dad and I'm the kid and that's the way it is. So I have to pretend like I didn't see all these bottles and keep looking for something to stop the bluster in my brain.

Something is banging into the side of the house. I open the window and look out, expecting to see a tree branch knocking against the tired siding.

It's the demon goat.

Bleeeeeaaat. He's looking up at me. Goddamned thing knew I was in the bathroom. "You following me, you little psycho? I'm gonna eat you one of these days."

Bleeeeeaaaaat. Mangala's creepy, horribly-not-right rectangular-pupil eyes stare up at me. He's frothing at the mouth, a clump of weeds dripping with slobber hanging out his bearded jaw. Oh my God, maybe he's rabid. That would explain a lot.

I look back at the open drawer. Goats eat everything, right? Do they like codeine?

We're about to find out.

I throw one pill. Beans him right between the eyes. He bleats and the half-masticated blob of green plops to the ground. He eats the pill.

"No way … this is too easy."

I throw another one. Eats it. The prescription says 300/30—the ratio of Tylenol to codeine. How much codeine will take down a goat? Considering Mangala ate not one but two plasticized canvas tarps last winter, was hit by the mail truck, killed a coyote that wandered into the yard, was terrorized by a pack of raccoons and still lived, I should probably give him the mother lode.

Six pills later, bastard is still looking up at me like a circus lion waiting for bloody slabs of top sirloin. He snorts, and pillows of white spittle fly from his sticky goat lips. He's looking at me sideways through a devil-spawn eyeball. I shudder. Those eyes, man. God was like, let's give this beast sideways eyeballs to fuck with the humans. I don't dare give him more. I only want to knock him out so I can get to my car in one piece. I don't *really* want to kill him. Okay, maybe I do, but that makes me sound like a dick. I'm supposedly the animal lover. The girl with the WildAid and World Wildlife Fund bumper stickers. I hide the bottle in the back of the drawer, hopeful that Dad won't notice six missing pills. Okay, eight. I took two for later. For me.

Dad's already back in his study, unspooling wire around neon puffs of dyed yarn. "I'm gonna head out."

"Hey, thanks for coming out. I'm sorry about Keith …"

"Nah. Don't be."

"You have a fantastic time up at that resort. Email me if you can. No—wait—don't. Unplug. Just have some time to yourself."

"Love you, Dad." Smooch for the road.

"Okay, maybe one email or text so I know you've arrived all right."

"Will do."

"Love you, Hollie. You're my favorite daughter."

"I'm your only daughter," I sing over my shoulder, closing his study door behind me. Technically, biologically speaking, that's the truth. I will never let him forget it.

Sitting atop my box of childhood treasures is a box of cupcakes. Confounded cupcakes hell-bent on reminding me of my suckage quotient. I don't want to admit that Moonstar's cupcakes are anything other than poop-flavored fat makers. She's—I don't even know what Moonstar is to me. She's a kid some friend of Aurora's dumped on her doorstep when the girl—birth name, Tanya—was eleven. After a few years of living with Aurora, she got mad because Aurora was going to marry my dad so she packed up and moved into a commune, had a baby at fifteen, gave the baby up for adoption, went back to school, got her MBA by twenty, and now runs a successful, international all-organic cupcake business. She's a millionaire several times over and looks like Hippie Barbie. I pretty much hate her.

And my father nags me about seeing her. "You guys are the closest thing the other has to a sister." Which is exactly why we hate each other. Not even the flaxen hair and sun-kissed, lightly freckled face and perfect little tight organic body can make up for the fact that her soul is silicone fake.

I'll leave the cupcakes on Mrs. Hubert's doorstep. She can feed them to her rotting cat or throw them at the paperboy.

As I step onto the porch, the rotting wood creaks under my feet. *Shit. Goat.*

I listen for the bell. Make my way down the four sagging steps. Listen again. Nothing but birds.

"Mangala ... where are you, buddy?"

No response. No tinkle of his bell, no bleat from his septic maw.

The codeine worked. I pull my keys out, just in case. The box isn't heavy but it definitely precludes my view in front of me.

Which is exactly what that calculating little soul-slurper was banking on.

I scream loudly, but to no avail. I can't get the gate to latch, so he chases me around the car. My parcels slide across the trunk lid, cupcakes flying and splatting open on the driveway. I launch myself onto the hood on the next spin around. But not quite in time.

His evil horns tear into denim. I'd scream for my dad, but it won't help. I'm on my own here. Just me and the demon goat.

Shit. "You little prick! These are my favorite jeans!"

I don't dare move. Damn bastard might try to finish me off.

Except he's distracted by the fluffy goodness dotting the driveway. He digs in, paper wrappers and all, the pink and yellow plumes of frosting—which, for the record, look amazing—smearing his muzzle and manky goat beard.

Wishing right about now that I had a sunroof so I could squeeze into the car and run over the wretched beast. Mangala looks up at me, his mouth chewing way too fast for a creature with many milligrams of codeine on board.

"Next time I'm giving you the whole bottle, you asshole."

Bleeeeeeaaaaat.

Chapter Eight
Revelation Cove

In the cab to the train station, I feel nauseated.

It's just nerves. Nervous nerves. Because I'm leaving everything that I'm used to and standing on my own two feet and no one is holding my hand or mumbling in my ear. Everyone else in the City of Roses is going about their lives and doing their Monday morning things ... I, however, am playing hooky. Two fingers down my throat when Polyester Patty was on the line, and voila. "Take a few days off. Could be contagious." I thank my sensitive gag reflex for delivering me unto another sin.

Tucked into my suitcase is some sexy lingerie and a new razor and body lotion that smells like summer, just in case. Perhaps Revelation Cove will reveal her secrets to me in the form of some newly single stud and he'll want to do more than talk about pressure dressings and why the new defibrillator batteries aren't up to snuff.

Keith texted last night about his shoes, so I filled a box and slid it onto the porch. He said he'd come for the TV on Wednesday when Mushroom Cap Joe could help him. I didn't bother to tell him I'd be gone, basking in otters and hot springs.

And I don't want to talk to or see him right now. My resolve is about as firm as a saltine cracker soaked in filmy chicken soup.

In a fit of panic at 2 a.m., I reread the resort's confirmation email. Something about a forty-eight-hour cancellation policy to avoid the nonrefundable charge equal to one night's lodging plus tax. Not enough hours left to cancel. As such, I'm stuck. That kind of stuck you get when you stick your head in between the bars at the zoo to get a better look at the lion but then the lion sees you and starts to pace on the other side of the enclosure and the only thing that's keeping him from eating you is the murky green pool that he can't quite leap across and the zookeepers are pouring oil on your head to try to get it unstuck from between the bars and everyone's talking behind their hands about how dumb you are and that you deserve to be eaten by the lion.

I should've emailed Concierge Ryan to make sure there are no lions.

Ridiculous. British Columbia doesn't have lions.

Do they?

I love taking the train. This one even smells nice, thanks to the fact that the dining room is just one car down. And I'd like to smooch Steve Jobs for the greatest invention this world has seen in the last one hundred years, besides antibiotics and PEZ: the iPod. I can drown out the world with audiobooks and music and podcasts. I can catch up on my monumental reading list, learn how to better market my nonexistent business, listen to the music I prefer instead of Keith's brain-melting detritus.

Thank you, Steve Jobs, for fueling these budding antisocial tendencies. My burgeoning crazy thanks you.

Three hours later, the cab ride from the King Street Amtrak station to Pier 69 where the Victoria Clipper boards is short but eventful. Like, pretty sure the driver was pretending we were in Baghdad, or maybe Boston. No seatbelts, vinyl seats I could not bring myself to look at after that first unfortunate glance. I might have stuffed the train's complimentary newspaper under my ass to prevent the transfer of communicable disease. Half a bottle of Purell later, I feel secure enough to present the Clipper ticket agent my credit card without worrying I will transfer microscopic pathogens to my wallet or onto her unsuspecting hands.

That's how the next plague is going to start. With unwashed, germ-slathered hands. It'll thin the herd. A lot.

When the giant catamaran motors out of Seattle toward Victoria, British Columbia, I am humbled by the power of such a big vessel. The whole concept of a boat this big skimming the surface of Puget Sound as if doing nothing more than giving it a wet kiss. Rainbows shimmer in the spray under a half-clouded sky, Mr. Golden Sun squeezing through stubborn puffs of gray and white to remind us that spring has sprung and he's doing everything in his power to make sure flowers bloom and bees buzz. I forgo the iPod for the duration of the trip, instead sitting outside in the chilly May afternoon on the water, the ferry's dull roar lulling my eardrums into a comfortable deafness, watching port towns and vast mountains covered in the planet's lushest greens appear and disappear along the water's edge.

This is gorgeous country. I am so lucky to live so close to such beauty.

We dock, and the excitement of being in another country sets in. Passport stamped, a "Welcome to Canada" grumbled out by someone who didn't really look like they meant it, which sort of spoils the moment because I thought all Canadians were supposed to be super nice. Plus, no one handed me a beaver or a moose or a flask of maple syrup. I thought that was part of the deal. Americans, when you go to Victoria, British Columbia, they don't give you syrup. You have to buy it in the gift shop next to the docks. And there are no red-coated, stud Mounties waiting for you, either. I thought there would be hunky Mounties waiting for me. I'd totally volunteer for a pat-down if it came to that. "What, me, smuggle cocaine? You'll have to search for it, you big brute."

Maybe not from the angry-looking woman with the very tight ponytail and paramilitary gear standing by the door.

I'm cutting it close. The email from Revelation Cove said my floatplane will be loading at the docks near the Victoria Inner Harbour Airport, across the way. Wharf Street. I can find this. Standing outside the Clipper office, a brisk breeze skips through about a minute apart. Like the sky is having contractions. Let's just hope the clouds' water doesn't break and let loose all over the busy sidewalks.

The sky isn't pregnant, Hollie. No one needs you to count them through the contractions until the ambulance arrives.

Again with the nerves. Especially now that I see those little tiny planes bobbing on the surface of the water. Without concrete under them. Just water.

So much water.

We'll be taking off—and landing—on nothing solid, on a surface that could just as soon swallow me whole, floatplane and all, than let me roost atop. Do we wear lifejackets? In case of a water landing? Because I'm pretty sure a water landing is absolutely part of this deal. Not like a big commercial jet where a water landing is *bad*. I'm willingly submitting to a water landing.

This flies in the face of all things sane. Pun intended.

Maybe this wasn't such a good idea.

Time for contemplation is over. I'm committed. I have to be Brave Hollie. "There could be otters, Hol. And cute boys. Get thee to the plane." I hope no one hears me whispering to myself or I might find out if the security guards in Canada's mental health facilities look as stern as the gruff Customs woman.

I hustle off the Clipper dock and move toward where I see floatplanes loading passengers and parcels. This won't be so bad. The planes look big enough. I count the windows alongside one: six. That means, what, twelve passengers? Looks safe. It's *got* to be safe. How many floatplane accidents have made the news lately? I'm tempted to Google it, but I don't know what the roaming charges will be on my phone, and as we all know, I'm on a self-induced budget.

Pretty planes. So pretty planes. Nice planes.

I feel like I'm talking down a pissed-off Doberman with a rubber band around his balls and a Cone of Shame around his neck. *Nice planes, niiiiice planes.*

People are boarding that one over there, a shiny white one with solid-enough-looking wings and sturdy pontoons and lovely green and blue stripes. Those folks look confident; the pilot looks fetching in his pilot-y getup. I have nothing to worry about.

I'm looking for the Revelation Cove supply flight, so I'm not to go through the regular airport check-in. The concierge emailed me the option of an extra night's stay or a complete spa treatment for agreeing to take the supply flight. Means they have space for another guest on their regular flight. The email also instructed that I'm to look for a cart full of stuff on the docks with my name taped to the side.

Like that cart full of stuff over there with a piece of cardboard taped to it that says "Hollie Porter."

I'm here.

And that floating air-slash-water vessel, the one where the rather tall, burly, bearded man in a beat-up red sports jersey is loading stuff into a very small, was-once-probably-red plane, is not like the pretty white and blue and green planes over there with the guy who looks like a real pilot.

Maybe this guy isn't the pilot. Maybe he's just a hired grunt loading what looks like the spoils of a Costco run.

"Excuse me," I say. Not loud enough. His head and upper body are still buried into the plane's rib cage. I try again. "'Scuse me."

The man extracts himself. Piercing greenish eyes. Very thick beard. A nose that looks like it met with a baseball bat one too many times. Total mountain man. "Hey, hi. Are you Hollie Porter?"

"I am. Is this the ... plane ... to Revelation Cove? Wait—duh— of course it is. You knew my name."

"Ryan," he says, thrusting forth a wide, calloused hand. "We talked the other night on the phone."

"Right, yeah. Cool." He's got something in his beard. Not sure if I should tell him.

"You're more sober today," he says, a smile broadening across his face. My cheeks combust.

"Yeah, I figured making my way through Customs trashed was probably a bad idea."

"Wise. They're prone to body cavity searches when things are slow." He hoists a giant bag of flour over this shoulder. "I just have to finish loading these things and we'll be off. Do you want to grab something to eat or use the washroom?"

"Washroom?"

"The toilet."

"Oh. No, I'm good." The plane wobbles a little as he tosses his monster-sized groceries into the rear. "Um, you've got … something … here." I point to my chin. He wipes a hand over his bristly mass.

"Gross. Ah, lettuce. Thanks." He flicks the offending shred into the water. "Way to make an impression, hey?"

"Happens to me all the time." I didn't want to make him feel awkward, but I knew I'd be staring at it the whole trip. Like when someone has a pimple that needs attention. You can't help but look. "So, uh, where's the pilot?"

Ryan stands straight, smiling again. Teeth unnaturally perfect and very white against the dark of his beard. His curly hair makes him taller than he is. I'll have to look up at him if I stand too close. And the shoulders are broad. His red jersey has a tear in the shoulder and the front is smeared with something black. Oh God, maybe it's engine grease. Maybe the plane has mechanical problems. Maybe the grease on his jersey is a sign.

And he's too big to be the pilot. How the hell is he going to fit inside that plane?

"Ryan Fielding, Revelation Cove concierge and pilot, at your service." He bows, an arm folded across his midsection.

"*You* are the pilot?"

"Don't I look qualified?"

I look over my shoulder at the other fellow in the dress blues with the wings pinned above his breast pocket. No, Concierge Ryan, you do not looked qualified to be the pilot.

I lie. "Yeah, okay."

"Ever been in a floatplane?"

"No."

"You'll love it." He loads the last item from the cart and reaches for my bag. "This the only one you brought?" I nod yes. "Good. Not a lot of space left here. Don't want to risk overloading Miss Lily." What happens if you overload it? Will she crash?

Are we going to crash? Did I pack too much lingerie?

He slams the flimsy cargo door closed. And then again when it pops open. And a third time. The fourth time he messes with it, it remains closed.

And my stomach is in my feet. This cannot be safe to fly in. He can't even get the door to stay closed.

"Don't worry about that," he says, gesturing to the now-latched door. "Miss Lily's very reliable. Even if she's not as pretty as her cousins, right, Lil?" He pats the top of the plane's wings.

"Right. Okay," I squeak. "How long is the flight?" Gulp.

"Little over an hour, depending on the winds. We'll get there just in time for a late dinner. You hungry?"

The roiling in my stomach has less to do with hunger than abject terror. "We'll see."

"You're nervous." He rests a hand on Miss Lily, bouncing lightly against the dock. Twilight is imminent—clouds along the mountainous horizon glow orange and pink. Oh my God, we're going to be flying—and landing—in the dark. "This old girl will treat you right. But you should know—these smaller planes aren't like the big jets. If there's turbulence, you'll feel it a little more."

"You can land in the dark?"

"I think so." He creases his brow, looks at the sky. Then laughs. "Yeah, I can land in the dark. I promise I won't let you down."

My legs are the consistency of Jell-O. I'm not a great flyer to begin with, but I clearly didn't think this through. Concierge Ryan chuckles at me and opens the cockpit door. If you can call that a cockpit. He kneels inside the aircraft, shuffles through a zippered bag, and stands tall again, offering a token in his outstretched hand.

A sample-sized liquor bottle is dwarfed in his palm. "Cheap but effective. Drink up. Our complimentary in-flight refreshment."

"I hope you have more where this came from."

"Is Hollie Porter a lush?"

"Is Concierge Ryan really gonna judge when he's asking me to get on an airplane that is likely held together with duct tape under that peeling paint?"

"No duct tape. I swear it." He holds crossed fingers over his heart. That smile again. Some dentist has made a fortune off those teeth.

Ryan snickers and helps me across his seat into my own. The passenger space is no bigger than the front seat of a pickup truck, except the dashboard, embossed with *De Havilland,* is awash in dials and gadgets and gauges and handles. So many. God, please tell me these mean something to Concierge Ryan. The propeller is motionless at the front, alarmingly close to where our bodies are sitting. Well, except for that engine between us. Just like a car. The windshield stretches to the sides of the aircraft, windows on each door larger than they look from the outside. I can see the water everywhere. There is no escaping the fact that I am on the friggin' water. In an airplane.

Ryan climbs in and slams his own door. It takes two good slams. This does not settle my nerves. He hands me a headset with a spongy microphone stretching across the front.

"So we can talk to each other," the earphone says. Wow. This is like being on a spaceship. Or what I might assume is a spaceship, you know, with the headsets and the mics and the scratchy, radio voices. "You ready? I'd like to get going before the orca start hovering around our landing spot."

"Wait—what does that mean?"

"Our local pod knows that we bring in fresh meat from the mainland in the form of tourists. If someone misbehaves or doesn't appreciate our in-flight hospitality, we let the orcas have first pick."

"That's totally not funny."

Ryan's laughing. "Little bit funny."

"Have you ever … landed on any sea life?"

"Nope. See, that's one of the things about being a pilot. They make you practice a lot. The metal bits, they don't taste very good. The sharks and orca, they're not interested."

"Sharks? There aren't any sharks up here."

"Sure there are. More than twenty species call the BC waters home. And sometimes we get makos, oceanic whitetips, even great whites."

I twist the lid off the whisky and swallow it in one long pull.

"Like I said, there better be more where this came from."

Between the seat sits an open duffel bag with an assortment of fun things: little white bags I'm guessing serve as barf receptacles, a tub of HandiWipes, and a bootlegger's bounty of those little liquor bottles.

I'll be fine. As long as I pace myself. I hope the mic doesn't impede my drinking.

The engine sputters to life, the propeller soon a blur that looks like it's only spinning around a few times. My eighth grade math teacher explained to us oh so many moons ago that spinning things look like they're standing still because the human eye can't capture each individual revolution. I soothe my spastic stomach by reminding myself that the propeller is going really fast. It just doesn't look like it.

Concierge Ryan maneuvers us away from the docks, waving at a few of his pilot buddies, and we glide into an open space. I guess this is the runway. Made of water. Kinda bumpy. So far, it feels more like a boat than a plane. I can do this.

A little farther away from the docks, the harbor opens up and the engine whines louder. Ryan explains something about thrust. I don't want to know. Just get me where we need to be without making me die.

I reach into the duffel between the seats. I don't even look to see what bottle I pluck from the cornucopia. Twist the lid, swallow the contents. Shit, tequila. That burns.

Speaking of burns, my nipples are better. In case you were wondering. They're not even peeling. Yet.

"Here we go," Ryan crackles in my ear. That thrust thing he was talking about, it's happening. I can feel the G forces against my chest as the plane picks up speed, skimming the surface of the not-placid water. Hey, Mother Nature, no wind right now, yeah? "Say goodbye to our fair capitol!"

The plane is no longer touching the surface of the water.

We're up.

Holy shit, we're flying.

And every bump and buffet of wind? Yeah. We're feeling it. This is going to be a long hour. I might need another drink.

My hand in the booze bag, Concierge Ryan smiles. "What's funny?" I ask.

"You might want to hold off. Just in case it gets bumpy. I have a strict no-barfing policy on board Miss Lily."

"What are the little white bags for, then?"

"In case we crash and need to collect clams to feed ourselves until we're rescued."

I let go of the unnamed bottle. I think he's kidding about the clams, but maybe he's right about the liquor. We're eight minutes into this journey. I'm already feeling the effects of those two other tiny shots. Such a lightweight. Or maybe it's because alcohol from two nights ago is still likely an appreciable component of my blood chemistry.

"So, Hollie Porter, are things better than they were the other night?"

I try—and fail—to remember what I told him. "I think so. I'm hoping this little vacay will set some things straight for me."

"I hear that. Sometimes getting away from the mad dash we call life is just what we need." He fusses with a couple of dials. Makes minor adjustments to the lever thingies on the dash. Reports something into his radio in response to someone else talking to him. "You said on the phone that you like otters?"

"Yeah. I do. Did I really tell you that?"

"You told me all kinds of stuff." He keeps eyes forward, but the grin on his face makes me realize my lips were loose. Ridley should've pried the phone from my cold, drunk hands. "I see you left the stethoscope-loving, knight in dented armor behind."

"God, I did talk a lot." I fiddle with my mic stretched in front of my face. "Um, yeah. We broke up. Two years together. It wasn't working out. I think we both knew it. I was just the one to say something first."

"I get that."

I don't know this man well enough to be having this conversation. "So, have you always been a concierge and a pilot? How does a person even get into this line of work?"

"Nah, this is my second career. But I've been flying planes for a long time. Sort of a love of mine. And once you see the resort, you'll know why this is such a killer job."

"Yeah?"

"Yup. Did you check out our website?"

"The pictures were great."

"That's nothing compared to real life. I think you'll have a fantastic time. If a change of pace is what you need, you'll find it."

A strong gust bumps into us, like a plump cloud has thrown her hip into the side of the plane. I have nothing else to grab onto except Ryan's denim-clad leg.

"You have to at least buy me dinner first," he teases. I release. It was instinct. Like when you stop fast in your car and you throw your arm up in front of the passenger. Your arm will do shit to stop the other person's forward momentum or save their brains from splattering against the inside of the windshield, but the arm throws itself up there in good faith.

"Sorry."

"No worries. Told you we'd feel the wind a little more. I promise you're safe. And with a sunset like that, how can you worry?"

He's right. The sun is skinny-dipping into the ocean now. It's so clear from this height. Like one of those mass-produced paintings all the kids do in first-year art college of the sun's fading light dancing across a shimmering body of water. Totally right here. I'd take a picture but my shitty phone won't do it justice. Plus I'm terrified to move.

"I hope we can find you some otters. If you're lucky, we might even see some orca. They pass through once in a while. And no, they don't really eat tourists."

"If you could get one of them to give me a ride on his dorsal fin, I'd be totally impressed."

"Sounds like you watch too many movies," he laughs. "We have a couple of small islands around our main island, and then if you go up and across the inlet where it meets the mainland, we've got every kind of wildlife you can imagine."

"Isn't that dangerous?"

"Nah, not if you're safe. We don't advise people to go up there without bear spray or at least a set of bells to scare off the critters, but the bears and cougar have little interest in people. They're still afraid of us, which is good. Not like in Vancouver where the bears try to share neighborhoods with people. That never ends well."

"Are you from British Columbia?"

"Nope. Michigan."

"You're American?" I say, surprised.

"Don't tell anyone. I have a rep to protect."

"What, they don't like Americans up here?"

"They like everyone who brings in tourist dollars." Ryan mumbles something else into his headset. Makes more adjustments. We're going a little higher. As the shine on the ocean fades, the thick blanket of nightfall drapes itself over the tree-dressed mountains. The deep green is fading into deeper shades of blue, hedging on blackness. I can't imagine being lost out here in the dark. It would be hard to see a hand in front of my face, let alone a predator hungry for a free meal.

"I've been in Canada off and on for nine years, so I'm pretty Canadian," he says.

"How long have you been at the resort?"

"Since it opened. Almost five years now."

"Nice. I think it would be awesome to live someplace so beautiful. But don't you get lonely being so far from civilization?"

"Only occasionally. I'm in Victoria often enough that I catch up with my buddies. Plus, with technology what it is, we're never really that out of touch with anyone, are we?"

"You married?" He holds his left hand aloft to show an unadorned fourth finger.

"Guess that makes us like twins, eh, Hollie Porter?"

I blush again. "Man, I really did talk a lot the other night, didn't I ..."

"It's okay. Your secret's safe with me."

His phone rings. When he answers, I want to tell him that he's not supposed to drive and talk, but are the rules different in airplanes? As long as he keeps one hand on that funny steering wheel, I'll be fine.

But it's really, *really* dark out here now. It's amazing how dark things are without the city lights to soak into the sky. Every few miles, a tiny spot of light will push its way through the void from a cabin or outpost along the shore. Compact wooden docks tether bobbing boats, their white sides just visible in the rising moon. Sometimes the little houses will have a floatplane out front, and as expected, no cars. I'm sure it smells fresh, fresher than anything I've ever experienced as a city slicker. Fresh like summer camp, with its trees and campfires and wet earthen walkways packed flat with dead pine needles ... but better. Do I dare ease down the window next to me? Not on your life. It's fine, sealed up tight the way it should be. I'll wait to smell the goodness once we're again on terra firma.

And that's when it happens.

My fucking door opens up and slaps against the side of the plane. I scream. Loudly. Pretty sure Ryan's eardrum is going to need a Band-Aid.

"Hollie! It's okay! It's okay. You're belted in. Just sit back ..." Ryan leans across me and tries to reach the handle for the bouncing door. He sits straight again. "Can you grab it? Just grab it and give it a solid tug."

"What? No! Jesus Christ! I am not leaning outside the plane to shut the damn door!"

"Listen to me—you're not going to fall out." He rests a giant hand on mine where it digs into the side of the seat. "Just reach over ... grab it ... then I'll give it the slam to shut it all the way."

I stare at him, eyes wide, asking *are you fucking kidding me*, but he's not. His return look is assured, confident. He's telling me it will be okay.

I close my left eye, peeking only with the right as I angle toward the bouncing, flimsy door. The seatbelt restrains me, cinching when I move too far forward. *You'll be okay, Brave Hollie. You can do this.*

As soon as I have the door in the almost-closed position, Ryan leans hard over my lap and reefs on it.

God, he smells good.

Shut up. Keep it together.

The door clicks. "Thank you," I whisper.

"See? Piece of cake. And you didn't fall out."

"If I'd known the supply flight was a stare-down with death, I might have taken the regular charter."

"Nah, this is way more fun. And this time of year, we're getting a lot of older folks coming up, so the charter ends up smelling like old-lady perfume. Plus, no drinkie-poos." He reaches into the duffel and offers me a bottle. "You earned it."

I don't hesitate. My heart thuds hard enough against the inside of my chest from this latest near-death experience. I *do* deserve it.

But I was so brave, wasn't I? Leaning out of an airplane to shut the door?

I feel strong again. Like I did when I told Keith and the Yorkies to pack it up.

I suppose I should be feeling some sort of sadness about my loss of that relationship. Do I?

I don't think I do.

Except for the rapid inhale/exhale going on in my chest. The twinkly stars in my peripheral vision. Ryan hands me one of those paper bags. "Breathe in and out. No hyperventilating on Miss Lily."

"You have … a lot … of stupid rules … on this plane." I breathe into the bag, and while I know this is a myth—rebreathing your exhaled air does not remedy hyperventilation—I need to calm my shit down.

"Tell me about your otters."

"Um, they're cute." Inhale. "And fluffy." Exhale.

"And?"

"And they take care of their babies."

"And?"

"And I don't know … I saw one when I was at the beach when I was little, and I fell in love."

"And?"

"And the older they get, the blonder the hair on their head is."

"Now that's interesting stuff."

His strategy worked. I'm not hungry for air anymore. I can breathe again.

"I do hope we can find you some otters while you're here. Things should be pretty quiet. A business conference this week wrapping up with a small golf tournament. Do you golf?"

"The planet has asked me not to. I do too much damage to the greens. And the trees. They weep for days after I've manhandled a nine-iron."

"You can take a lesson. Or maybe a kayak class? You can kayak between our island and the next one over. Do you swim?"

"How cold is that water?"

"Like, from a glacier."

"Then, no. I don't swim."

Ryan laughs at me again. "You don't sound very outdoorsy for someone who likes otters."

"I don't like freezing my nips off, either." As soon as the words are out of my mouth, I regret it. I've totally just opened up the can of worms for him to dig in and bait up.

"Speaking of … how are the girls?" He gestures to his chest. "All healed from the nachos?"

"Shit, I can't believe I told you that." My turn to laugh. "Yeah … they're fine, Concierge Ryan. My nipples will live to see another day."

"The single men of the world are grateful."

I can't even look at him but then I do and we start laughing and yes my nipples were singed but I survived and now a total stranger knows my weirdest secret and I really need to talk less openly with people I've never met in real life.

"See that up there?"

I sit a little straighter, trying to make myself taller than the plane's dash. Up ahead are lights. Lots of them. "That's where we're going?"

He nods and shuts off his mic to me so he can communicate with the other voice in his ear. We pass over the resort and circle back, so I'm given a 360 view of the resort and surrounding island. It's far bigger than I expected, a full eighteen-hole golf course along the western side, the greens lit by lanterns that sparkle in the distance. The lodge itself is huge, not at all a wee, quaint little lodge with a dozen or so cozy rooms. This is full-on luxury. I count four chimneys extending from various pitches of the roof, and lights from inside blaze through the expansive windows, lighting the walkways and paths and endless porches around the periphery. A dock extends off the eastern side, tethered small boats and canoes, stacks of kayaks, and the proper charter plane—obviously Miss Lily's bigger and younger sister.

The mic clicks on in my ear again. "We're going to circle back and come in along the eastern side, along those docks."

I give him a thumbs up.

"It's like landing on a runway at first. A bit bumpy, but then smooth under the pontoons. It's still gonna be a little wobbly until we slow down. You ready?"

"As I'll ever be!"

"Welcome to Revelation Cove, Hollie Porter."

CHAPTER NINE
TABLECLOTH IS MY BEST COLOR

Wobbly, my ass. I clenched so hard around that door handle, afraid it would fly open again, my knuckles froze in the four minutes it took us to actually coast to a stop. The mic was on during the descent, and Concierge Ryan talked me down, but *still* ... wow. Maybe I should see about taking a boat back to Victoria when this adventure is over.

Ryan repeats the process at takeoff in reverse. Once he's out and the plane is tethered, only then do I dare move. My ass is asleep. I try to look sturdy and completely in control when I step first onto the pontoon, black water licking the sides like fingers from hell reaching for my ankles, and onto the dock.

"Do you need help carrying this stuff?"

"This? Nah, you're a guest. Don't you worry. What you need is to get checked in and hop into a warm tub." I raise my eyebrows at him.

"Do you say that to all of your guests?"

"Mostly the over-sixty crowd. They're more my speed. The mature woman knows what she wants." He leads the way up the lantern-lit wooden docks toward the spectacular lodge.

"I'm not over sixty, though."

"I've made an exception for you. Considering my plane almost kicked you out midflight."

"So chivalrous, Concierge Ryan."

"Well, it is my job, being concierge and all."

He pushes open one of the massive wooden double doors that look straight off a Middle Earth movie set. Inside is everything you'd hope it to be. Not some backwoods hunting lodge, Revelation Cove's resort is full of raw wood, exposed beams, lush carpets accenting well-polished hardwood floors, modern, comfortable furniture with not a speck of flannel or cheap '90s-era faux Indian print (my dad bought a whole living room set in the dark woodsy colors. Showed every ice cream stain). The walls are adorned with art, some reflective of local natural environs, some modern. No animal heads stare at me, glassy-eyed and sad their lives were cut short. The ceilings are massive, unreachable. This main entry is like every other fancy downtown hotel, open plan, airy, inviting. The aroma of something delicious wafts through—someone's baking. Cookies? Bread? My mouth waters. Down one wall leading into undiscovered territory is a series of framed sports memorabilia. Jerseys for an undetermined sport. One looks like the red torn thing Concierge Ryan is wearing.

"You like sports?" Ryan says, nodding at the far wall. He drops my bag in front of what must be the check-in desk.

"Sure. I guess. I've been to a few Trailblazers games with my dad."

"Basketball girl, then."

"Not really. It's fun because Bob—my dad—he gets really into it. There aren't a lot of sports in Portland other than the Jailblazers."

Concierge Ryan laughs. "Harsh. I've heard about that team's reputation. Ever been to any Winterhawks games?"

"Baseball?"

His mouth drops open. "Oh, Hollie Porter, I'm not sure if you can stay here at Revelation Cove." He picks up my bag from the floor.

"What? What did I say?"

"It's hockey, little American girl. Don't let anyone around here know that you're not a hockey fan. You're in Canada, remember?"

"So your jersey—hockey?"

He holds a stretched finger to his lips. "Ssshhh. Yes. Hockey. Detroit Red Wings. Later when you're settled in, I'll show you our jersey collection and give you a primer in case someone corners you and asks about your favorite team." He leans in and lowers his voice behind his hand. "Probably best to be a Canucks fan around here. West Coast fans usually like the Canucks or one of the LA teams. I can give you a primer on the Original Six, in case one of the old-timers wants to talk Bruins or Blackhawks."

"It's all Greek to me. But I've heard of the Canucks. I can handle that."

"You should know they have goalie issues. Which is why they can't win the Stanley Cup."

"Is that bad?"

"Don't you remember the riots a few years back?"

"Yeahhhh ... I think so. We talked about it at work—everyone making jokes about the Canadians rioting. We figured they threw beer and doughnuts at each other."

"Ryan, you're back," interrupts an older woman scooting in behind the counter. "Who have you dragged in with you?"

"Miss Betty, this is Hollie Porter. She'll be staying with us for a few days."

I stretch an arm across the gleaming marble counter and shake hands with Miss Betty. Her skin is soft, the lavender of her lotion floating toward me. When she smiles, her whole face smiles, the lines deep from a good life lived. "Welcome to Revelation Cove. Let's get you checked in and on your way to relaxing and away from this brute of a man. He smells like grease."

"Hollie Porter, I look forward to seeing you soon." Ryan bows again. "You're in good hands here. Find me tomorrow and I'll give you a personalized tour of the grounds." He winks and walks away. Before he reaches the door, he turns back toward us. "Miss Betty, can you send a few of the guys down to the dock? Lil's belly is full."

Miss Betty smiles as Ryan pushes the door open with his rear and disappears into the night. She checks me in and shows me to my room, asking me about the flight, how I fared, if Ryan was well behaved.

"Perfect gentleman," I say. She smiles and slides the cardkey into the door lock. The room's interior is even more breathtaking than the website photos promised. The queen-sized bed with the rough-hewn timber headboard, a round wooden soaker hot tub on the patio, windows that look out across a green lawn and manicured beds and blossoming trees sloping down toward the blackness of the water. I can see the dock. Ryan is down there, much smaller from this far away. Three other guys, one pulling a cart not unlike the one left behind in Victoria, move down the dock and greet him, handshakes and shoulder slaps all around. Friends.

What are those like?

"Are you hungry, Miss Porter?" I'm starved, actually. "We have room service, or the dining room is open until midnight. Come on down when you're ready, or we can send something up. Whichever you prefer."

Miss Betty opens an antique armoire and places my bag inside. "We have fresh terry robes here if you decide you want to take a swim. The outdoor pool is heated year-round. It also closes at midnight. We don't allow the little ones in after 9 p.m., so you don't have to worry about getting splashed." She opens another cupboard in the bathroom next to the tub and calls out. "Fresh towels here. And if you run out, there are plenty more at the front desk. And of course, be sure to help yourself to the soaker tub. Only thing is, remember to take your cardkey. The door to the patio has a lock, so once you're out there, you'll need your cardkey to get back inside."

"Okay, thank you, Miss Betty."

"Come down to the front desk anytime and one of our staff can show you all the wonderful activities we offer. Enjoy your stay, dear." She slides out of the room, her movements no louder than the footfalls of a cloud-walking cat.

I flop onto the bed, and despite the slight minibottle buzz pulsing through my veins, I feel awake. Tired, but awake. I should order room service. I don't want to sit in the dining room and look like a dork because I'm alone. That's a hurdle I can tackle tomorrow.

I order the cheapest thing the menu offers—club sandwich on focaccia, extra pickles, sweet potato fries. The minifridge in the room has soda and more of those blasted little bottles. I crack one open. What the hell. I'm on vacation. *I'm on vacation!*

And there are no Yorkies and no stethoscopes and no possessed goats or frizzy-haired troll dolls or wide-hipped, power-hungry supervisors.

Mona and Herb would be so proud of me. I'm not rotting in the soul-sucking 911 dungeon listening to people die on the phone. I'm living. Letting it go. That's what the emergency dispatcher employee assistance liaison told us to do—when we walk out the door, we leave the sadness, the tragedy, the suffering and heartache behind us. Like a coat we check at the door.

I like the idea of leaving it all behind. In fact, looking through the gauzy curtains at the sprawling, moon-kissed mountains across the water, I don't know if I ever need to go back. If this is living, I think I might like it.

Maybe I can get a job here. I know how to answer phones. I can clean toilets and change beds. If it means I don't have to go back to an empty life ...

This is avoidance behavior. The liaison talked about this too. Some people use alcohol or drugs or even sex to avoid dealing with the skeletons prancing about in their closets. Thing is, my skeletons are dressed in feather boas and expensive heels and they won't share. Even my skeletons have more fun than me.

God, what a whiny bitch. Seriously, Hollie, there are people with real problems. Pretty sure you know that clean water will flow through the tap when you turn the spigot and no one is going to sneak in during the night to steal you as a plaything for their pillaging army.

Self-pity is a fickle cow. She makes you feel worse about feeling worse.

This calls for more spirits of the liquid variety.

The sandwich arrives quick-quick. I tip the delivery guy and chomp it down—the sandwich, not the bellhop—to soak up the wee bottles of avoidance I've sucked back. Belly full, it's time to carry on with this whole living theme and check out the soaker tub on the patio.

And in the spirit of being awesome and brave, I'm going in the buff. My old swimsuit I didn't have time to replace is baggy and gross, and it makes me itch. No one can see me, I'm sure—the patio is protected on all sides by tall potted greenery and the frosted glass railing, plus it's a mere four steps from the outer door.

I smile in the bathroom mirror while piling my hair atop my head. I feel so … dangerous. Except my teeth need whitening. Like the commercials say, I might not get a man if my teeth are yellow.

"You don't need a man, Hollie. That's what batteries are for." My reflection is talking to me. Or else I'm talking to myself. Yeah, probably that.

Tiptoe, tiptoe, out on-to the pat-i-o.

Mmmm, the water steams when I pull the lid back. I'm hunched over, one arm over the boobage in case someone actually *can* see me. With my luck, security cameras are going to pick this up. I should've asked about security cameras, but then that might have made Miss Betty nervous that I was a bad guy. She seems sweet. Maybe she's not the suspicious type.

One leg over the side. "Ohhhhh, that is delicious." Both legs in. Body submerging, inch by inch. It's hot but not too hot. The outside air goosebumps my exposed skin until I'm immersed to my chin.

I could clean toilets for a living to have this life. Although I'm guessing the staff doesn't get access to such luxuries. Then again, Concierge Ryan doesn't look like an abused resort worker, not like the folks we hear about on the news subjected to indentured servitude with endless shifts and meager pay and roach-infested, leaky cabins with bed bugs. Ryan and his very crooked nose look well fed and well adjusted, though maybe in need of a date with a razor.

I should seriously see if they're hiring. I need a calmer, death-free job. And this soaker tub. Forever.

Eyes closed, I practice reflective breathing. Concentrate on the sounds around me. A distant owl. The muffled laughs of people down the way. (Man, I hope they can't see me. Maybe I'm the reason they're laughing.) Eyes open again. Pretty sure they can't see me.

Another attempt at tub-aided meditation.

The water lapping at the sides of docked vessels. No seabirds—it's too dark. Crickets. Frogs. The whiny buzz of an early mosquito in my ear, close enough for him to try to tell me a secret before I drown him with the swipe of a hand. The slight smell of chlorine from the tub's water. Not too heady like in a swimming pool, but enough to know that creepy crawlies from prior soakers have been chemically eradicated.

I need to text my dad. Thank him times eleventy million for this great gift. My dad. What a guy. My eyes burn a little thinking about what an awesome father I have, that he gave me this present at the perfect time and now I'm here instead of sitting at home, feeling sorry for myself.

I need to do better. I need to be a better daughter and do something to make him proud, to show him that I am as amazing as he raised me to be. When he was my age and found himself strapped with a mewling infant and a vanishing wife who left nothing but a lipstick-smeared note written on a cigarette pack, "Sorry, I can't do it. You'll be great," with no phone number or forwarding address, he didn't cave. He dropped out of medical school and reenrolled in nursing courses. During a time when men were laughed at for becoming nurses. But he knew he could rely on good pay. Good benefits. Good retirement.

A good life for his motherless daughter.

This is why I suck at meditation. I have the attention span of a flea that forgot to take his ADHD meds.

I soak until my fingertips are pruned and my nails are bendy. Dummy me, in my excitement to hop naked as a babe into the tub, I failed to grab a towel. It's okay. I'm a woman of action. I'll jump out and run into the bathroom for a quick shower to scrub my hair of its travel grime.

One. Two. Three!

"Shit! Cold!"

I twist the doorknob. It's locked. *It's locked.*

In that moment, the warmth of panic settles into my stomach, Miss Betty's kind warning replaying in my ears: "Remember to take your cardkey. The door to the patio has a lock."

Oh my God, no way. No bleeding way. I'm out on the patio. Naked. No towel. No fluffy white complimentary bathrobe plucked from the antique armoire. No cell phone.

No cardkey.

To prevent hypothermia while I work this out, I splash back into the tub to consider my options. I'm on the second floor, so I can't exactly jump. I don't want to scream for help because it has to be pushing 11 p.m. The lanterns along the docks and pathways out front are dimmed. A quiet hush is settling over the place. Folks are turning in, their warm, cozy beds swallowing them in pillowy, down goodness. Those same people have clothes.

Whereas I have none.

Because I'm a goddamned genius.

I stand on the shelf inside the tub, hands squished across my boobs, squeeze in between the tall plants, and stretch over to see how far it is to the ground.

Too far to jump without breaking something important. Break a bone, end of vacation. Wouldn't that be the irony to end all ironies if Concierge Ryan and Miss Betty had to call for medical help to have my naked, broken body transported back to civilization?

No. No jumping.

A vined trellis extends up the side of the building, stretching from the patio below all the way up. Must be four floors here. I could climb down the trellis. Those vines don't look thorny. It's dark enough, I might be able to sneak past unnoticed, dash around to the front, and maybe … somehow … find some clothes.

I soak for another ten minutes. I am ridiculously pruny now. I don't know if the folds in my fingertips and the pads of my toes will ever flatten.

I have to act. Before they lock the front door and I'm super screwed.

Now or never, Hollie.

Out of the tub, slowly, slowly. Oh dear baby Jesus, it's cold. I swear I see snow until I realize they're billowing cherry blossoms from a nearby tree. It feels cold enough to snow.

I don't have time to think about if there are spiders or other multilegged, antennaed friends hiding inside the trellis. I give it a solid tug, a tight shake to see if it will support my weight. Seems sturdy enough.

God, if anyone's down below, they're going to see parts of my body only my gynecologist should see. One rung at a time, toward the ground. It should only take a few steps to be close enough to jump. Please don't let there be guests on the ground floor enjoying their soaker tubs too. *Please.*

The ivy is pokey. Not like thorns, but still pokey. I'll have splinters to withdraw. And me without my jump kit.

I'm down. Onto the grass. I hunch into a ball, as if tightening like a turtle will make me invisible. When we were kids, we thought if we squeezed our eyes shut and rolled our bodies like roly-polies, no one could see us. I now know that this is untrue.

Eyes must remain open. I have to find a way to move past these patios, up the sidewalk, through what I hope are unlocked doors, and pray that Miss Betty is still at the front desk.

Tick tock, Hollie. Ain't gettin' any younger over here.

I am the wind, dashing past potential onlookers, up the sidewalk, on the balls of my pruned feet, freezing pavement under me, an unforgiving breeze patting my buns. God, I hope they're not jiggling as I run. I should really re-up that gym membership.

Front doors—unlocked! Open quietly. Poke head in. It's quiet. Lights are still on and distant voices float down the hallway—people laughing—but not close enough to pose an immediate threat. I throw myself inside and fly behind the check-in counter, praying Miss Betty will find me first, or better yet, there'll be a warm, fresh stack of towels hiding behind on a shelf.

On hands and knees, I scuttle along the length of the counter. No towels. Not even a box of Kleenex.

"Excuse me," a man's voice says from above. I flatten against the desk. I consider pushing the garbage can out of the way and crawling into its cubby, but then the person would know I'm there and oh my *God*, he might come around the counter. "Is someone there?"

"No. I … I don't work here." Maybe he could get me a towel.

"Can you get someone who does?"

"Sure. I can send someone." As soon as I find some clothes. "Where shall I have them find you?"

"I work here. What can I do for you?"

No. This is not happening. Concierge Ryan's voice is approaching from the right. And I am still naked as a newborn, ass blowing in the breeze, freezing nipples on full salute.

"Someone's back there," the other voice says.

"Stay where you are!" I shout. "Nobody move!" Ryan does not oblige. He moves around the side of the check-in desk, where he can now see me.

"Hollie Porter?" he says. "Are you … naked?" My hands are just not big enough to cover all the parts. I'm squished as tight as I can against my bent legs but this floor is super cold under my … yeah. That.

"I need a towel. Or a bathrobe." I look up. A very handsome, tall, blond man is looking down at me. Smiling. Widely. "Seriously! Both of you stop looking at me!" I yell. "I got locked out. I forgot that the patio door locks and I didn't take my cardkey."

"And you didn't think to take a robe out there with you?" Ryan smiles.

"No, *Ryan*, I did not. Now are you going to get me something to cover up with or what?"

"I don't know. I'll have to go find something."

The guy standing over the top of the counter is laughing. "Aw, get the poor girl something to cover. She looks cold."

I look down to make sure he can't see my nipples.

"I'll be right with you, Ms. Porter. This gentleman asked for help first," Ryan says.

"No, I'm okay. We just were wondering if we could get some ice. That's all," Mr. Handsome Blond Man says.

"Sure, sure, I'll bring some in right away. Hollie, do you need ice too?"

"Very funny."

"Good luck, Lady Godiva," the resort guest says, the sound of his feet tapping away from the counter.

"Now, what did you say you needed again?"

"Ryan whatever-your-name-is, if you don't get me a towel or something to cover up this instant, I will tell every travel review site in the world that your hotel is infested with bed bugs and seedy lowlifes."

"Really? You'd do that? That's sorta mean, even for you."

"Please … help me. I'm freezing here."

"I can tell." I look down again. My boobs are covered. He points to my exposed arms and legs. "You have goosebumps."

"All the more reason to help me."

"I'll get you a towel. Hang on," he says, shuffling away.

Nine minutes later—and I know because there is a clock above the check-in desk—he comes back. With a hand towel.

"That's the best you could do?"

"I still have a party going on in that room. I had to get their ice. I grabbed that on my way through the kitchen."

"This won't cover anything."

"It will cover the front. Just walk along the wall," he says, that smile still solid on his hairy mug. He maneuvers above me, fiddling with something on the counter.

"Don't you dare look down or I'll tell your boss."

"You're pretty brave throwing all these idle threats around when you're the naked one needing *my* help."

"What are you doing?"

He reaches a hand toward me, eyes averted. "Making you a new cardkey."

"Oh." I take it. "Thanks."

"I'm going to walk away now so you can escape. Access to the stairs is the second door on the left. Don't s'pose you want to take the elevator. Cameras and all. Can you remember that?"

"I'm cold, not mentally deficient."

"And not at all a smart-ass," he says. "Have a good night, Hollie Porter. Find me tomorrow when you're … dressed."

I wait for him to leave, sitting quietly, hoping that the lobby will remain quiet and unoccupied long enough for me to sneak out. If I keep my backside against the wall, the towel is just long enough to cover the other stuff.

On tiptoes, I slink toward the hall. Open the door. The one that leads to the stairwell.

Only it's not the correct door. Instead, I've opened the one that leads into a meeting room, filled with drunken businessmen, one among their party on the small stage, microphone in hand. Upon my entry, everyone freezes. Mic feedback screeches through the silence.

"Sorry. Uh, wrong room."

Mr. Handsome Blond Man is sitting at the table closest to the door. His face erupts into a heart-melting smile. Within a few seconds, there are many smiles. On way too many male faces.

As if planned all along, I run at the table and do my best yank-the-tablecloth routine. But as I'm not a practiced magician or tablecloth-puller, the lovely flower arrangement and unfinished drinks and water glasses and dessert plates launch and clamor upward and outward, thankfully taking the attention off me. The tablecloth wraps around my body as I fly out of the room.

Goddammit, he said the *second* door. That was the first.

"I hate you, Concierge Ryan," I mumble upon opening door number two. The one with the little sign that says "stairs."

"Wait!" A voice behind me. He's going to want me to pay for the damage I've just caused. I don't stop moving. Up the first flight of stairs, my tablecloth gown damp from whatever I toppled in my circus act.

Cardkey in my teeth, I bolt toward the top step on the second flight. "Wait! Don't go!" he says. I stop, fully expecting it to be Concierge Ryan ready to chew me out.

"What?" I turn on him, one hand on the doorknob, the other clutched very tightly around the top of the tablecloth. It's not Ryan but Mr. Handsome Blond Man.

"That was a hell of a stunt."

"I'm very sorry. I just needed the tablecloth."

"Yeah, I knew that. It's okay."

"I'm sorry I interrupted your party."

"Are you kidding?" he laughs. "You were the highlight of the evening."

"What, in this old thing?"

"Dullest party ever. I think some of the guys were hoping you were the surprise entertainment."

"People really do that?"

"Not here. But a guy can hope," he says.

"Totally sexist."

"You're telling me if you went to a party with a bunch of your female coworkers, you wouldn't get excited if some muscled stud walked into the room pretty much naked?"

I think briefly about my coworkers. Strippers and Les? Troll Lady? Polyester Patty? I do not need to have this conversation wrapped in a tablecloth in front of a total stranger.

He moves to the landing and extends a hand. "I'm Roger."

I tuck the cardkey under my tablecloth-dress hand. "Hollie Porter."

"Yeah, I caught that earlier. From Ryan."

"He's the devil."

"Nah, he's a good guy. And a hell of a hockey player."

"How would you know?" There's no ice rink at Revelation Cove, as far as I'm aware.

"He played in the NHL for a few seasons."

"He did?"

"Yeah. Cool guy. Don't be too mad at him. He's just giving you shit."

"He brought me a *hand towel*."

"Well, you're clearly a resourceful girl. You have quite the fashion sense here," he says, gesturing to my ensemble.

"It's a gift."

"How long are you staying?"

"Four days. Maybe less, maybe more. I haven't decided yet."

"Well, it would be a great pleasure if you'd honor me with your presence at breakfast tomorrow."

"What?" *Is he asking me out? Now?* "I don't even know you."

"What do you want to know?"

"Um, enough to be certain you're not a crazed serial killer who preys on girls wrapped in tablecloths in hotel stairwells."

"I'm a boring businessman here for a conference. Tomorrow we're playing golf. I'm supposed to go back to the mainland by Friday but I might stay the weekend, that is, if I find something to keep me here."

"That's a terrible pickup line, Roger."

"I'm not good at it."

"Mm-hmm."

"Come on, Hollie, have breakfast with me. Some poached eggs, fresh salmon and bagels, Miss Betty's secret-recipe blackberry jam … I promise, that's all. If you like me and are sure I'm not going to drown you in the inlet, you can drive the golf cart tomorrow and get drunk like a proper resort bum."

I squint at him. "This is really weird."

"Why? You're adorable. You have an obvious fire about you. I'm not going to walk away and forget the last fifteen minutes haven't happened. It was too much awesome."

What harm could breakfast do? He's not asking me to marry him or have his gorgeous blond babies. "Fine. Breakfast."

"Perfect." He claps his hands together. "Say, nine? Is that too early? We can go later if you need your beauty sleep."

"I'm plenty beautiful. I don't need sleep to help me with that."

He laughs at me. "I think we're going to get along splendidly, Hollie."

"No one says 'splendidly.'"

"I think I just did. I want to impress you with my verbal prowess."

"Breakfast, then."

"I'll meet you at the front desk at nine."

"Fine."

"Looking forward to it. Thank you again for crashing our party."

"Anytime," I say, finally turning the knob and moving down the hall toward my very warm room.

After a long hot shower and a thorough brushing of my knotted hair, I cozy into the queen-sized bed and, looking at the vacant pillow next to me, wonder what Mr. Handsome Blond Man looks like when he sleeps.

Chapter Ten
Sampling Local Delights

My wardrobe choices are limited. I brought three dresses but only two that might pass for dinner apparel and enough clean everything else to get me through four days without having to do sink laundry. Something else I will have to work on now that I'm single—buy clothes that don't make me look like I've given up. No more baggy T-shirts printed with superhero logos or cartoon otters. I'll have to start shopping in the women's section again rather than raiding the men's clearance rack with the change of seasons.

I did have enough forethought to bring a summery dress with matching sweater. Still means tomorrow I'm back to a Batman T-shirt and Levi's. I don't want to make a bad impression on my breakfast date, though.

Considering I've not seen the resort in the daytime, I'm early. I want to scope it out, get a feel for the territory before I submit to breakfast with a total stranger. "What a lovely little dress," Miss Betty says. "I thought girls nowadays forgot how to wear those." When she smiles, her green eyes twinkle. No mention of my shenanigans last night. Maybe she didn't hear.

She shows me to a quaint table against the expansive floor-to-ceiling windows, through which is an unrivaled view of nature in her finery. So taken by the indescribable natural beauty before me, I am suddenly very glad that my room is on the opposite side of the building and that I did not make my naked trek past these windows. The whole resort community would've seen my parts had I sprinted past here. Seems I'm not the only person looking for an early start to the day. Across the way near the quiet fireplace sits a couple I'm pretty sure might consummate their love on the table if they run out of scrambled eggs. He wipes the corner of her mouth with his napkin; she leans over and licks jam from his lip. They entwine their arms to sip what looks like champagne. Like it's a wedding rehearsal. And judging by the rock on her left fourth finger, it probably is. Maybe even the honeymoon.

Keith and I, we were never happy, romantic saps. We met when one of his supervisors told him there was a single dirty-blond girl working in dispatch. (For the record, dirty blond is the color of my hair. I am not necessarily dirty. I shower regularly. I do watch occasional porn. Is that what he meant by dirty blond? How the hell did he find out?) Keith started hanging around dispatch. Asked me out. We moved in together four weeks later because he lost his lease when his roommate got engaged to a hot swimsuit model from Brazil. (She was smokin' hot. Even I wanted to touch her.) The rest, as they say, is history. But not the kind of history you buy albums for or write about in your journal.

I think we were just wasting time. Keeping each other warm.

That couple ... they look really *in love*. She's glowing. He's so attentive. He pours her more orange juice. She cuts his ham. They take turns talking. She looks up something on her phone, holds it for him to see. He laughs, grabs her face, and kisses her. Again. He smooths her hair when it falls over her shoulder and threatens to dangle in her hollandaise sauce. After a busser clears their table, he pulls a flower out of the tiny vase and tucks it behind her ear. She smiles, her teeth an advertisement for whitening strips. Her diamond glistens so brightly, I'm almost blinded when it reflects the sun streaming in through the windows adjacent to their table.

He pulls her chair for her, she yanks on his shirt and lays a long, smoldering kiss on his lips. They walk out, so attached to one another's bodies that it's miraculous they haven't melted into one mass of flesh. Like the Human Love Blob. The table next to their vacated one holds another couple—she's an animated talker, using her hands to illustrate her point. He grabs one and kisses the tattoo that sits on the fleshy spot where her thumb attaches, as if the tattoo is there to remind him where to kiss her. She blushes.

A young family in the dining room's center hosts a curly-haired, oatmeal-covered baby tossing handfuls of cereal at his mom. The dad pretends to nom on the kid's chubby little hands. When a Cheerio ends up on Momma's face, Daddy grabs and eats it. She clutches Dad's hand, and he squeezes her fingers. The look between them … it's foreign to me.

Like they're home. Home to each other. Not strangers in the same boat. Like if they were in a boat, he'd give her the sole life vest and jump into the raging sea to kick them to shore, even as the sharks swarmed underneath and threatened to eat his legs, one toe at a time.

With my luck, I'd be the one to answer that 911 call.

"Good morning, Miss Porter," Roger says. I jump.

"Hey. Hi." I stand.

"You're early."

"A little."

"Hungry?"

"Very."

As if I weren't nervous enough. This is the first "date" I've been on in … years.

Like a dope, I marvel open-mouthed at the scene on the other side of the double-paned glass, hoping my addled brain remembers soon how to make small chat. I could pretend he's one of the 911 callers, but that's ridiculous. He's not in distress. I don't have to talk him off a ledge. I have to relearn how to talk to men, a feat compounded by the fact that this one is devastatingly handsome. Wow, leagues from Keith.

Why am I sitting here again? Has there been some weird identity swap?

"Something else, isn't it?" Roger asks.

"Yeah. Unreal. I don't know how I'm ever going to leave."

"First time here?"

"Mm-hmm. Oh my God, are those deer over there?" I point to a smattering of soft brown dots across the water.

"Probably. If you sit here long enough, you'll see a little of every-thing. It really is a gorgeous venue."

"You've been here a lot, I take it?"

"We have a businessmen's association conference once a year and then a lot of us visit more often. It's relatively close to Seattle and you can't beat their all-inclusive golf-and-stay deals. Plus, wait until you taste Miss Betty's secret-recipe jam. You'll be hooked."

"That good, huh?"

"I've tried to talk her into mass producing and selling it in my stores, but she won't have it."

My stores. He's rich. Roger is rich. And no ring on the left hand.

He's probably a stalker. Or maybe he really is a serial killer.

"Your stores?"

"Yeah, among other things, I run a chain of independent grocers and fruit markets in the greater Seattle area. We've just expanded down I-5 into Portland. I'm here this week trying to get investors on board for moving into the California markets. That's where the real money is. Big state—lots of organic eaters, healthy folks."

"I'm from Portland."

"Oh, yeah? What part?"

"Northeast originally. I live over by Laurelhurst Park now. Maybe I know your store."

"Maybe. Ever heard of FruitBasket or the Monday Merchant?"

"Those are *you*?"

He laughs quietly. "Those are me."

"Nice. I've started going to Merchant because your selection is better than Trader Joe's."

"Don't say that too loud. One of their Western reps is just a few tables away." He winks. "So, Miss Porter—"

"Just Hollie."

"Okay, Just Hollie, what do you do?"

"I'm an emergency services dispatcher. But I don't know for how long."

"Uh-oh, what happened?"

"Nothing happened. It's … it just might be time to move on."

"To what?"

"Not a clue. Maybe finish college. Four years late."

"Hey, getting it done is the important thing, at any age. I finished my MBA five years later than my classmates because I did it at night. And I only did it because banks wanted those three little initials behind my name to give me loans."

"I'll bet those loan officers feel stupid now."

"I was a risky investment."

"Not anymore, though?" My meaning is double-edged. I think he gets it.

"Not anymore." His grin confirms that he does.

A young, pretty, long-haired waitress dressed in what must be the Revelation Cove uniform arrives at our table. Roger orders for us both, and I don't protest because he's interesting. Might be nice to let a real man take charge for a few minutes. Wondering if he likes to take charge in the bedroom …

Hollie Porter, you mind your manners.

What? A girl has needs too. Don't judge, you mean, uptight inner dialogue.

When the Mimosas arrive in stemmed glassware, Roger proposes a toast. "To Just Hollie's future, whatever adventures may come her way."

"And to Roger and his many stores. May your produce always be freshest."

Clink. Sip. Flirty smiles.

We eat. We laugh. We talk, about nothing particularly important. Superficial life stuff. Getting-acquainted-with-a-new-person stuff. I'm doing okay, not stumbling face first into taboo topics. No politics, no religion, no contentious current events or tumultuous relationship rehashing.

And most importantly? No medical talk.

He's funny and he laughs at my (lame) attempts at humor. Roger is thirty-one, clearly financially independent, and comfortable in his own skin. He's not pretentious or self-righteous. He listens when I talk and asks insightful questions. He's not overbearing or argumentative. For the first time in a very long time, I feel present, like I'm important to the person across the table, that what I say matters. He wipes a crumb off my cheek, picks up my napkin when I drop it. Not creepy or too touchy-feely, just ... comfortable. When his conference cronies stop by the table to confirm their tee time, he's friendly and introduces me to faces and names I won't remember past today.

Despite the weird luck of the first twelve hours of my journey, the sun's out, the Mimosas are flowing, and Roger has a smile that makes me feel like I'm the only person in the room.

At the front desk, we're waiting for keys to the golf cart. The one he wants me to drive. Not sure if it's safe for me to do so three orangey-Champagney drinks later, but if I steer us into the inlet, I'm pretty solid that we'd laugh it off and order more drinks. Concierge Ryan likely won't be happy with me destroying resort property, but isn't that what insurance is for?

In the course of our five-hour golfapalooza, I only drive over one guy's foot, and he seems liquored enough to not be too mad. I manage to keep the golf cart free of the surrounding water, which is actually quite simple because the paths are wide and well demarcated. To get to the water, I'd have to crash through some shrubbery and drive along a short rocky beach covered in foraging seabirds. When the tide goes out, the smell of seaweed flies our way on the occasional wayward current. Fat white clouds slink by, pleased with how the day has turned out, sun bright, storms somewhere far away and not our joint concern.

It's so idyllic, it doesn't seem possible that I'm here.

But I am here. And though the air is occasionally crisp, chilled enough to remind us that May along British Columbia's coast is not exactly bikini weather, it's pleasant. Roger points out a pair of eagles as they track and dive after a midafternoon snack, their huge black and white bodies thrusting toward the water's surface, yellow talons outstretched for the big grab. Roger's golf buddy, a stout, pleasant fellow named Jorge, sneaks toward a tree and gestures toward a sleeping owl. A *big* sleeping owl.

It's one of my nature shows, *in real life*.

Roger shoots a terrible game way over par but not once does he scream at the ball or blame the breeze or pound his club's head into the green. A real contrast from the one time I made the mistake of golfing with Keith. This is not a sport for people with short fuses. As he proved with epic flair that day.

Why am I thinking about Keith when I am the belle of this ball, where this new, very good-looking man has no problem with his advancing affections throughout the day, offering a hand to me as I step from the golf cart, wrapping a loose arm around my waist while we wait for Jorge to take his turn, pushing an errant hair behind my ear so it doesn't stick to my eyelashes. When the refreshment cart ambles through the green's pathway, Roger pays for a round for all of us, not once questioning or taking cash from his cohorts. Keith would've pulled out his cell phone and broken down everyone's portion, down to each person's contribution to an embarrassingly paltry tip.

Stop comparing, Hollie. Roger is not Keith.

This is a new day!

Or it was, but now the day is over, the golf carts are put away, and the clock is tiptoeing toward yet another meal. "Feel like a quick swim?"

Swimming? Really? Can't we just stare into one another's eyes over a nice bottle of local wine?

"Now?"

"Do you have other plans?" he smiles. Warm and fuzzy erupts like a soda bottle left in the afternoon sun.

"No other plans."

Swimming. In my bathing suit. My four-year-old, very saggy, wildly unattractive bathing suit. "We could do that."

"Go change. I'll meet you in the lobby in, say, twenty?"

"Sure. Yeah. Okay, sounds doable." Panic. *Thud thud thud,* says the heart. Shit. Things were going so well too. Now he's going to see my third-world bathing suit and all bets are off.

Unless … Concierge Ryan is standing behind a desk across the lobby from the check-in area. On the phone, he waves as I approach.

I wait, impatiently, knowing the twenty minutes is evaporating and I *might* need to trim the tarantula right quick before exposing it to the world.

He hangs up. Finally. "Hollie Porter, how has your day been? Enjoying the links with your new friend?"

"Yeah, yeah, it's great. Hey, quick question. I, uh, I need a bathing suit."

"What, no more streaking through the resort?"

"I'm serious."

"Did you check the gift shop?"

"You have one of those?"

"Follow me." He grabs a set of keys and moves from behind the desk, down the hall past the wall of framed jerseys. I am ashamed to notice that his ass looks really nice in his tight black slacks. He's cleaner than yesterday, although the beard is still firmly attached to his face. The crisp white cotton of his monogrammed *Revelation Cove* button-down fits his physique well. Hunky. He must work out. I should live up to the promise I made to myself last night when my flabby butt was jiggling in the elements and see about the gym facilities here.

But eww. I'm on vacation. Exercise can haunt me when I get back to my crappy life.

The gift shop is a tiny little thing, no bigger than my apartment living room and packed to the gills with all kinds of Canadiana. Wool First Nations blankets, fleece pullovers with wolves and killer whales, key chains, shot glasses, Revelation Cove-embossed memorabilia, snacks, golf shirts, ball caps, winter hats, scarves, leather purses, journals, beaded necklaces and silver, hand-tooled earrings, collector's spoons and thimbles, even CDs and books from local creatives. And about four bathing suits to choose from, none of them particularly breathtaking.

How am I going to land a stud wearing poochy foam cups and a cellulite-shielding skirt?

"If there's nothing in here, you can always check the lost and found," Ryan says, his smile like that of a little brother. If I had one of those, I'm sure this is what his obnoxious face would look like after he hid a spider in my bed.

"You can keep those to sell in your used underwear and VCR repair shop, thanks," I snipe.

Ryan chuckles. "VCR repair will be big business again someday. You just wait."

I hold up one suit that has neither foam nor skirt. Black, it's slightly lower cut on the thighs than I'd prefer, but it's the sexiest of the lot. Which isn't saying much. If I had more than a handful of minutes left, I could probably fashion something sexier out of a pillowcase, a shower cap, and some stale jellybeans.

"This one, I suppose," I say to Ryan. I look at the tag. "Holy shit, seriously? Sixty-five bucks for *this*?"

"Quality doesn't come cheap. And think about the memories you'll make being clothed for this dip in the water. It's a far different experience than what you had last night."

"Are you always this insufferable?"

"If by insufferable you mean charming and irresistible, then absolutely yes." Ryan takes the hanger out of my hands, holds the suit up against me, and nods. "Perfect. Will keep you chaste."

"You're a Neanderthal."

Ryan winks and walks to the counter where yet another young woman works behind the counter. "Tabitha, this is a gift for my friend Hollie."

"That's not necessary, Ryan. I can pay for it."

"You're newly single, remember?" I look at him, aghast that he'd mention this in front of the shop girl. "All I mean is, let a guy treat a girl. Broken hearts are the worst. Besides," he leans closer, "we can't have you flopping around the joint in your birthday suit. Once was grand, but this is a family establishment." Tabitha smiles at him—and I can't figure out if she's smiling because she heard about last night or if she really wants Ryan to notice how cute and perky she is. The longer the smile lingers, which is the whole time we stand before her at the cash counter, she does not at all try to hide that those starry, dreamy eyes are for Concierge Ryan and his crooked nose. In spite of the cliché, I actually roll my eyes.

"Thank you." I yank the suit out of his hand and stomp out of the shop.

"Don't do anything I wouldn't do!" he calls after me.

I'm going to do everything you wouldn't do and it's gonna be awesome.

I'm a couple minutes late meeting Roger in the lobby, but he's made good use of the time. In his hands he clutches two sweating, ice-cold bottles. "Local brewery. Well, local as in Vancouver. Canadians make excellent beer. We're trying to get some of these guys to import to us."

The healthy swallow is to prepare myself for the imminent reveal of my not-so-sexy bathing suit. I'm glad it fit, especially given the duress under which it was acquired, and it's certainly better than the piece-o-shit I brought with. But still. When Ryan said chaste, he wasn't kidding. Even trying to hike the hips up a little just makes me look like an escaped nun on her first post-convent bender. Not exactly Aphrodite. So we'll just get in the water and work with whatever else I've got. At least the bodice pushes up my boobs. Maybe he'll notice those instead of the 1920s-era action going on around my thighs.

Roger is an enthusiastic swimmer. When he dives under, I quickly disrobe and lower myself into the heated pool before he can get a whole glimpse at the ensemble. Boobs above water and I should be okay.

Our first beers finished, he pays a pool attendant to go to the bar and bring out another round. After the day's Mimosas, I'm already feeling bloated. Adding beer to this is not helping. I sip only, afraid I will be a gaseous mess in another hour. And farting is only safe in a jetted hot tub with other people present to shoulder the blame.

Roger does a few laps, showing off his fine, muscled form. And fine and muscled, it is. His skin is tanned, surprising given that he lives and works in one of the rainiest cities in the country. Maybe he's one of those vain fake-and-bakers.

Or maybe he's just come back from a buying jaunt to Central America where he spent some of his time donating to orphan charities or building schools. Maybe he's back from an activism trip to Africa where he fought to stop the hunt of elephants for their ivory. Or maybe he's back from an excursion aboard an exploration vessel to seek out new and amazing products from the indigenous people of the South Pacific.

Wherever the tan came from, it looks good on him. Good enough to lick.

I will attempt no laps for fear of drowning halfway across. I've been blessed with a naturally quick metabolism, but the last time I ran around a soccer pitch, I was seventeen. After we were handed the final loss of an abysmal season, I hung up my cleats and haven't broken a sweat since, unless you count pushing and boxing my way through the Black Friday crowd at Nordstrom Rack.

Under water, something—or someone—pinches my rear. Roger emerges, shaking free the water from his now-shaggy hair. As we're in the shallow end, he leans against the wall, knees bent, and pulls me onto his lap. It feels weird to be held by someone else, a little awkward because I've only known him for not even an entire day. That feeling of being a thirteen-year-old French-kiss virgin surges—when Andy Andrews, the boy with the name so nice, they named him twice, asked me atop the play structure at the school if I'd ever French kissed. Before I could answer, his tongue was down my throat.

And although Roger from Seattle is no Andy Andrews—shit, unless Roger's last name is Rogers—this still feels a little scary.

Oh my God, I don't even know his last name.

Let go, Hol. It's okay. You're on vacation, remember? Relax. Relax into him.

I do, silently hoping that I won't feel if he's excited under my thigh. It's been a long time since I've felt another man's ... excitement ... I know I'm not cheating on Keith, because we broke up, but it's a little soon for me to know if Roger's happy stick functions after two beers in a warm pool.

Apparently it does.

Which prompts me to delicately slide off his lap, my best flirt smile pasted on my face to hide my nerves. *Why am I so nervous?*

Because I haven't had loads of experience with men, despite my obvious charm and pleasing affect. And he's a bit older than me. Six years, but still. That's six years longer that he's had to work the system. Or perhaps many systems.

What if he has herpes? God, I'd never live that down. First sign of a lip lesion, Keith would freak out and accuse me of cheating and thus likely infecting the Yorkies by my mere presence. Even though I'm not cheating because we broke up.

I'm single.

I'm doing what single people *do*.

"You okay?" Roger asks.

"Yeah! Yeah, just the combination of a long day in the sun, the alcohol, this warm pool ..."

"And of course, my intoxicating presence."

"Certainly there's that."

"You want a ride?"

"On ..." Oh God, he's not asking me to. In the pool. Here. Is he?

He smirks. "On my shoulders. Arms around my neck. I'll pull you around the water. It's very relaxing."

"I'm good. You swim. I'm thinking I'll just float. Over here. By the warm vents."

"Dinner soon, then?" He raises an eyebrow. "After such a spectacular failure on the golf course, you at least have to let me buy you dinner to prove that I'm not completely inept."

"You get points for effort," I say.

"Please, no more points. I'm already so far over par, the PGA would ban me from their approved courses if they got wind of it."

"And rightfully so. A par-three doesn't mean ten strokes later." Roger laughs. Glad my dad golfed for a few dark years so I know what the hell par means. Something to do with how many times you're allowed to try to get the little ball in the little hole.

But how Roger's looking at me right now, I hope he's not calculating my par score. Breakfast + lunch + dinner = three strokes. Then the hole?

I'm going to ignore that little voice in my head screaming at me that I'm behaving like a girl of questionable scruples.

"I could be coerced into joining you for dinner."

"Really? Now I have to resort to coercion?" Roger erases the distance between us, wrapping an arm around my waist. His mouth is close enough that I can see the tiny lines in the surface of his lips. Plump lips, but not too much. Not like the weird kid in the back of the class who ate paste and boogers. His lips were really big and flesh-colored and made him look like a *Star Wars* creature. Roger's aren't like that. At all. And especially not when they make contact with mine.

All those mushy words romance writers use: warm, soft, moist.

All of those. Yeah. Oh, and nice. A little tongue, but not too much. Breath minty. Conscientious, this one. Scruples be damned, he's a good kisser. Those extra six years he's got on me have been well spent, and his body squishing against mine might just be worth the risk of herpes.

I should be playing coy. Saying no.

We all know *no* isn't my strong suit.

I really want to say yes.

His excitement is rising. Between us. I should be embarrassed, but I'm not. Not really. It's a confidence boost to know that I've still got it, that Keith didn't suck all the life out of me. Roger is a successful, handsome, accomplished individual who could likely have any woman he wants—and for all I know, he has had every woman he wants—but right now, his arousal is pressed against my lower half, and my lower half is sorta diggin' it.

What the hell! *I can have any man I want. Look at me go!*

Our interlude is brief, interrupted by the cleared throat of a dad with a floatie-clad toddler on one hip, his other hand clutched around fingers belonging to a wee, curly-haired girl in a tutu bathing suit.

"Family venue and all that," I whisper, hiding my flushed face against Roger's cologne-spiced neck.

"Maybe we should see about that dinner," he says, arms scooping me from the water. He carries me to the stairs and I sit, hoping he will dash out first so I can avoid him seeing this swimsuit in all its glory.

Why do I care? He just had his erection pressed against my stomach. I'm guessing he won't care about the suit at this point. And my legs still got it. The minimal cellulite naturally present doesn't wink when I walk nor does it harbor the scary purple veins painting Dr. Aurora's legs. Troll Lady warned me about growing a dispatcher's ass—see? This little vacation is already better for my health. Let someone else's cellulite go forth and multiply in my vacant chair.

Roger holds a robe open for me. I step into it, and we walk toward the patio doors, his arm draped over my shoulders. "How long do you need to get ready?"

"Forty-five minutes? I need to dry my hair. Maybe wash the chlorine out," I say, pulling a soaked strand to under my nose.

"Shall we meet in the lobby again, or would you like me to escort you from your room like a proper gentleman?" He's asking for permission to come to my room. That could be dangerous. Deliciously dangerous.

Roger holds the door for me. The warmth of the lodge's interior is welcome considering the sun is going to bed and the wind is coming out to play. "I'm in room 212. Meet me there in forty-five. Enough time to get yourself presentable," I say, tugging his lapels to bring him closer. The toes of our sandals are touching, and he doesn't hesitate to plant another kiss, this one teasing, just to the side of my lips.

"There's more where that came from but first, food," he says.

"Food first sounds good."

He splits off and moves westerly, away from me, around the back of the front desk/office area. I'm floating, trying to remember when I've felt this stupid over the attentions of the male variety. It's novel, this tingly-twittery feeling in my gut. Something I never experienced with Keith. We were a relationship of convenience. No spark, no sizzle. Then again, the guy had a lot to live up to—my ideal-relationship bar was set pretty high from watching too many romantic comedies and reading too much Jane Austen as an angst-ridden teenager. My own Mr. Darcy almost happened when I went on my first date at fifteen. Jory Angel. I'm not even kidding. That was his name. I liked him because he wore torn jeans and a leather biker jacket and his dad's cologne and he didn't give a shit what any of the other kids said about his wild black hair or his strange name or the tattoo he kept hidden from his preacher daddy. Held back a year, Jory got his license before the rest of us, so he drove us to the movies, no parent chaperone, and then to the now-defunct ice cream parlor with staff in old-fashioned red-striped shirts and straw boater hats, and then to the movie theatre still under construction where we squeezed through the security fencing and ran up and down the bare concrete inclines where the seats would eventually go, and then to his father's tiny church where we broke in and he played the piano for me while I stretched out on a pew … it was pretty perfect.

Keith had a lot to live up to. I almost feel sorry for him. Almost.

"How was the water?" I'm yanked from my reverie.

"What?"

"The water. You're dripping on the hardwood." Concierge Ryan and his beard are smiling back at me.

"Oh. God. Sorry. Water's great. I love this place."

"It seems to love you too," he says, nodding toward the hallway Roger disappeared into.

"It's just for fun."

"Is it?"

My smile dissolves. "What business is it of yours?"

"None. I'm just making conversation."

"About my love life?"

"No, no, I'm just messin' with you. Don't get your knickers in a knot. Well, if you're wearing any. I never know with you."

"Do you harass all your guests, or did I just win this lottery?" I lean over his concierge desk counter and grab one of the resort brochures. "You need to add this to your marketing stuff—'Concierge Ryan is here to make sure you never live down your dumb mistakes.'"

"Aww, Hollie Porter, it's all in good fun. Don't be so sensitive."

"I thought men liked sensitive women."

"Roger seems to."

I squint at him. "Do I detect jealousy from the gentleman?"

Ryan smiles and shakes his head. "Let's just say I've worked here a while, and I think you should be careful. Don't give up the prize to the first horse across the finish line."

"What, no hockey metaphor?"

"I can conjure one if you want it."

"Roger tells me you're a hockey player. Or were. What happened? You get chased off the ice because you were chasing the coach's daughter?"

The look on his face darkens, the smile evaporating. *Shit.* Maybe it did have something to do with a woman.

"You have a pleasant evening, Hollie Porter." Ryan walks away, without looking back, without a parting joke.

Hollie, you're an asshole.

Chapter Eleven
Hooker Shoes

The little black dress fits—just barely. I guess the breakup diet hasn't kicked in yet. But because my heart isn't shattered into forty-two pieces and embedded in my chest wall, I should be careful that this breakup diet doesn't go in the wrong direction, as in, I'm having so much fun being broken up that I balloon like a blue whale in a krill swarm.

God, my chin doesn't look like a blue whale's, does it? I examine every angle in the mirror. No double chin. Yet. Nurse Bob has one. Granted, he's fifty-two and likes his beef jerky too much, but still.

Wide bracelet to cover Oliver Otter. Matching earrings. Drop of perfume behind each ear. Thank you, *Cosmo*, for teaching me how to be a girl. My poor father.

A knock sounds at the door.

I grab my stuffed otters and give them a kiss. "Wish me luck," I whisper.

Roger's cologne wafts through the open doorway like a sex cloud. He oozes pheromones. If my girl parts were in charge—and the wrestling match between sex and sanity begins as soon as Roger and his bouquet of flowers cross the threshold—I'd strip off his clothes and see just how much mojo I've still got.

But I'm a civilized girl with a personal moral code to uphold and not nearly enough alcohol left in my bloodstream to make me this brave.

"You look beautiful," Roger says, stepping close. He kisses the end of my nose.

"Thank you."

"Anything in here pass for a vase?" He wiggles the bouquet in front of me.

I grab the pottery vase/pitcher from the small dining corner table. "These are lovely. Where'd you get them?"

"My sources must remain protected."

As I fill the vase with water, Roger sneaks in behind and wraps arms around my waist, his chin resting on my shoulder.

"How is it you're single, Miss Porter?"

"How do you know that I am?" I tease.

"Because you don't seem the type. And no ring."

I don't want to have the *I just broke up with a knob* conversation. Roger smells and looks too good to waste a single moment talking about Keith and his Yorkies. "Just lucky, I guess." Pitcher's full. I'm not sure if I should move. He hasn't yet.

"Lucky for me." He turns me around, taking the filled vessel from my hands and setting it on the counter. He's not as reserved as he was in the pool, one hand on my cheek pulling me toward him, another on my lower back, precariously close to the top of my ass. My heart's stampeding with enough vigor, I'm sure he can hear it—or see it through the low cut of the dress.

He doesn't bother to look but instead kisses me, harder and deeper than the soft tease of earlier. It's hot, yeah, but seriously, if he keeps going, he'll discover I had my tonsils removed.

When he pulls away for a breath, he's wearing more lipstick than I am. I laugh and reach for a tissue.

"You've got ..." I twirl a finger around his lips and move so he can see in the mirror.

"I suppose we should eat," he says. "You seem hungry." Judging by the fact that he's speaking to my scant cleavage, I don't think he's referring to my stomach.

And I am hungry. Indeed, he is hot. If I get drunk tonight, I will probably show him the remarkable landscaping I've done on the panty tarantula. She's more like a panty daddy-long-legs now. But I need to behave. Remember that men like Roger *can* have any woman they want, and I don't need to be that easy vacation lay he won't remember to call next week when the floatplane carries him back to his own version of real life. But do I want him to call me?

What is it you want, Hols?

He doesn't order for me this time, which is good—he chooses the lamb, something I refuse to eat. One strike against Rog. There's no conceivable reason why human beings should eat baby animals. This includes sheep and cows. I'm not an environmentalist, but I have issues with eating baby *anythings.*

I go for something cliché, given the environment—smoked salmon, although I may live to regret it if I can't get to a bottle of Listerine soon. Maybe just more whisky. Dinner on a date is about so much more than a satisfying meal. One has to consider a number of factors: too much onion or garlic? Bad for kissing. Too much greenery or carbs? Fodder for the fart factory. Too spicy? Could be looking at embarrassing bowel upset. I also avoid green tea and any-thing caramel. Both have resulted in disastrous ends to first dates when my stomach decided that such ingredients are offensive and should be expelled through the lower route immediately, without delay. Nothing says romance like taking an explosive shit in some stranger's bathroom.

"We should eat. Might need our strength for later." Roger ges-tures toward the door. My gut flip-flops. *Strength for later …*

I'm nervous throughout the entire meal. I do my best to be clever and adorable, even when Miss Betty walks past the table, lips pursed at Roger, not a word spoken. Does she not approve? Does she think I'm a naughty girl because I'm sitting in this rather reveal-ing dress with the only pair of sexy shoes I own, purchased solely because Moonstar the Non-sister had her business launch and emailed me specifically to tell me it was semiformal and Converse would thus not be allowed through the door? They're *cupcakes,* psy-cho. Who needs heels for cupcakes? Apparently Moonstar.

Roger's talking, but I'm only hearing half of what he says. Not because he's not interesting—although he does talk about work quite a bit—but because I can only think about what will happen once the plates have been cleared. I jab at the asparagus spears with my shiny fork and shovel in a few meager bites of couscous, wondering if I am really ready to get naked with someone I only met twenty-four hours ago.

And then I remember he's already seen me naked. Which is awkward.

Maybe it's one of those stories we'll laugh about in a few years while aboard his private yacht, sailing through the Caribbean. Probably a not-safe-for-our-kids story. Kids. Kids?

Whoa. This is not right. I'm already planning our future.

I need another glass of wine.

Midsentence, he pauses and pulls a phone out of his pocket. "Oh, hey, I gotta take this. You okay if I excuse myself for a sec?"

"The wine and I will be just fine," I say, topping up my glass. The bottle feels light. Might need a new one soon.

A sec turns into ten minutes, and I've finished glass number two, pouring number three from the bottle I went ahead and ordered, my nervous and anxious and antsy giving way to mellow and tingly and daring.

But now I have to pee. And I have to try to look completely stable en route to the bathroom so Roger doesn't think I'm a drunkard.

When he returns to the table, I quietly announce that it's my turn for a moment away. "Ladies' room." As I stand, Roger does too. Chivalry is not dead!

I feel loose, like my joints are held together with rubber bands. Is the wine stronger here in Canada? It's not a bad feeling, I'll admit, but I'm afraid my inhibitions might be taking a little siesta, especially as I examine myself in the bathroom mirror, posing this way and that to find my best angle for seduction. My left side is definitely stronger. That boob is bigger too. "Sexy beast, yo," I say to my reflection.

Back through the lobby, I don't notice those two little carpeted stairs until the heel of my shoe snags, and by then, I'm ass up on the ground, ankle screaming at me that it's not supposed to bend that way.

The pain surges strong enough that I almost reintroduce the evening's wine selection to the floor. Several hotel staff rush to my sprawled form.

"I'm fine, I'm fine. Thank you. Dummy me, I just tripped," I say to the sweet-faced boys as I pull my dress down to make sure everything's covered. "No, I'm sure. I'm a bonehead." The two lads gently help me up but the twisted foot is very much not interested in cooperating. Shit. This can't be good.

Down I go again. "Maybe you guys can help me to a chair?" Miss Betty rounds the corner.

"Oh, dear! What happened?"

"I just stumbled. I'm used to wearing flat shoes," I laugh because I'm so embarrassed and I don't want to cry. Even though crying is very probable. The pain … *the pain.*

"Oh, Hollie, you poor thing. Is anything hurt? Can you stand?"

"Seems I may have twisted something," I say, feeling stupid. Again. "I'm sure it'll be fine in a minute. I'd really like to get off the floor."

Concierge Ryan materializes from the kitchen.

Why is he always here when I'm making a fool of myself?

"Ryan, oh, good. Seems Hollie took a spill. That ankle looks angry already," Miss Betty says. A small crowd is now gathering around the broken, drunken girl.

"Up you go." Ryan kneels and scoops me off the floor. One of the boys hands Miss Betty my shoe. She holds it as if it's hazardous material.

"Put me down," I say.

"Not until we see if you've broken something." He carts me over to a couch in the sitting area on the opposite side of the lobby.

"It's not broken. I'm just a dumb-ass who shouldn't wear heels. And I know what a break feels and sounds like. I'd be screaming my head off."

"Probably, but a sprain can be bad news too, sometimes worse." As he sets me down, he asks Miss Betty for scissors and the young staff member for ice. Lots of ice.

"Why do you need scissors?"

"May have to cut off the foot."

"You're a child."

"Your stockings. Unless you think you can ease them down on your own, right here."

"What, because I like being naked in public? Is that where you're going with this?" He shrugs and smiles but says nothing. "Cut them. There's already a hole in the toe." I wiggle my big toe and wince against the lightning bolt shooting up my leg. "Shit, can you go tell Roger that I'm out here? I don't want him to think I've run away."

"Would that be a bad thing?"

"Ryan, please, just go tell him."

"In a sec."

Bullshit. I'll go myself. I swing my legs over the side of the fancy leather settee. As soon as my throbbing foot hits the floor, the electric shock up my leg tells me I won't be doing the two-step—or any other related physical activities—for the remainder of the evening.

"Sore?"

I nod, the tears making it hard for me to speak. Tears because it fucking hurts, tears because I feel like an asshat, because I was maybe going to have a careless nice of reckless sex with a hot stud of a man … and now I'm not and stupid Ryan had to be the one to rescue me.

I hate being rescued. It's lame and weak and damsel-in-distressy and I'm not that girl.

Miss Betty hands over scissors and Ryan snips away at the sheer black stockings, careful to not touch the cold steel against my throbbing ankle. "Ooooh, pretty colors already."

"Seriously?"

"Do you think it's broken?" Miss Betty asks.

Ryan pushes and prods. "Ow! Stop!" I slap at him.

"Nah, but definitely a decent sprain," Ryan answers.

"Should I call Dr. James?"

"You guys have a doctor here?" I ask.

"No, Dr. James lives three islands up. He's our on-call guy during the summer months," Ryan says. "He's coming over later in the week. We can have him take a look if it's still swollen."

"And what the hell am I supposed to do until then?" I say.

"Ice, ibuprofen, rest, and wrap," Ryan says.

"We have some crutches you can use, dear." Miss Betty disappears again. I can't even think about crutches. I feel nauseated again, my upper lip sweaty. Hot and cold flushes through me.

"I think I need to lie back for a minute," I say.

"Are you going to throw up? This couch is really white, and that wine you were drinking was really red."

"How do you know what color wine I was drinking?" I cover my eyes with the back of my arm, willing the spins to slow down. Goddammit, my ankle hurts. Fucking shoes. I shouldn't have worn the shoes.

"Hollie?"

Ryan stands. "Hey, Roger. Yeah, our sneaky streaker here twisted the hell out of her ankle in those stripper shoes."

"They are not stripper shoes." They are, a little bit, but every girl needs a good pair of those. Mr. High-and-Mighty. "You're a judgey asshole for a concierge. I'm a paying guest. You should be nicer to me."

"And here I thought maybe she'd met some dashing young man in the lobby and abandoned me forever," Roger says. I peek out long enough to see him leaning over my lower half. His eyes travel up my now un-stockinged leg and his finger extends to touch the balloon growing around my ankle.

"Jesus! Don't touch it! It hurts!"

"Sorry. Wow, that looks bad. That might need something stronger than wine," he says.

Miss Betty returns with not crutches but rather a wheelchair. Out of the corner of my eye, I can see multiple people standing around, looking curiously in my direction. Stupid doesn't begin to touch how I'm feeling.

I force myself to sit up. "I need to go back to my room. We're making a scene here."

"This should be soaked in ice, Hollie. If there's one thing I know, it's this," Ryan says.

"Yeah, Ryan, tell her about that knee of yours. It's seen its share of scalpels and ice buckets, huh?" Roger says, slapping Ryan on the shoulder. Ryan's return smile is tight.

"What's wrong with your knee?" I ask.

"Nothing today," Ryan says. The young staffer returns with enough ice to satiate a polar bear—a bucketful and two long icepacks.

"Last game he played with the Canucks, he got slammed into the boards. Poof. Bye-bye, knee."

Ryan stands and glares at Roger for a beat. Miss Betty looks at Ryan and pushes Roger back so she can squeeze through. "No talking hockey. Hollie needs looking after. Roger, you go have the server pack up Hollie's dinner so she can eat it in her room. Ryan, let's get her upstairs and soak this ankle."

In that weird moment, I'm glad for Miss Betty's take-charge attitude. The pain is a lot and I don't want to cry in front of all these strangers.

I submit to the wheelchair but only because there is no bloody way I can walk yet. My own personal entourage escorts me upstairs— Concierge Ryan pushing the wheelchair, Miss Betty carrying my shoes and purse, the young staffer with the ice.

They set me up on the small sofa, a little awkward because I'm still in the evening's hot-date attire and the dress is not covering as much leg as I'd like. I hope Miss Betty doesn't think I'm a hussy.

"On the count of three, we're going to ease your foot into the bucket," Ryan says. "You ready?"

Miss Betty, as if reading my mind, hands me a small knitted throw from the back of the sofa to cover my lower half. "You're gonna be cold in a minute, sweetie."

I relax as much as I can so Ryan can ease my leg downward, the ankle disappearing into the melting ice. I chomp down. I wish they would've given me a shot of whisky or at least a leather strap to bite on. When the tears start rolling down my cheeks, smearing the mascara and leaving visible tracks in the foundation, I feel a little exposed. Again.

Why is this becoming a pattern? *Revelation Cove—come here so we can expose you to yourself and the world.*

"There, there, Hollie, it'll be okay. You want to hold my hand?" Miss Betty sits next to me and wraps her warm, soft hand around mine. Ryan excuses the young staffer and moves into the bathroom closet.

"He has a nice butt. Too bad I hate him," I say through the tears.

Miss Betty laughs at me. "Well, I don't know about his bum, sweetie, but you don't hate him. Ryan's a good boy. Works hard. Never complains. He cares about the people who come to stay here."

"I gotta take this out. It hurts so much …" I feel lightheaded again.

"No, no—keep it in the ice. It'll go numb in a minute," Ryan says, walking toward us, towels in hand. In one swift movement, he opens the minifridge and pulls out a few small bottles. "Drink this. Oh, and ibuprofen." From his pocket he pulls one of those foil packets the doctor's office hands out.

"I don't think I should mix these."

"It's not gonna kill you to mix ibuprofen with a few ounces of whisky."

"How do you know?"

"If it did, half the players in professional sports would be dead."

"I thought you weren't supposed to drink."

"We don't do it before a game, but once we're home and away from the trainers … sometimes whisky is the only thing that works." He breaks the seal on a bottled water. "Chase it with this, if you're so concerned. I wouldn't steer you wrong, Hollie Porter."

I swallow the tablets with the liquor and half the water. My belly is sloshy, which means eventually all the liquid consumed this evening is going to need an exit strategy. I start crying again.

"Awww, it'll be okay," Miss Betty coos. "Does it hurt so much?" She looks up at Ryan. "Maybe we should take her to the mainland, to a proper hospital."

"No! I'm fine," I snort. "I … this was supposed to be a fun get-away and I had to go and screw it up, just like I screw everything up."

"Don't you worry about a thing, Hollie. We'll help you out. When the swelling goes down, Ryan here can tape up your ankle just like the pros do. Gotta get those boys back out on the ice, right, Ryan?" She smiles. He chuckles at her. I wonder how long they've known each other. They seem close. "And what else do you have to do but relax? I have lots of books and we can set you up downstairs so you're not lonely."

A knock at the door. Ryan's face changes.

"Oh God, that's probably Roger and I'm a mess." The ankle is, surprisingly, less painful. Sort of numb, just like Ryan promised.

"Do you want me to send him on his merry way?" Ryan asks.

"No, it's fine. Just … whatever. I don't care at this point. Let him in. You guys have other guests to tend to. I'll be fine."

Ryan opens his mouth as if to say something but then doesn't, moving to the door. Indeed it is Roger, my tinfoil-wrapped dinner in one hand, a bottle of red wine and two glasses in the other.

"How's the patient?" he says, striding in territorially. "I brought medicine." He waggles the wine bottle.

"She's already had a shot of whisky and ibuprofen. Probably no more wine tonight," Ryan says.

"Well, thanks for your esteemed opinion, Dr. Ryan," Roger says, a smile on his face but an edge to his voice.

"That decision is up to Hollie," Miss Betty says. "We'll go now but I want you to phone down to the front desk if you need anything." She pulls a pad of paper and pen from the nightstand. "Here's my direct line, and here's Ryan's. Don't be shy about asking for help. Oh, and I'll send one of the bellhops upstairs with the crutches so you can get around the room."

Miss Betty pats my cheek and then moves to the door. "Ryan?"

"You sure you'll be okay?" he asks me.

"Yeah, I'm fine. Thanks for your help."

"Ice machine's down the hallway. I'm sure Roger here can get you a fresh bucket, right, Rog?"

"Sure, yeah, no problem."

"Keep it elevated. I'll come by in the morning and see if it can be wrapped until Dr. James arrives."

"I'm sure we can cover it, Ryan. It's not like she broke it," Roger says dismissively. He doesn't know me well enough yet to be speaking on my behalf.

"Thanks, you guys. I appreciate your help," I say. Ryan nods and follows Miss Betty out the door. I'm again alone with Roger, which is what I wanted in the beginning of the evening, but everything has changed in the last hour or so and now I'm feeling very sorry for myself.

"You hungry?" He points at the plate resting atop the small dining table. "It's probably still warm."

"Not really, but thanks. Sorry I screwed up the evening."

"What? Nah, you didn't. We can hang out here. It's nice. I haven't seen these smaller rooms. Very quaint."

"Yours is bigger?"

"I always book the suite on the top floor. Great views. We can go up there, if you want." He puts a hand on the wheelchair, his eyes sparkling with mischief. I find it annoying given current circumstances.

"You know what, I'm actually in a lot of pain, so I don't know if I'll be the best company tonight."

He sits next to me on the small couch, his hand on my knee. "I'm being a jerk. I get nervous when someone is injured. I'm used to being the person who can fix everything." He grabs the icepacks. "Let's do this—I can help you settle on the bed and we can order a movie, lady's choice."

That doesn't sound too terrible. Although I'm not excited about pulling the ankle out of the bucket. Ryan was right—the numbing works. Then again, the wine and shot of whisky, not to mention the comedown from the adrenaline, is making me really tired.

I let Roger help me onto the bed, and as expected, the throbbing starts anew as soon as the freeze wears off. He cracks the icepacks and wraps the whole ankle with a towel to keep everything in place. I feel helpless. This is not my idea of a great first date.

"Roger, you don't have to do this. I feel like an ass."

"Don't worry. I got no place to be." He raids the couch cushions and sets up a nest on the bed. Throws the remote onto the duvet. "They've got pay-per-view." He clicks through the guide, and I'm a little nervous when I see him heading into the adult channels.

"We could watch something naughty …" He wiggles his eyebrows at me. I'm guessing my response doesn't meet with his expectation when he retreats into the lower digits.

"Wait—" He stops on the National Geographic Channel. "Perfect."

"Really?"

"Yes. Really." Damn, yeah. This is my vacation, and I will not allow some pervy new guy dictate my viewing menu.

"You're a wildlife junkie, huh?" he says, smiling.

"I am, I guess."

"Favorite critter?"

"Otters. You?"

"I've been to Africa and saw the big cats on a nature reserve in Kenya. That was pretty crazy. I like animals, but I'm so busy, I don't have any of my own. Seems cruel to have a cat or dog I'm never home to take care of."

"You should try fish. Good starter pets."

"Oh yeah? But who will feed 'em?"

"Your maid," I tease. He laughs and stands to pour wine.

"How's the ankle?" He hands me a glass. I likely won't drink it because I actually do want to stay conscious—and clothed—tonight. One sip, and I give it to the nightstand.

"Comfortably numb."

"You feel like a shoulder rub?"

"Would it be weird if I said no?"

"Not at all. Just trying to help the little patient." He takes a healthy swig of his wine and settles into the cushions next to me. The drowsy is taking over, even with the documentary about Brutus the domesticated grizzly. I've seen it before but I love that bear. I want one. He and Chloe the Cougar could protect my family of otters from scary predators. We'd be our own wildlife sanctuary.

Two hours later, Roger is snoring next to me and I'm awakened from my own little impromptu nap by a pissed-off bladder. Oh, this is not going to go well. I'm still wearing the tiny black dress, not exactly great for hopping around, but what choice do I have? If I strip, darling Rog might take it as me wanting to see his parts naked too. The G-string and strapless bra aren't unsightly by any means, but the evening hasn't at all turned out the way I'd hoped, and I'm not feeling super sexy with the ballooning, purple ankle and eyes puffy from wine and tears.

But I have to pee. Or else I will die.

Worse, I could piss the bed and that will be the end of me at Revelation Cove.

I unwrap the towels around the now-tepid icepacks and am happy to note that the swelling has gone down somewhat. I can do this. I can hop to the toilet and do my business. I am not at all interested in having Roger watch me pee. Too much information, too soon.

One hop, two hops, three hops, floor.

I cringe and turn back to the bed. Roger is blissfully unaware that I have vacated the space next to him, so I'm off, on hands and knees, onto the very cold tile of the bathroom floor.

I don't think I've ever been so much in love with a toilet.

My phone is sitting on the counter. *Don't look at it, Hols. Leave it.*

Of course, I pick it up. Keith has emailed. "TV's out. Left next month's rent too—until you can get a roommate. Polyester Patty said you have the stomach flu? But you're not at home, so I hope you're having fun wherever you are. I won't narc on you. Love, Keith."

Shit. I lied to my boss. Eighty-sixed my relationship. Skipped town. This Brave New Hollie isn't working out the way I'd hoped.

"It's been three days, Hol," I whisper to myself. Three days. Only a million more to go before I figure out who I am.

Chapter Twelve
Smells Like Maple

The knock at the door comes early. I wake to find myself clothed and vaguely remember throwing my very unsexy pajamas on after the magical trip to the toilet. Roger is in his khakis but his shirt is off, revealing the tan pecs and abs I noted poolside. Before Roger, I've only ever seen flesh like that on magazine models. Pasty Keith wasn't a sight for sore eyes in the bathing suit department.

Again with the comparisons.

Knock knock knock.

I try to stand. Remember immediately why that is a bad idea.

"Roger … Roger, can you get the door?" I nudge his shoulder. Grab a tissue to wipe eye boogers clean before he wakes to mascara blobbed around my eyes. And I'm going to need toothpaste before too much conversation happens.

"Huh? What? Heyyyy, good morning, beautiful," he says. I can't help but smile. No one's ever woken up and said that to me. Perhaps Wednesday will be better.

"Can you get the door? Pretty please?"

"Sure, sure." He jumps up but doesn't bother with such a silly thing as covering his upper half. When the door opens, it swings wide enough for me to see the disapproval on Miss Betty's face. I wave, hoping she will notice that I am in fact fully clothed in PJs embossed with baby otters and starfish. See? No boobies anywhere, Miss Betty!

She bobs her head politely but simply hands off a set of crutches.

Why do I feel like I've been caught with my hand in the cookie jar? Damn Catholic relatives and their genetic guilt. I didn't even *taste* the cookies. And it's not lost on me that the cookies look delicious even after a lame night's sleep in a stranger's bed. He looks as good as he did when he zonked out last night.

That is so not fair.

Roger helps me adjust the crutches to the correct height. I sneak into the bathroom and rinse with a half-liter of mouthwash, followed by a quick slathering of lip gloss. Pull my hair into a messy, supermodel-ish bun. Roll the waistband of my PJs so a little tummy shows. Not perfect but neither is planting my face into the hardwoods on a first date. If he stayed the night without any action, he must be okay with not perfect.

Upon opening the bathroom door, my yay-this-guy-might-be-awesome is met with a dose of reality. He's fully dressed, shoes on, phone against his ear, looking out the window. He hangs up and moves across the room, dimpled smile in place. "I have a surprise for you."

"For … me?"

"How soon can you be ready?"

"Half hour? I just need to clean up a little …"

"Nothing here needs cleaning up. You're radiant," he coos as he steps closer. God, he smells so good. His lips brush mine. I'm surprised to find his breath minty. Again. Must have a secret stash somewhere. "I want to make last night up to you."

"But you didn't do anything—"

"I know. And I had so many things planned for you." He kisses me again, longer, more intense. It overrides the throb screeching from my ankle. "I'll meet you downstairs in thirty. Wear something comfortable." His finger along my cheek sends shivers to all the right spots.

I practically chew the ibuprofen Ryan left in the bathroom. Face on, hair tamed, I'm in the lobby with moments to spare. Roger moves like a god from the dining area, a huge basket in hand, emanating confidence and health. Clearly he is a man who takes care of his body. Such a contrast from what I'm used to.

I pinch the side of my leg to make sure I'm awake. Not even the swelling around my toes is enough to convince me this is real, that rich, beautiful Roger is walking toward *me* with that basket, that glow, that look of warmth. All for me.

"You ready?"

"I don't know. Where are we off to?" I try to peek into the basket. He taps my hand away.

"Come on, broken princess." He opens the resort's front door and we are assailed with the absolute glory of the mid-May sunshine. The sky is a sinful blue, not a cloud in sight, the scent of new growth heavy in the morning air. Roger leads the way, slow as I am on these ridiculous crutches, down the pathway and onto the docks. The doors of one of the float planes—a nicer one, not Miss Lily—sits open, a two-tiered step stool on the dock awaiting passengers.

"Where are we going?"

"Would you, Miss Porter, be my guest for an aerial tour of the local islands, followed by a delectable lunch on one of the many fantastic beaches?"

Eyes wide, I laugh. "Are you serious?"

He extends a hand to help me onto the plane. "Your presence would be a gift."

No way this is real. But I'm going to go with it and pretend that it is until something loud and bloated with reality wakes me from the dream.

Which happens way faster than I expect. On board the floatplane, a far nicer model than the supply plane, I am met with the grin of our pilot. "Good morning, Hollie Porter," Ryan says. A damp curl bobs haphazardly against his forehead.

Roger slides in after me, sitting very close, arranging the crutches along the plane's floor. "Is he really the pilot?" I whisper.

"Are you displeased?" Roger says into my ear. It tickles. Of course I'm not displeased. I couldn't care less if Concierge Ryan is flying the plane, as long as Roger keeps breathing into the side of my face like that. His breath is like … like sex-fairy dust. My mind races with the possibilities of landing on an island, ditching our beloved pilot, and exploring the wilder side of Roger's nature.

"You kids ready?" Ryan says, his headset in place. I guess we don't get headsets this time.

The takeoff is definitely smoother in this aircraft—remind me to take one of these planes home. No more Miss Lily. Hell, maybe by week's end, alternate arrangements for transport home will be necessary.

Stop, Hollie.

You can take the girl out of the relationship but you can't take the relationship out of the girl. Or something like that. This is dumb, thinking so far ahead. I need to be in the moment. Live in the moment. Enjoy the moment.

Because at *this* moment, Roger's arm is wrapped around my shoulders, his hand is clutching mine, and I'm in a plane flying above some of the most spectacular landscape I have ever seen, next to one of the most spectacular male specimens I have ever had the pleasure of touching. My tummy is aflutter with nervous energy— the good kind, not the *shit I'm going to hurl* kind. New romance! New adventures!

I feel like such a big girl right now. Look at me go.

Like a proper tour host, Concierge Ryan does a fine job detailing island histories—old First Nations settlements, long gone, fishing and hunting activities for locals and tourists alike, common wildlife, local lore. I let go of the initial awkward feeling and sink into Roger's smile, his hard but supple body curled against mine, the attention he gives me every time I get excited about a herd of deer or a gaggle of Canada geese.

I could so live up here.

Ryan announces that he's going to take us down onto a beach the locals call Brigand Bay. Just as with takeoff, this landing is smooth as silk. Despite Ryan being a pain in the ass, my faith is restored, especially when he pulls us along the shore and jumps out in waders to escort both of us onto dry land. I try not to notice how, when he carries me, it's as if I weigh no more than a dandelion's feathery seed before he hands me off to Roger. The two men move quickly to organize our picnic: checkered blanket spread, food displayed, Champagne popped. Roger pulls a very fat wallet (do rich people call them wallets?) from his back pocket, pulls several brown Canadian hundreds, and moves down the beach to Ryan. A quiet conversation ensues, sealed with a handshake and a smile. Ryan pulls his own pack from the plane's interior and disappears around the corner of the beach.

We are alone.

Roger feeds me fresh Brie on water crackers, my first caviar (and likely my last, but don't tell), smoked salmon and crusty French bread and the sweetest bubbly I've ever tasted. He tells me stories of his days on the rowing team at the University of Washington and laughs loudly when I tell him the crazy trouble we'd get into during my (unfinished) days at Oregon State, the pranks we play on Troll Lady at work but how I totally had nothing to do with Elvis's haircut. Conversation about everything—and nothing—perfect.

So, so perfect.

He rubs the back of my hand, tracing the bones down each finger. Asks about Oliver Otter and in response to the *Enhydra lutris* banner shares his own list of impressive Latin names: *Phoneutria*, or Brazilian wandering spider, sometimes called the banana spider (this one apparently because they had a castaway in an order shipped to a FruitBasket store); *Gorilla diehli*, the Cross River gorilla of West Africa, of which there are only a few hundred remaining and thus is this year's chosen beast for company-wide fundraising activities (of which he has many, including literacy programs for inner city schools, back-to-work grants for the homeless, and round-it-up initiatives in the retail stores from which the extra pennies go to support local kids' sports teams); and Sangiovese of the species *Vitis vinifera*, the most planted, most delectable grape used in Italian wines.

"Like this one," he says, corking a bottle of red pulled from the basket.

Hello, Universe? Can I keep this one? Pretty please? I promise to get regular Paps and dental check-ups, I'll stop filing my taxes late, and I won't lie about my weight on my driver's license ever again. Fine. Yes. I'll stop feeding codeine to demonic goats.

PLEASE.

Let me keep Roger. Or at least, let me sleep with him.

I am ashamed at how naughty I am. Until the little devil who perches on my left shoulder in her overpriced shoes and fresh manicure giggles and implants images of a naked Roger in my sex-starved brain.

Two hours in, my ibuprofen is wearing off, though the ankle pain is dulled by impressive volume of wine and the happy-making endorphins surfing through my veins. Thus, I'm comfortably numb. Thank heavens. And despite the midspring temperatures, a slight sunburn pinks my cheeks.

Roger's phone buzzes. "It's Ryan. Are we ready to go yet?"

"I suppose. You?"

"There's one thing I want to show you first." Roger texts back to Ryan. "I'll have him clean this up while we go."

"How far?" I nudge the crutches.

"I will be your chariot, milady."

Roger hoists me onto his back and we move down the beach, in the direction opposite where Ryan disappeared. I'm excited to see what awaits—the little girl in my head hopes it will be otters. The big, naughty girl hopes it involves Roger's hands on the parts of my body that are supposed to stay covered by clothing.

Alas, no otters. We do make it to a more secluded beach area, the trees and foliage denser. Roger sets me on a log, his forehead hinting at a sweat given the workout of carrying me across the rocky sand. He moves through the bushes, foraging, plucking from the branches and from the greenery that melts into a greater forest behind us. "I want to show you the variety of berry plants on these islands. We hire special pickers to harvest for a number of our specialty jams." He offers a flat hand with different-shaped leaves. "There are no berries yet because it's too early, but these are the plants they come from."

We're here because he wanted to show me plants?

This is why we're here in this secluded, romantic spot in the middle of nowhere?

He identifies the varying leaf structures for a salmonberry, a red huckleberry, tall Oregon grape that is used primarily for flavoring but can be toxic. Another one I don't catch the name of. "Wow. That's ... fascinating."

"Oh God, I'm boring you, aren't I? I get excited about this stuff. I am so sorry," he says, brushing off his hands. "Come here. Let me make it up to you." He buries his hands in my hair, wrapping their warmth around my neck.

Now *this* is what I'm talking about.

We're moving right along, hands under shirts, his fingers toying with the edge of my bra's padding, our conjoined breath rushing quickly toward the top of the mercury. When my hands fidget with the button on his shorts, I realize I may break every Good Girl Rule taped on the walls of my fickle head.

Roger stops kissing me, pulls back for a moment, and cranes his head to listen.

"What? Why are you stopping?" I say, chest heaving.

"Do you hear that?"

"Hear what?" I ask, biting at his lower lip. And then I do hear it—the sound of water. Like, being poured from a water bottle?

Clutching my upper arms, Roger turns. "Who's there?"

Ziiiiiip.

You've got to be kidding me. Ryan emerges from the bushes, guilty smile on his damned hairy face.

"Were you ... peeing? In the bushes?" I say, adjusting my shirt.

"I am so sorry. I thought you guys went the other way. I—I made my way around the entire island and was coming back to clean up the lunch stuff. God, seriously, Roger, Hollie ..."

"No, it's fine," Roger says, his smile tight. The vibe rolling from him does not say that Ryan urinating on our very intimate moment is okay, but he's quiet as he hoists me onto his back and moves in the direction of the plane.

Ryan leads the way, looking back only once. I swear I see a smug smile. I want to smack it off.

As we round the bend, Ryan hollers loudly and takes off at a sprint. He moves pretty quick for such a big guy. His arms flail wildly and he continues yelling—at the large family of raccoons that have descended upon our lovely picnic. The black-masked bandits think little of the crazed hairy beast running at them. Roger's laugh is infectious, and we stop, waiting for Ryan to chase off the marauders. Their wobbly, chubby bodies disappear into the thicket, but left in their wake is the sad reminder that a once-beautiful picnic existed here. Even the red-checkered blanket is now covered in their wee raccoony footprints.

The laughter only abates after Roger sets me down and reaches to help Ryan clean up. It is then that he finds his wallet. And the formerly fat lump of cash is remarkably ... thinner.

"What the hell?" he says.

A smile creeps across Ryan's dumb face, a completely irrational and contrary response given the look on Roger's. "Did you have hundreds in there?"

I look up the beach and a straggler raccoon sits staring at me, noshing on something. Something brown and not at all food-like. Holy shit. He's eating ... money?

"Roger, the new Canadian hundreds smell like maple syrup," Ryan says. "Looks like you've been robbed by nature's original bandits." Roger's face is very, very far from looking amused at this particular moment. Oh God, Hollie, don't laugh.

But seriously, the fat raccoon eating the money because it smells like maple syrup?

"What kind of a country makes their money smell like pancakes?" I ask. And then I lose it. Fall backward off the log onto the hard beach. I can't not laugh. I try to right myself, remembering immediately that my ankle is still fucked up. "Roger ... oh, Roger, I am so sorry for laughing."

He looks between Ryan and me, dumbfounded. I'm not sure what to expect—in the very few days I've known this man, I have no idea how he reacts when he's mad. And then his face, it softens. A smile breaks. He laughs too.

"Sorry about this, man," Ryan says, kneeling to clean up. More bills are tucked under the basket, red fifties untouched by the enterprising raccoons. "Here ..." Ryan reaches into his back pocket and hands over the hundreds Roger gave him a few hours ago.

"No, no, it's all right. It's my own fault. I should've left my billfold in the plane," Rog says. And there you have it, folks—rich people call their wallets *billfolds.*

Ryan cleans up the dead food, empties the wine bottles; Roger shakes out and folds the soiled blanket. I'm still on the rocky beach when I see them. Candy bar wrappers. Ripped to hell by crafty raccoon hands. At least three wrappers, staggered up the beach toward the bushes, as if they were placed there.

On purpose.

Did Ryan *lure* the raccoons to our picnic? Because I know for a fact there were no Snickers bars in the picnic basket. Ryan skips up the sand and gathers the wrappers, and when our eyes meet, I'm sure that look is of guilt.

Roger carries the basket and my crutches toward the plane, giving me a moment alone with this scheming concierge. I balance delicately on one leg. "Did you—did you lure those raccoons to our picnic spot? With your candy bars?" I slap at his clutched hand, the wrappers in his closed fist.

"What?"

"You did, didn't you ... you left those candy bars for those little buggers to find us."

"I did no such thing. I didn't need to lure them anywhere. The Brie was stinky enough to attract wildlife from the next province."

I point a finger in his face, inches from his bristly beard. "I. Don't. Believe. You. Roger doesn't *eat* garbage like candy bars. So they had to come from you. And you knew the money was in there and that it smelled like maple and that they would eat the money—"

A megawatt smile interrupts my conspiracy theorizing. "Believe what you want, otter girl." Without missing a beat, he grabs and throws me over his shoulder like a sack of potatoes. I pound on his rather solid back, and in response, I get a firm smack on the ass.

"Ow!"

"Behave," he says. "Didn't your parents ever teach you it's not nice to hit?"

As he places me into the plane's belly, I point at him again. "I'm onto you, Concierge Ryan."

"Did I miss something?" Roger asks, one eyebrow flexed.

"Hollie was just telling me how much she loves Snickers bars," Ryan says, slamming the plane's door closed.

CHAPTER THIRTEEN
SPA DAY

I hop around the room, dressing in yoga pants because they don't hurt going over my stupid foot. To compensate for the haphazard wardrobe choices, I spend extra time on the face and hair, just in case I see darling Roger midmeeting. I have the whole day to psych myself up for our dinner date. I deserve to have my girl parts played with. Finally. And I'm confident—given earlier cursory gropings—Roger Dodger knows a lot of fun ways to play with said parts.

Two nights in a row, I've gone to bed with my virtue intact. Soon after arriving home from Brigand Bay, my hopes for a quiet dinner and not-so-quiet dessert were dashed when Roger announced he had a work-related function to attend. "Which is why I chartered our little excursion today. You're not upset, are you?"

I shook my head, feeling sorry for myself. "What about tomorrow?" God, forty-eight hours in and already sounding clingy.

"Meetings all day, babe. How about an early dinner? That'll give you time to recuperate a little, yes? You really should get off that ankle for a while."

"Yeah. Sure. I guess …" Mental math: Tuesday night, sprained ankle, no nookie. Wednesday night, business dinner for business-y types, still no nookie.

"Let's meet in the lobby at five, order dinner to be delivered, and then we can hobble upstairs to my suite and watch the sun go down. Sound good?" Roger kissed me hard, pulling my body against his. When I felt the strain against his chinos, I sensed victory.

My plan, however, did not work. Hands cupped around my cheeks, he whispered, "See you in twenty-four hours."

"Unless you get done early … you can always pop by."

"I'll keep that in mind," he said and squeezed my ass.

I tried to wait up for him. Dinner arrived at my door—a huge, multicourse, expensive affair—complete with more flowers and a note that read, "With every bite, think of me. Xoxo, Roger."

But the second glass of wine on top of a very full stomach, I had enough wherewithal to text my dad, thank him again and promise a call Thursday, and drift off.

In hindsight, I did need the rest. I slept like I haven't in months—years?—no Yorkies licking my mouth or assailing me with their rancid farts. No Keith snoring or making that weird "puh" sound from his side of the bed. The romance. It overwhelms us, Precious.

And now it's Thursday morning, bright and early, the sun is dancing through the gauzy drapes, and the wind is subtle and fresh. 'Tis a new day, another opportunity for me to embrace this big-girl life. The crutches and I are getting along a little better, even though the ankle still hurts like a mother. For the first time in countless days, the face in the three-mirrored bathroom vanity is smiling.

Wow. So *that's* what that feels like.

Concierge Ryan is at the desk talking to some folks with luggage at their feet. I sloth it through the lobby, careful of every step. I've made enough of a fool of myself around these people for three lifetimes. And I want him to see me, see my radiant glow of "I am awesome and you're not" and know that I'm watching his every move.

"Good morning, Miss Porter. I trust you had a restful evening," Ryan says when the traffic has cleared.

"Like that's any of your business."

"It is my business. It's my job to keep our guests happy."

"Mm-hmm."

Miss Betty appears from around the corner. "Oh, dear Hollie! How's your ankle, darling?" she sings.

"A bit sore, Miss Betty. Thank you for asking."

"And your chartered flight yesterday? Did you enjoy that?"

"Yes. Concierge Ryan is an excellent pilot. And so good with the local wildlife." I give him a pointed look.

"Oh, really? You saw wildlife? You didn't mention that, Ryan."

"Just raccoons. Attracted by the Brie."

"A right smelly cheese, that is. I tried to warn Mr. Swinyard that it might not be a good choice, but sometimes it's best for me to just stay quiet," she says. "Well, I'm off to grab some brekkie. Be back shortly."

Swinyard. Roger's last name. It dawns on me that I didn't know that until this very second, and here I am, willing to show him my boobs. Well, now I know his name. Which makes me not a floozy. Right? Right! I'm a modern woman, an empowered She-Ra of the twenty-first century and I can have meaningless sex with anyone I want! Even men for whom I don't know their last names.

"So, what is Hollie doing today? Any new plans to entertain us?" Ryan taps a Revelation Cove ballpoint pen against his lips. Again with that Cheshire smile.

"Har har."

"We could get you on staff—pay you an entertainer's rate. Better yet, I could moonlight as a bookie—'what will Hollie do next' could be our main game and guests could place bets on your hijinks. Wait! That's what we call the game! Hollie's Hijinks!"

"Did you graduate from third grade? Because I knew a kid exactly like you—when I was *eight*."

Ryan laughs, clearly enamored by his own riveting sense of humor. "Let me see your foot."

"Are you going to laugh at it?"

"Probably. But then I can wrap it for you so you can bear weight and get around a little better." I stare at him as he leans on elbows on the marble countertop so we're eye to eye.

"You have long eyelashes," I say. "Freakishly long. Like a wolf."

"All the better to see you with," he snarls. "Come on. In the office with you." He opens a small door I didn't even realize was there. He has to duck to get through the narrow frame but the office behind is tiny and quaint, like I've just walked into some English granny's tearoom. "Have a seat." I do, settling on a seafoam green chaise while he fumbles in an oversized medicine cabinet. It's an antique icebox, repurposed to hold medical supplies. "This tape is professional-sports approved," he says, tossing a few rolls my way.

Concierge Ryan, scissors and supplies acquired, kneels before me. "Oooh, that's a good position for you. On your knees, at my disposal."

"What would Her Highness of Hijinks have me do?" he teases. "Man, I hope you've shaved. I don't want to bleed on you if I get poked."

"Yeah, because last time I checked, I'm a porcupine." I tug on my pant leg. The purple is settling into my skin rather nicely.

"That is a thing of beauty. My trainers would be so proud of you."

"Yeah?"

"Definitely. Can you skate?"

"Mostly on my face," I say.

"Why doesn't that surprise me?"

I watch as he unspools a length of cushioned self-stick tape. He wraps my foot in a cloud-like pillow of cotton wool and sets to taping it in place. When he's finished, it's a masterpiece.

"Nicely done. Even the stethoscope-clad goober would've been impressed by this handiwork," I say.

"Glad I could oblige, miss." He scratches at his beard. It makes a mountain-man sound, all scratchy and rugged and … manly.

"Do you always wear the beard?"

"Playoffs, baby. Oh, man, we gotta have The Talk still, don't we … if you watch any of the Stanley Cup games, you'll notice all the guys have beards. It's a superstition. Once your team is in the playoffs, you can't shave until the team is either eliminated or wins the Cup."

"So your team is still in it?"

"Nope. Got eliminated last night, actually."

I place a hand on his shoulder. "You sure you're gonna be okay, Concierge Ryan?"

"Talk about a smart-ass," he chuckles. When he stands, his knee makes an ominous pop.

"Dude, sounds like someone else needs a wrap job." I point at his leg. "Care to continue Roger's story from the other night?"

"About the knee?"

"The very one."

"Just not sure which story old Roger Dodger was feeding you ..."

"What's that supposed to mean?" The tease is replaced with tension. "What is your deal with him?"

"Nothing," he says, looking away as he cleans up his supplies. He's not saying something, and I have no idea how to read him. Does he not like Roger? Does he know something about him I don't know but maybe should? "You hungry?" he asks, breaking the silence.

"Yeah. I could eat." Crutches tucked under my armpits, I touch my toes to the floor. The wrapping really helps. I can put a tiny bit of weight on the foot without wanting to vomit. "Hey," I say. Ryan turns around, hand splayed on the open door. "This feels much better. Thank you."

"Follow me."

Into the kitchen. A guy in a tall white hat hollers orders at a crew of at least ten other cooks. It smells divine. Ryan finds a stool and plants me at the quieter end of one of the stainless tables. "Eggs okay?"

"Perfect." I hope he can't hear my stomach growling. All this fresh British Columbian air is turning me into an eating machine. "Scrambled is fine. Toast too. And I keep hearing about Miss Betty's magical blackberry jam."

"Coming right up," Ryan says. The chef doesn't seem to mind that the concierge intrudes upon his kitchen, using up two of his cooktop burners to make breakfast for some random guest. The relationships here are casual and friendly, like a giant family. I'm envious.

Within a few moments, Ryan slides a plate of fluffy eggs with green onion and fresh, diced tomato, two slices of decadent, thick toast, and fresh fruit. I'm going to try to remember to breathe while chewing.

"Omigod, so good," I say, mouth full. "If this concierge thing doesn't work out, you should totally cook. In fact, just quit and I'll hire you. I hate cooking."

"You can't afford me," Ryan laughs.

The kitchen is filled with the smells and sounds of any other busy restaurant kitchen, minus the screaming, demanding chef, the cowering sous chef and lower specimens relegated to stirring pots and washing plates. Something is simmering for later—the smells are so many, I don't know where to begin—just imagine how hungry you've been on your hungriest day. Now think about all the favorite aromas that make your mouth water. That. Plus baking bread.

I can't wait to see what's on the dinner menu. And if I play my cards right, I might be on the dessert menu.

Ryan takes my plate just as I'm about to hoist it in front of my face and lick every remaining crumb. "Get enough?"

No. "Yes," I lie. "That was amazing."

"They were eggs. You must've been really hungry."

"Everything always tastes better when someone else prepares it."

I follow him out of the kitchen, waving to the chef in quiet thanks for allowing us to interfere with his operation.

"What's on your agenda today, Hollie Porter?" Ryan walks slowly next to my hop-skip gait, a toothpick bouncing across his lips.

"Dunno. Dancing is off the schedule. Miss Betty said something about books the other night. What about you?"

"Gotta check out the vineyard."

"Does it involve long-distance walking?"

"Sometimes ..." He looks at me sideways.

"Maybe I should keep you company."

"Not sure if that's such a good idea."

"How come?"

Miss Betty sneaks behind the check-in counter with her own plate of breakfast goodies. "Miss Betty, Hollie wants to come with me out to the vineyards today."

"Oh? But do you think that's wise, given her ... condition?" she says to him, nodding at me.

"Are you sober?" Ryan says.

"What?"

"Have you been drinking this morning?"

"God. No. I just had breakfast. You saw what I ate."

Ryan turns to Miss Betty. "She's not drunk right now."

"What are you talking about? I wasn't drunk when I tripped and did this!" I say, suddenly feeling like that boozer girl everyone whispers about.

"No one's suggesting you were," Ryan says.

"Then why are you asking if I'm drunk?"

"Miss Betty is concerned about your condition. I figured that's what she meant."

"You assumed *that* instead of thinking maybe she was talking about my ankle?"

"Well, you have hit that minibar pretty hard, judging by how much I saw left in there the other night. Plus, two of the three nights you've been with us, you've had some sort of ... interesting event. Maybe you're ..." He tips his thumb into his mouth to simulate drinking.

"You know what? You're impossible. Forget it." I turn to Miss Betty. "I'll need some books to read. And you have a spa here, correct? Maybe I'll book a massage. Or a facial. Something completely sober people do."

"Suit yourself." Ryan slides behind the front desk and extracts a set of keys from a hook. He kisses Miss Betty on the cheek. She brushes him away.

"Your team lost. Time to get rid of that beard or I'll call management," she teases after him.

I'm glad to see him go, even though I notice—again—how nicely his slacks fit him. But it doesn't matter. He's an obnoxious mongrel who wouldn't know how to treat a woman if she gave him an instruction manual with an audiobook and full-color illustrations. He has to be a total lost cause if he's still single—he's gotta be pushing thirty—and living this far from civilization? He's probably doing womankind a favor keeping himself out of circulation.

Miss Betty shows me the "library," i.e., a shelf of well-loved paperbacks other travelers have left behind. The choices are limited—vampire fare, a cheesy detective novel with a busty woman and a revolver on the cover, a few other titles I'm embarrassed to admit I've already read. So much for a day of literary escapism.

I grab one, something about forgotten kisses or maybe a butterfly, judging by the cover, and tuck it into the waistband of my yoga pants. Not like I have an extra hand. I don't want to make an ass out of myself—again—so I decide a walking tour of the facility is in order, to get better acquainted with the lodge. Maybe find some secret spots to maul Roger in between courses at dinner tonight.

The pretty girl from the gift shop yesterday is at the spa's front desk. "Hey, you're the swimsuit girl. How'd it work out for you?"

"Fine. A little uptight for my taste, but it covered all the right parts."

"How's the ankle?"

"Sprained."

"We heard about your fall."

"You people need hobbies."

"Safety first. Plus, when you live with the same people for months on end, news gets around. Gossip central. And things certainly got more interesting when you checked in."

"Fantastic. Glad I could amuse you."

She laughs quietly and leans closer to me. "Honestly? Everyone thinks it's awesome that a live wire is here. We get so many newlyweds and nearly-deads that this place could use a little shaking up."

Which makes me wonder, quite embarrassed at the thought, "Are there … security cameras … around the outside? Of the building?"

She gives me a quiet, lip-closed smile and nods yes.

"So, you guys saw … the other night …"

"Just a quick bit when you ran around the front of the lodge. And you do have a great body," she says, her hand on my wrist. "Ryan made sure the footage was deleted so no one would put it on YouTube."

"Wonderful."

She thrusts her hand out to me in introduction. "I'm Tabby. And I think you need some pampering."

"Hollie. And yes. Pampering would be nice." I'm mortified all over again, the idea of untold numbers of staff watching my naked ass run across the front of the lodge.

"Let's do this. I have an opening for a massage right at nine, which is," she looks at her watch, "in eight minutes. Perfect. Then I'll give you a facial and do your makeup, no charge. Just because I need someone to play with, and you need someone to be nice to you."

Her kindness almost makes me want to cry, this girl named after a cat. But then I remember that I have a chance at redemption with Roger tonight. Some pampering might be just what I need to get relaxed and in the mood, to let loose and be twenty-five instead of listening to that nasty hag in my head who reminds me that good girls don't do it on the first date. Technically, bitch, this will be the third date.

Which means all bets are off.

Chapter Fourteen
Who Doesn't Love a Surprise?

The massage—oh, how my muscles melted into blobby blobs the consistency of beached jellyfish. Mike—Steve—whatever his name is—his hands should be insured by that place that insures Gene Simmons' tongue and David Beckham's legs. Even my ankle feels better this afternoon, thanks to Mike/Steve's special attention to the muscles in my calf. He force-fed me what seemed like a gallon of water afterward, "to flush out the toxins locked in your muscles," and then scrubbed me down with lavender-infused towels. I smell so good right now, I might make out with myself.

Only I won't. Because Roger's hands are far better suited to doing egregious damage to my girl parts.

Tabby continues the Hollie Holiday by practicing her makeup skills on my face. Says she wants to head south to Hollywood after college and break into the makeup artist biz. Even pulls out her phone to show me photos of the fantastic makeup she's done on some of her staffer comrades.

"You ready?" she says, hands on the back of the chair.

"Ready." She spins me around slowly, and I'm taken aback by the face in the mirror. It's me, only better. I look … *pretty*. I haven't looked pretty in a long, long time.

"Don't cry! Your mascara!"

"You should be doing this for famous people."

"I know, right? Some of those stylists are ridiculous. I could do so much better!"

"No, I'm serious. This—you have a gift. I look …"

"Amazing." Mike/Steve the masseuse steps up next to Tabby. "She does killer work, eh?"

Oh, these adorable Canadians and their *eh*s. "Indeed. Quick. Someone take a picture. I'll need proof later that I looked so girly."

"Hot date tonight?" she says, handing my phone back.

"God, I hope so. After the week I've had, I need something so immoral, it borders on illegal."

I try to tip her, but she curls the money back into my hand. "Keep it. Go to the MAC counter as soon as you're back home and buy yourself some treats. You've got a terrific canvas here. Don't let it fade away."

"How'd you get so wise?" I laugh. "You're, what, twelve?"

Tabby hugs me and sends me on my way, but not before she presents me with the crutches bedazzled with ribbons. "Like a parade," she says. "Pretty crutches for pretty Hollie!"

I never want to leave here.

I feel like a supermodel as I move through the lodge. A little girl smiles at my very fancy crutches. When I round the corner to the front desk area, Miss Betty's face lights up. "Welllll! I see that Tabby got her claws into you," she sings. "You look so marvelous, my dear."

"Like a girl, right?"

"Very much like a girl," she says, patting my cheek.

"Round two for the hot date."

"Tonight, dear?"

"Yup. I have one dress left. After that, it's Levi's and yoga pants for the duration."

"Hollie, you could wear a burlap sack and still look lovely. Appreciate this," she points to all of me, "while you can. It doesn't last forever, sweetie."

"That's what everyone is saying. You guys are making me paranoid."

"How's the ankle? Those crutches working out for you?"

"You like my ribbons?"

"Very fetching."

Another guest taps his cardkey on the counter, his not-so-subtle plea for attention. I wave and hop-skip to the elevator, sort of wishing meanie-face Ryan were at his concierge desk arranging whale watching excursions so he could see how cute I look.

I am absolutely down to the last winsome thing I brought with. It's almost five—perfect timing. With the simple swipe of a credit card, Tabby has made me a vision—even painted my exposed toes of the sprained foot. Like magic.

Standing in the bathroom, I test the ankle. I can tolerate more pressure than I could last night but the zing of pain rockets up the side of my leg with too much weight. I hear my dad from the soccer sidelines after I've taken a hard hit. "Toughen up, Princess! Play now, cry later!" I am very much in the mood to play now, cry later.

I hope Roger is ready for what's coming down the elevator for him.

By five thirty, I'm still waiting. One white wine spritzer down, I don't want to get carried away. *Stay with the game plan, Hollie.* It's not like he could've stood me up, unless he left the island. I consider hobbling over to Miss Betty to see if Roger has checked out, but I don't want to come off as desperate.

By quarter to six, I am feeling exactly that. Maybe his meeting ran late.

At the maître d's podium, I ask for a table for two, leaving word with him that Roger Swinyard will be looking for me and here's five bucks if you can make sure he finds me thanks so much.

Another white wine spritzer. Fifteen more minutes.

And then I see him at the podium. My heart skips a beat. Twelve beats. If it doesn't restart soon, we'll have to test the defibrillator I'm sure Concierge Ryan has tucked under his mighty desk. Roger looks absolutely edible in the dark slacks and light blue buttondown. Whatever he does to maintain that tan, it looks criminal on him. My mouth is already watering, and there's nary a crumb of food on the table.

I push my chair back to stand, my hand raised to get his attention, when a gorgeous blond, her dress so tight I can see the outline of her liver, steps next to him and wraps an arm around his middle.

My hand drops.

There has to be some weird mix-up.

"Daddy, let's eat at this table!" says a miniature version of Roger who materializes from behind the statuesque blond, her hand firmly gripped around Roger Junior's. A fourth member of their party, yet another tiny clone, this one of the woman, grabs Roger's unoccupied hand.

He makes eye contact with me—those sheepish, sheepish eyes telling me, *Oh fuck I've been caught please don't say a word*—and then follows his picture-perfect family to the best table next to the roaring fireplace. The woman hugs him before sitting down, the rock on her left fourth finger big enough that it's wondrous she can lift her arm without mechanical aid.

I slide into my chair, my face raw as if freshly slapped.

We never talked about past relationships because I didn't want to reveal that the split from Keith was so new. He clearly didn't want to talk about such things because he's a cheating, lying son of a bitch.

Oh my God, he has kids. Two beautiful little kids who look at him like he's some sort of god. The way I look at my dad, like he can do no wrong.

Only Roger is doing so much wrong, lying to their mother, disrespecting their very existence by rubbing his boner on my naïve, ridiculous body.

The wine glass is empty before I can warn myself otherwise.

"Is this seat taken?"

I look up, eyes wide. A man's voice is not what I expect to hear, given this unnerving plot twist, but the voice does in fact belong to man. If it weren't for the crooked nose, I'd not recognize him.

"What?"

"This seat. May I occupy it?"

"Yeah. I guess."

"You look breathtaking tonight."

"What? Yeah … Tabby. She's great." Another foolish glance over my shoulder at Roger's table shoots one more arrow into my chest. His wife is doing her best to mark her territory, her fingers ring-deep in his hair, their smiles warm and affectionate.

"Lying bastard," I whisper to no one. To Concierge Ryan. Because he's there and his face is clean and his green eyes are staring back at me with what I expect is pity. "Don't look at me like that."

"I just don't think it's right that this work of art should go unappreciated." He gestures at me.

"What do you want?"

"Dinner might be nice."

"Did you know? About Roger?"

"Do we need to talk about that? Maybe we should have that hockey talk. I can get more wine." He sniffs at my glass. "You drinking spritzers?" He motions to a waiter, points to the wine glass, and holds up two fingers.

"He's married? How did I not know this?"

"Would you look at that …" Ryan is looking out the tall windows. "There's a unicorn over there, dancing with his leprechaun friends."

"I can't believe I didn't figure this out." I'm replaying the last two and a half days, searching for clues, even the slightest hint, that Roger was a married, cheating douche nozzle.

"Oh! And Santa just arrived! Look at that rainbow!"

I slam my hand onto the tabletop, startling the silverware. "What the *hell* are you talking about?"

"Nothing. Just trying to get your attention off matters who don't deserve it."

"You knew."

"Knew what?"

"You knew Roger was married."

"Hollie Porter, it is none of my business what goes on with the guests here."

"Bullshit. Why didn't you tell me?"

"What would I say? Don't hump the good-looking business stud with the fake tan and glistening teeth because he's a lying scoundrel?"

"Yes. Exactly that."

"As I recall, I tried to mention something along those lines the other day and you shut me down. Told me to stay out of your love life."

I glower at him. "I don't even know you. This … this is not happening."

"You do know me. I'm friend, not foe, Hollie. Let's have dinner. I can tell you everything you ever wanted to know about the N-H-L."

My laugh is cruel and acidic. "I don't want to know anything about your stupid hockey or why you looked like a mountain man three hours ago and now you don't or how your nose got to be so damn crooked."

"You don't have to be mean," he says, sitting back as the wine arrives. "I'm just trying to help."

"Maybe I've had enough help from you for a lifetime."

I shove back my chair and grab for the crutches, trying not to look like a clumsy asshole as I hop across the fancy dining room filled with fancy people eating fancy food with their cherubic off-spring and fashion-forward wives.

God, you are such a fool.

I need to go home. This was a mistake. Revelation Cove—no, my *life*—has been one fucking disaster after another since I stepped foot out of my apartment. That's what I get for listening to my drunken self.

I don't stop at the front desk to ask Miss Betty why *she* didn't tell me about Roger because this place is filled with traitorous liars. They probably all knew about it. Tabby said it herself—it's gossip central around here. I wonder who won the wager about if Roger would nail the dumb tourist before his 36-24-36 wife arrived.

The sun hasn't set, though it is low in the sky, painting the chubby gray clouds in the purples and reds and pinks of late spring.

Seabirds across the way are tearing apart something on the shore—looks like a dead fish. It's dinnertime. I should be tearing apart my own fish, though with a little less violence, giggling at the clever things my dinner date has to say, enjoying the adoration of being the only one in the room who looks this good on crutches.

Instead I'm down on the dock in front of the lodge, stopping only because I can go no farther without falling into the water. The tears have made a ruinous mess of Tabby's handiwork, I'm sure, but who cares? All of this fawning and special treatment was just a big fucking joke. Now everyone's tee-heeing over clinking shot glasses, watching the pathetic Hollie fall apart on the closed-circuit security television.

Among the row of small boats moored to the dock, canvas tarps covering passenger compartments, one remains open. I don't think—I act. Perhaps a float in a boat is exactly what I need right now. Time away from Roger and his magazine-spread family, from Concierge Ryan's piteous face, from the knowing glances of staff who saw me going gaga over that ridiculously handsome man because *oh my God someone who isn't Keith is paying attention to me.*

Frailty, thy name is woman.

Shut up, Hamlet.

Chapter Fifteen

Orcinus orca

O n my ass, I manage to slide into the boat without too much
pain. It's unsteady, and my sea legs are nonexistent, but it's
not like I'm planning a cross-Atlantic tour. I just need to float. And
think.

This boat has oars. And under the bench I find a bag with a
Revelation Cove fleece pullover and some emergency supplies. I
won't need the sunscreen tonight but the spray bottle of mosquito
repellent is most appreciated. Not like anyone's going to inhale the
lavender Mike/Steve scrubbed into my pores. Adding DEET to the
perfumery won't make a bit of difference when no one's tongue will
be licking parts usually covered with decency.

I should do it. I should untie that little rope and push myself
out into the water and paddle across the way to that other island
where the birds are making mince of the fish, where no humans
are lying in wait to laugh or point or cheat on unsuspecting twenty-
somethings with more shoes than sense. It's not that far. It's not
dark. The emergency bag has a crank flashlight and granola bars,
plus the dock and the front of the lodge have plenty of light, so I
can easily scoot across and scoot back.

I untie the rowboat and give a shove against the dock with one
of the oars. A quick scan of the area reveals I am, as yet, still alone,
though I can hear laughter rolling over the greenway slope from outdoor diners. Lacking marine expertise, I bonk and volley my hijacked
vessel through the other white boats, to the end of the dock, and into
the open water. Within ten or twelve pulls, I break a sweat—this is
harder than it looks, especially with leverage from only one leg—but

it feels good to be doing something other than watching Roger gloat or sitting in front of Concierge Ryan with his *I told you so even though I told you nothing because I'm a giant hairy jerk* face.

The shore across the way isn't that far. I'll make it in just a few minutes. Easily. Maybe there will be otters. Where there are fish and birds, there have to be otters. Right?

If I'm careful, I can pull up without scaring the winged diners away. They're having at it. From the only sequined handbag I've ever owned in my life, I pull my phone and try to take a photo of this crazy swarm straight out of a Hitchcock film. My first foray into wildlife photography!

Kerplunk.

Something splashes. I look around, willing it to be a seagull come to say hello, hoping it's not one of those sharks Concierge Ryan said live in BC waters.

"Don't be stupid," I say to myself and the silence.

Because letting go of an oar to take a photo of shithawks eviscerating a dying fish is not stupid at all.

Especially when the oar is now floating away from your boat, rather swiftly, its wide head bobbing as if to wave goodbye.

"Aren't these things supposed to lock in? Shit!" With the singular remaining oar, I struggle with the current that seems to be conspiring against my efforts. Round and round we go, swirling away from the birdy buffet, away from the dock, away from Revelation Cove and its hidden dangers of the male variety.

I'm going to have to paddle harder and faster, switching from one side of the boat to the other, if I don't want to end up in the middle of this inlet, alone, as the moon steps over the mountainous summits and settles in for the evening.

But that's exactly what happens. No amount of paddling is going to get me nearer to that dock, not with one oar. My only option is to steer toward the lost paddle, which now has a considerable lead in the current carrying us away from the speck of civilization.

I did not appreciate the true width of this waterway upon my initial floatplane arrival. Perspective is everything, and the drift downstream is providing me with a view I did not anticipate. Beauty of epic, overwhelming proportions and postcard pretty? Totally. Terrifying with a side of *oh my dear God I could die out here and no one would know*? Little bit.

I pull the second—only—oar into the boat, conceding that this water is stronger than I am. If I can get closer to shore, though, I might be able to ease along the quieter water or even use the subtle licks of wave to push me onto the rocky beach. Except the beach at my present location is nonexistent—the side of this latest island is trees and rock, straight into the water, as if dropped from the heavens. And it's far away. With one oar, by the time I get close, I'll be onto the next treed, rocky outcropping.

I clutch onto the oar—now my most precious commodity—and consider my options. If there's a knife in the emergency kit, I can slice up the canvas and use Tabby's ribboned décor to fashion makeshift oars out of one of the crutches.

Brilliant!

Excited, I spill the supply bag contents onto the boat bottom. Sweatshirt, tiny first-aid kit, bottled water, five granola bars, a can of some gooey stuff for repairing holes, three oily flares.

No knife.

Deflated, I stuff the contents back into the bag. If I can't turn this not-so-pleasurable craft around, will I sail to … to where? Victoria? The Pacific Ocean? Nah. Someone will find me before then, right? Shit, they better. I will run out of granola bars after five meals, granting only one bar per meal. I double-check the bag's outside pocket for spirits to warm a cold soul. Not a drop. Probably best. Getting drunk out here as the sun abandons me is likely not the wisest course of action.

As if any of my actions lately have been wise.

But wait! I have a phone! Of course! I can call the resort. Yeah, I'm going to eat a crow pie so big, I'll be shitting black feathers for a year once Ryan or some other staff member launches a rescue. But it's not really a rescue—it's just … helping. I lost an oar. Perfectly benign. Could happen to anyone. I had a dispatch call once from a kid who lost his oar on the Willamette River, and easy peasy, the river patrol helped him back within just a few minutes. No sirens, no flashing lights.

At this point, Ryan should expect something like this from me. Ryan and Tabby have both said it—I've been a source of nonstop entertainment since my arrival. Hell, since before my arrival. I made him giggle when Ridley and I drunk dialed the resort, right? That's it—when Ryan sighs and huffs at me for being a crazy pain in his ass, I will remind him that my antics have been solely for his enjoyment, that the sedate Revelation Cove hasn't seen hilarity of this scope, I dare say, ever. I'll be taking that free night's stay and in-room breakfast now, thank you.

But this pep talk to fortify my resolve against Ryan's sure-fire annoyance is for naught when the screen of my phone flashes two alarming little words: *no service.*

Well. This is a problem.

Panic is the wrong emotion here. I have to dig deep, channel Calm Hollie who talks husbands through birthin' babies on bathroom floors, who talks to scared babysitters afraid someone is in the house to chop them up, who talks Mona through Herb's diabetic fit while we wait for EMS to arrive.

Calm Hollie is calm.

Lying back against the forward bench, I listen as the water laps the side of the boat, watch overhead as stars peek out of their hidey-holes and burn hot to shine through thickening cloud cover. This is a peace I've never experienced, and while arguably magnificent, I've never, ever been this alone.

When I left Portland for pastures less complicated, wobbling adrift in unfamiliar waters was not exactly what I'd envisioned. Especially not on a night when I look as good as I likely ever will. Then again, I had no idea I'd be slimed by a dude who sells organic bananas and exotic vegan marmalade for a living. When it's a man whose wife cheats, he's a cuckold. What do they call the young woman in the midst of a premature midlife crisis almost duped into giving up the treasure to a cheater-cheater-pumpkin-eater?

Desperate. Foolhardy. Lame.

If my phone had service, I'd find an online thesaurus and search for all the words to describe what a total ass I am.

But I have no cell service. Which means no thesaurus to chip away at what remains of my limping self-esteem.

I cannot panic. All I can do is wait.

I pull on the oversized fleecy, mothball-smelling sweatshirt and flatten the canvas tarp over my bare legs, careful not to rest too much weight on my angry ankle. The tiny part of my brain that governs adult-like, logical behavior tells me that the stars are too numerous to count but that doesn't mean I won't try.

Within a few moments, the gentle lullaby of the rocking boat coaxes my wine spritzer-infused body with waves of sleepytime. I could sleep. If I lie still, I won't tip the boat. And I'm hugging the oar to my chest because it truly is my last remaining lifeline.

Something brushes under the boat. Seconds later, a wet *whoooooooooosh* explodes alongside my floating oasis. My heart rockets into my throat. Holy fucking shit, it's gotta be a shark. He said there are sharks. Twenty species? Or was it two hundred? The shark can sense my fear and now he's going to go *Jaws* on my ass and knock my boat around until I fall in and then he and his little shark babies are going to have an all-you-can-eat night at the Hollie Buffet.

I sit up, so, so carefully. "Please not a shark ... please not a shark ..."

The enormous black dorsal fin just feet from the rowboat does not belong to a shark.

It belongs to a killer whale. Orca. *Orcinus orca.*

Free Willy has come to visit. And with him—it has to be a male, judging by the height of that fin, easily taller than I am—he's brought friends. Another black fin, this one with more crescent in its curve, punctures the surface of the water, followed by a third, this one much smaller.

A baby.

A baby!

They're either checking me out, or I will be their sprite's next hunting lesson.

Let's hope for the former.

I sit up straighter, knuckles white around the oar's neck. I've watched a thousand documentaries on these gorgeous beasts but I am ... I don't even know what I am. A million emotions at once slam into the lopsided, wormy cabin in my head that serves as the nerve center.

"Holy mother of holy holies," I say to the breeze.

Whooooooooosh!

The male is back close to the boat, so close that he rubs it as he exhales wet breath into the sky, his nudge not entirely gentle. My face is awash in misty whale spit.

"A whale spit on me!" I laugh out loud. "Ohhhh, you are so beautiful!"

The gallop of cardiovascular muscle against cartilage and bone in my chest is almost painful, and I have to remind myself to breathe. Like the orca, I have to breathe or I will sink to the bottom of this inlet.

The female skyhops about ten feet from the other side, her dark eye inquisitive as she bobs out of the water. She clicks, a sound almost like a playing card against bicycle spokes or a thumbnail down a grooved surface.

"Hello, my darling gorgeous creature. Is that your baby? Can I see your baby?" She disappears into the blackness to circle around, showing off the white on her fluke's underside as she dives again. The male is particularly curious, again rubbing against the side of the boat, jarring the simple wooden vessel hard enough that I'm afraid he'll tip it, so close I could touch the grayish saddle over his wet onyx back if only I'd reach out. Which I won't do. Because as breathtaking and life-changing as this moment is, I am scared to the point that my stomach might have to be surgically returned to my abdominal cavity.

As though waiting for a thunderclap, I count between resurfacings, between blows around the boat. When I get to eleven-one-thousand, I think they've left me, gone on to chase seals.

"Did you leave? Come back ..."

I ease into a standing position. Maybe if I'm taller, I can better see the white-against-black contrast if indeed they're under the boat.

Nothing. The water has returned to its quiet former self.

Whooooooooooosh!

The exhale behind is just enough of a shove for me to topple backward into the water.

Beyond the bone-numbing, choking cold, all I can think about is the fact that I AM GOING TO BE DINNER if I don't get my half-naked body out of this fucking water. In the instant I'm submerged, something akin to a whistle slams into my eardrums, audible even over my flailing arms. The whales—they're talking to each other! And I hope it's not about their favorite recipes for harebrained city girls.

My damaged ankle shrieks as I kick to stay afloat, as I struggle against the inky drink to hoist my top half over the boat's side, a hundred screams stuck in my panicked throat.

If I struggle too much, Daddy Orca might pull me under and throw my oxygen-deprived form skyward for Mommy and Baby to slap around until I'm no longer a threat. That's what they do—orcas play with their food until it isn't flopping anymore. They seem to love the challenge of undoing what was once alive before sinking those impressive white teeth into blood-warmed flesh.

Get out of the water get out of the water get out of the fucking water!

Now is not the time to worry about the pain, present or future. Now is the time for action.

Hands locked around the middle bench, I yank myself up and over, praying I won't topple the rowboat, eyes squinted tight, waiting for that chomp that will remove foot from ankle, calf from thigh.

The chomp does not come, but the clicking Mommy Orca skyhops again, not five feet from the opposite side of the boat, as if to check on me. I'm on my belly across the narrow bench, legs bent at ninety-degree angles to keep them free of enterprising daddy orcas, my body drenched from stem to stern, hair dripping and heavy, my skin goosebumped so hard, it's painful like a thousand acupuncture needles stabbing into my hair follicles.

"Thank you for not eating me," I whisper. The baby skyhops alongside, his (her?) head and eyes so breathtakingly beautiful, I need that damn thesaurus again just to find the words. "Omigod ... omigod ... thank you ..."

Daddy Orca circles around, the exhaled blowhole mist wafting past, surprisingly warm against the chills vibrating violently through me.

This time when I start the count, I stop when three dorsal fins protrude at intervals farther and farther away. They're leaving. And they didn't eat me.

I wish they'd come back.

Not to eat me, of course. But because they have each other, and I'm alone and I want to see the baby again, just one more time.

That was, on the spectrum of human experience, ranked equally as most frightening and most exhilarating.

No one's going to believe me. I fell into the water with three killer whales and *lived to tell.*

My body is near convulsions from the very real cold, cold that I've never had the displeasure of experiencing ever before, not even when, summer between fourth and fifth grade, my dad's work schedule got weird and because of his I'm-a-terrible-daddy-because-you-don't-have-a-mommy guilt kicked in, he sent me to a summer camp that was likely a training stop for Al Qaeda where the lifeguard everyone called The Kraken threw scared kids into the unheated pool just to listen to their screams. I was cold then, but not cold like I am now.

And as if cold weren't enough, the oar, the only remaining oar, is floating away from me, likely to find its mate.

Holy shit.

Holy shit.

Holy *shit.*

Things just got fucking real. I could die of hypothermia out here. The canvas is the only thing left remotely dry—the fleece sweatshirt is so heavy with the inlet waters, it's nothing short of miraculous that I was able to right myself in the boat. The cotton wool around my ankle is five pounds of waterlogged goo and some of the tape has lost its sticky, now hanging off like the frills on my father's fishing flies. In a weird twist, the cold in the wrap is helping to numb the pain in the sprained muscles. A tiny blessing in disguise.

Teeth chattering and hands shaking, I scramble for the flares. Maybe someone will see it, see this little boat floating all by itself in the darkness, and hop in their own boat, zoom-zoom-zoom on out to save the dumb American girl with only enough brain cells to fill a shot glass.

I don't know how to use a flare.

I pluck the plastic cap and a string dangles from the top. I can't read the instructions along the flare's side—it's too dark, and not even the limited illumination from my phone helps when I discover the instructions are in French. *Magnifique.*

Out of options, I pull the string and turn away as the flare sputters to life, a blaring red flame tearing from its ignited end. Startled by the intense heat and aggressive overflow of nuclear-grade light, I accidentally drop it—*plop.* Into the water. It burns for a while longer, maybe a minute, before fading out, its oily husk spent and now nothing more than litter in this pristine landscape.

No rescue will befall me if I freak out and drop the damn thing in the water. And what I *really* need is one of those flares they used on the *Titanic.* The kind that shoot into the sky.

Oh my God, the *Titanic* sank.

Please tell me this is not the *USS Hollie.*

"There are no icebergs, Hol … no icebergs," I say.

If ever there were a time to cry, it's now.

So that's exactly what I do.

I cry for all the stupid things I've ever done throughout the whole of my life, from bad boyfriends to risky haircuts to slumber-party piercings that got infected to the time I took a ride down a winding country road in the bed of a pickup truck driven by a drunk friend to trusting that brief romance with the senior football player who promised if I sent him a shot of my boobs he'd erase it but of course not before posting it online so everyone could make fun of Hollie's Invisible Hooters to quitting college because I lied to my dad and used my student loan funds to hire a shady private investigator to find my missing mother to letting my best friend talk me into dangerous shit and never being able to say no to her and then grieving after she dumped me and moving in with Keith and his Yorkies and on and on and on. I'm so skilled at cataloguing the stupid shit I've done in my life, if this were an Olympic sport, I'd be gold medalist times infinity.

And now I'll have to get a roommate. With my luck, it will be some weird chick with strange taste in lovers and food with plantar warts she will share simply by walking on the same floors and showering in the same tub. If I can't find a roommate, I'll have to go back and live with Mangala the demon goat and try to keep my dad from setting me up with Manjit's cardiologist son.

And then I remember that my otters are back in Room 212, alone, wondering where Hollie the Human is and why she hasn't returned from the date to cover their little plastic otter eyes with a washcloth while Hollie does godless things to the perfect body of that lying sack-o-shit everyone calls Roger. If that's even his name. My otter friend doesn't know that Hollie the Human is floating oarless away from her, that this could be my last night on the planet known as Earth, the heartless, hurtful rock that it has become, and no one knows where I am or will figure out that I'm gone until it's too late and the sharks do surface from the depths to pick clean my bones.

I laugh at myself through the cascade of tears. Such a drama queen.

Things could be worse. It could be ...

"And you had to go and think it, didn't you, you stupid shit."

Raining.

CHAPTER SIXTEEN
RESCUE HERO

The patter of drops on the canvas tarp covering my shivering, aching body curled in the boat's bottom eventually lulls me to sleep. I don't know how long I'm out—when I wake to scraping along the boat's underside, I check my phone for the time only to find it wet, and thus dead. Of course. A thin fog has settled over the water's surface and the rainclouds have obscured the stars, but the scraping, I'm relieved to find, is not another orca.

It's the shore.

Land ho!

Somehow, during my slumber, the boat drifted east and the wooden bottom is rasping against a rocky shoreline. I'm so thrilled to not be in the middle of the inlet that I spring from under the tarp and hop one-footed into the holy-shit-that's-still-effing-cold water to pull the boat a few feet onto solid ground.

I went to summer camp. I can do this. The rain has lessened, though everything is still damp and weepy. Starting a fire will be tough with no dry wood. I've got fire via the two remaining flares, so I could burn the boat, but that seems counterproductive. I might need it again, even without the oars.

A crack-snap in the distant greenery startles me. Yeah, definitely won't be burning the boat. Might need to make a hasty getaway.

Shit, can bears swim? Of course they can. They eat salmon and salmon are in water ergo bears can swim.

As can cougars. That's how they get to these islands. They swim between them, paddling with their giant, mightily clawed feet in the glacial water to check out the eats on nearby menus.

I grab the crutches out of the boat's belly and slap the metal shafts together like a ginormous city-dwelling dork. Maybe the sound will scare off whatever is coming down to sample my fleshy parts. I almost pee my already soaked G-string when a huge owl throws itself out of a nearby tree and flies low above the short beach, soaring over the water until its form is swallowed by mist.

I should probably not camp on the beach itself—still too cold and nothing but the canvas tarp for protection, which will do very little in the way of keeping skin and muscle attached to bone in the event of inquisitive bear or cougar. Not like sleeping in the boat will offer much more protection, but it's all I got.

I do my best to drag and shove the boat completely out of the water and am so grateful that no one is nearby with a camera to videotape just how completely ridiculous this must look. Me hopping around like a maimed bird, bare knees and calves coated in dirty sand and tiny pebbles and a slime that I hope to dear baby Jesus is kelp or other sea-belched greenery, oversized sweatshirt filthy and sopping and oh so heavy. Perhaps in response to my body having bigger problems, i.e., survival, the throb in my twisted ankle has calmed. Maybe it feels sorry for me, like, "Man, Hollie, this is really fucked up so I'm going to chill and maybe you can find us a way out of this before the grim reaper knocks on your forehead."

Thanks, ankle. No, really, I mean it.

I hope the tide doesn't come in too high, or else I will be floating again within just a few hours. Another reason why I should stick close to my vessel. A captain never abandons her ship. Especially when the ship has the sum total of five granola bars, the only stash of civilized nutrition before unraveling the fabric of the barely there little black dress to use as thread for a handcrafted, broken-branch fishing pole baited with owl pellets.

Five granola bars. Five meals. Maybe more if I can exercise self-control.

Yeah. Right.

I eat two and a half. But all this rowing and fretting and swimming and almost dying with orcas has expended my energy molecules, spent them like a redneck lottery winner's wife in a bedazzled gun shop. I chug one of the bottled waters, unaware of how thirsty I am until there are only a few slurps left.

Man, I hope that inlet water is drinkable.

When the rain starts up again, so do the shivers. I turtle back under the canvas to await dawn, frozen fingers crossed that no mommas of any sort will come along with their wee charges for a midnight snack.

I tuck the canvas tight around my fetal-position body, trying like hell to keep the water from seeping in and expediting the hypothermia that is bound to set in soon. Except with my homemade cocoon, there is little fresh air getting in. Although the trapped exhaled carbon dioxide is good for warmth, it's not so great for my body's insatiate need for fresh oxygen. Which presents a problem if I'm to keep warm and dry.

A problem exacerbated when new scratching sounds begin on the outside of the boat.

I have to look. I should at least be prepared to use a crutch to defend myself. Maybe I should take the crutches apart and use the sharper ends of the dismantled metal shafts.

Scratch scratch. Chatter chatter.

I know that sound.

I poke my head out and come eye to eye with a rather large, very fluffy raccoon. Not sure who jumps higher, me or him, but he hisses and backs up. He's not alone—scattered about the beach is a whole troop, and while they collectively startle when I sit up straighter, I am soon forgotten in favor of washing the dead crabs they're fighting over.

Crab. Where'd they get that? I can eat crab.

I watch them chew and squabble, fighting over the claws and juicy innards. Two juveniles come to blows over a leg but one is clearly tougher and waddles off to another part of the beach to dig into his spoils. Too bad no one has any butter or garlic, or I might fight the little fella for it myself. So raccoons eat more than maple-smelling, hundred-dollar bills. Go figure.

Without warning, the sky lights up and the rain explodes from the clouds. So much for tonight's smorgasbord. The raccoons are off into the brush just as the thunder detonates overhead.

As if I weren't wet enough already.

Back under the tarp.

I don't sleep because the thunder is too loud and too terrifying, and I swear the lightning is striking the beach all around me and I will emerge from my pretend tent to find this island completely alight and the beach will be inundated with creatures trying to escape the fiery wrath of the sky's temper tantrum.

Between rumbles—*one one-thousand, two one-thousand*—grrrrrrrrrr-BOOM, says the sky—something else rumbles toward me. A sputtering put-put, like a motor.

A motor!

From a boat!

I pop up from under the cover, my hand serving as windshield wiper against the torrential downpour, desperately trying to see if that is indeed a boat coming closer to my little harbor.

When the light flashes across my face, it's not from the sky but from a bulb!

"Hey! Heyyyyyyy! Over here!" I wave. Not sure if the mariner can hear me over the elements.

The rowboat's bottom rough against my naked skin, I scrabble to my knees, no longer worried that I am absorbing even more water. If it's a boat, I need to be saved. I really, really want to brush my teeth. And punch Roger in the throat. Maybe not in that order.

"Heyyyyyyy! Help!" The bright light lands on my face, blinding me, and a small horn sounds.

At last. Saved.

The wind has grown ferocious, and I can see the waves buffeting the boat's side. I'm unable to see much else through the darkness secondary to the flashlight's glare, but a voice yells back at me, "I gotta drop the anchor! I'll come to you!"

I huddle again, waiting for my rescue to be completed. Maybe it's a kindly fisherman caught in the storm and he'll help me back to his nearby cabin where his portly wife will put on tea and wrap me in a woolen blanket and say things like *Dear, dear, look what the cat dragged in, poor wretched creature.* Or maybe it's a passing tourist, a family of vacationers, en route to their own cabin or maybe even to Revelation Cove, and the unexpected tempest took them by surprise too, and inside their warm boat, they will have cocoa and a bathroom with one of those portable toilets, and a bag full of dry socks and spiced rum for just such occasions.

"Hollie Porter? Is that you?"

Or maybe it's none of the above.

"Hollie? Are you okay? Can you walk?" I slowly reemerge from the canvas, wondering if I should play dead.

"Yeah," I wave. "It's me."

Concierge Ryan, outfitted in rain gear and looking like the Gorton's fisherman, struggles through the waist-deep water, a long rope in hand as he jogs toward a tree growing out of the rock face.

"Anchor's down but I gotta tie off, just in case. Are you hurt?" he yells. I don't bother to respond—he won't be able to hear me until he's closer.

Within a minute, he's standing over me, his large frame a shield from the rain but only long enough for him to bend over, throw the tarp aside, and hoist my soaked body over his shoulder.

And back into the water we go.

He helps me on board, and I'm grateful to find a cabin on this boat—a built-in couch and a kitchenette. It's drier than what I had going on in the rowboat, and I spy a very thick blanket draped over the back of the captain's chair.

He doesn't even wait for the door to slam behind him before the ranting begins.

"Where the hell have you been? What were you thinking, taking a boat out without telling anyone, without even a life jacket? Do you have a death wish? Are you really that stupid? You could've died out here and no one would've known! Do you know what kind of liability we'd be looking at? The resort could be shut down!"

I stare back at him, shivering so hard my teeth ache in my head. "You got anything to drink?"

"What?"

"Drink. I'm thirsty. And cold."

"Are you going to answer my questions?"

"Drink first. Dry clothes second. Talking third."

He pulls off his funny yellow hat and rain slicker, steps out of his waders. Everything wet is hung from hooks, shedding water into a long basin rather than on the thin carpet under our feet.

"How's your ankle? Is it okay? Are you hurt?"

I can't answer. Too cold. He moves past and cranks on a small heater. From a plastic bin, he pulls out sweatpants, yet another Revelation Cove fleece pullover—this one dry—and some thick wool socks. "You can change in the forward cabin. Just pull the curtain. I won't peek. And put your wet stuff in the shower stall so it doesn't get all over the bed. We have to sleep somewhere tonight."

We're sleeping here tonight? Why aren't we sleeping in our respective beds back at the resort, those dry, high-quality, cushiony, insect-and-raccoon-free beds?

As the question floats into my head, a strong wind slaps the side of the boat, knocking both of us just enough off balance to look cartoony.

"It's too foggy. Water's choppy. I don't want to take a chance. We're anchoring here for the night."

I'm not going to argue. I don't want to take a chance, either, given that I've already spent time in this body of water. My jaw is killing me from the chattering. No more midnight swims.

"What time is it?"

Ryan looks at the tiny digital clock next to the steering wheel. "Around 2:30."

"When's sunrise?"

"Why, you gotta be somewhere?" he says. I squint at him. "We should get that wrap off your foot. You're dripping on the carpet."

I look down. Certainly enough, a small puddle has formed under me. "Sorry."

He grabs a roll of blue industrial towels and rips off a few sheets. "Do you need the crutches or can you hop?"

I don't answer with words but rather by hobbling into the forward cabin, sliding closed the curtain with as much annoyance as I can muster. I'm burning my few remaining granola bar calories with this incessant shaking. I have to get out of these clothes. I fear for the integrity of my teeth. Shit, I was on Keith's dental plan. I won't have dental insurance until the next open enrollment at 911. If I still have a job.

Why do these questionable life decisions keep coming back to kick me in the girl balls?

I plop the sweatshirt and little black dress and the wad of cotton wool from my now very purple ankle into the shower bottom as instructed, although it's less a shower than a fiberglass rectangle wide enough for an emaciated six-year-old. "How the hell do *you* shower in this?"

"Very carefully."

I peek through the curtain, wise to not pull it away from the wall enough for him to see I'm still butt naked. He's making tea.

"Do you take honey?"

"And whisky."

"You can't have any booze until we get your body temperature back to normal." I know the medical rules of mixing alcohol and potential hypothermia. Those St. Bernards with barrels of brandy? Pure myth. Alcohol can make hypothermia worse, and St. Bernards never carried brandy to rescue snowshoers.

I will get dressed and sit in front of the heat and warm up and I won't die of hypothermia nor will I be a midnight snack for enterprising, curious orcas, and then I can have some whisky.

Although if this boat's rocking doesn't ease up, I might barf up that whisky.

"You okay? You need help?" he asks.

"I think I can handle putting clothes on."

"That hasn't been my experience with you so far."

"Here we go again," I say, throwing the curtain aside. The sweatshirt is huge and the T-shirt smells like old cologne and storage, and the sweatpants—pink—I just hope they're clean and not from one of Ryan's boat girls. If he has boat girls.

Does he bring his lady friends out on this boat? Oh God, am I wearing coochie pants?

Whatever. Beggars can't be choosers.

He's stirring honey into a mug, holding firmly to the handle so it doesn't slide off the counter. "Have a seat. Wrap up in that blanket. Your lips are purple."

I didn't even have a moment for vanity. I'm sure I look like a supermodel right now. Whatever. That blanket is thick and wool and has my goosebumps written all over it.

Ryan hands me a steaming mug. I sip too quickly, scalding the tip of my tongue.

"So is this the part where you restart your yelling at me for stealing one of your boats and putting myself in danger?"

"Do I need to?"

"You started it, so I thought we'd finish and get it out of the way."

"It's not often that I have to go searching for guests in the middle of the night."

"How'd you figure out I was gone?"

"Miss Betty went upstairs to check on you after the incident with Roger. You sort of disappeared, so she got worried. When you didn't answer your door, she let herself in to make sure you weren't locked out again or that you hadn't fallen, you know, with the sore ankle," he says, gesturing at my leg. "When we couldn't find you, we counted the boats. Sure enough, we were one short."

"A broken one. I lost an oar within just a few minutes."

"Yeah, well, you didn't get the oar locks in right."

"I'm not Popeye."

"Clearly. Or we wouldn't be out here right now." He finishes preparing his tea and sits next to me on the couch-bench thing. His hands dwarf the coffee cup. "Why'd you leave?"

"Do you have to ask?"

"You looked amazing tonight. We could've had a nice dinner, a few laughs. I could've explained everything you never wanted to know about hockey—"

"Hockey? Really?"

"You didn't notice—my beard's gone."

"And that has to do with hockey?"

"Remember? Playoff beard. My team lost. I shaved."

"I thought you shaved because Miss Betty threatened to tell your boss."

Ryan chuckles and shakes his head, eyes diverted. "Yeah, there's that."

"Is hockey what happened to your nose?"

"You really don't like my nose, do you."

"I never said that."

"No, but you haven't missed an opportunity to flip me shit about it."

"It's … unique."

"If by unique, you mean broken and improperly set between periods three different times, then yeah. I'm unique."

"Your teeth are lovely, though."

"These were expensive." He flashes a cheesy grin. "They'd better look good."

A moment without conversation settles between us, but it isn't quiet. The wind screeches like depraved harpies trying to shred the windows. "So you bailed on dinner because of some guy who doesn't deserve the air he breathes."

"That's not a very nice way to talk about paying guests, Concierge Ryan."

"I've been at this for a while. I see these guys all the time. Saw 'em when I was playing hockey. Give a man a little power, a little money, and he thinks he can have any honey who smiles pretty at him."

"And I happened to be a honey who smiled pretty."

"What do you expect with a guy like Roger?"

"Is that even his real name?"

"Yeah. And he really does own those grocery stores."

"He seemed nice, though. I guess I should've known better."

"Why would you?"

"Because why would a guy who looks like that be interested in me?"

"Uh-oh, are we heading into one of those I'm-not-pretty-enough conversations?" He looks at me sideways.

"You should talk with that nose of yours."

"See? Again with the nose. I'll have you know I earned this." He points at his nose. It's not *that* bad. In fact, without the Grizzly Adams-ish beard ... those green eyes are something kind of crazy.

"It's not that I'm not pretty enough—I do fine with what I've got. But he's successful and rich and he's just not the type I usually attract. Did you see his wife?"

"Plastic. All of it."

"And you would know that how?"

"Hollie, I've played professional athletics. Been in and around the hockey world since I was a young, hormonal, pimply-faced man-child with no idea what to do with the attention the girls and women were throwing at me. I've seen my share of plastic babes."

"So you're a manwhore?"

"Nah, not me. All I'm saying is that I've seen my share of guys like Roger Dodger."

"Still ... he would've been fun."

"Really?"

"Did you see his abs?"

Ryan laughs under his breath at me. "No, I did not see his abs."

"I haven't seen abs like that outside of a magazine or movie screen."

"Really? Working at 911, don't you have your share of firemen and cops?"

"Hardly."

"And Keith the paramedic has no abs, I take it."

"If abs could be built with Cheetos and cheap takeout, then he'd be Mr. Olympus ..."

"You're hanging out with the wrong crowd, then, Hollie Porter."

"Which is why I will never drunk dial your resort ever again," I laugh. "You clearly know way too much about my life."

"Hey, I'm just a willing listener, doing what I can to make my guests happy," he says, his smile warm and wide. "It's not my fault loose were your lips."

"Thanks, Yoda."

"The Force is strong with you, young Padawan."

"Oh my God, you sound like Keith."

"Noooo, not Keith! Wait—wait—where's my stethoscope?" He pats his chest.

I reach behind me and grab the small, rather ugly throw pillow and threaten to smack him with it. Instead, I stop midswing and look at the pillow's circa-1975 cat face. "This is the ugliest pillow I've ever seen."

"Don't be mean. That is a classic."

I swallow the rest of my tea in one long pull. The undissolved honey in the bottom is sweet on my teeth.

"You warming up yet?" he asks.

Actually, I am. The shivers aren't gone, but the chattering of my teeth has subsided and I don't feel like I'm going to crack like an icicle against a fence post. "I think I might need more tea." Ryan nods and reaches for my cup. "Wait—you have a potty on board, right? I don't have to hang my ass off the boat or anything?"

"In the closet across from the shower stall, a Porta Pottie, just for the lady."

As Ryan moves the few feet to the kitchenette, the boat rocks with a little extra force. I grab the arm of the couch. "We're not going to tip over, are we?"

"Nah. The wind's coming at us from the side. Anchor's down. We're going to get rocked around a little bit." When he returns with my refilled tea, he lobs a banana onto my lap. "I'm guessing you're hungry."

"Yeah, the granola bars in the emergency kit—"

"You didn't eat those, did you?"

"Uhhhh, yeah …" Ryan grins. Again. "What? Are they rotten?"

"No. You're not dead or throwing up yet, so looks like you're fine. I just don't know how long they've been in there."

"Nice. Real nice. Not only do you torture your guests, you try to poison them."

"*What* are you even talking about? How have we tortured you?" He's laughing hard enough now that he has to put his own cup down. "God, you are something else. I don't think I've ever met anyone like you, Porter."

"What, you mean, crazy?"

"Spirited. Feisty. Authentic."

"Those are euphemisms for crazy, obnoxious, likely unstable."

"Your words, not mine." He nestles my mug into a cup holder on the ledge behind us so I can open the banana. In a few bites, it's gone. Damn, I am hungry. "Let me see that ankle."

"It's feeling better. The little dip in the water helped, I think. Froze the shit out of it."

"You went into the water?"

"Dude, you missed it!" I straighten out my leg onto his. "I went into the water with *orcas*."

"No way." He gingerly pulls the roomy wool sock off my foot. I'm so glad Tabby painted my toenails earlier. At least that part of the beauty regimen remains.

"They came around—Daddy Orca popped up first—effing *huge*—and when I was standing to get a better look at Mommy and Baby, he came up behind the boat and scared the shit out of me. I fell into the water."

"And they didn't show any aggression?"

"No! It was amazing. I swear to God … probably the scariest and awesomest thing I've ever experienced."

"'Awesomest' isn't a word."

"It is when you're talking about swimming with wild orcas."

He presents his balled hand for a fist bump. "Then you win the Awesomest Award for the day. And I think the cold water helped. The swelling's down, but the bruising is really, really pretty. Quite a masterpiece."

"I've been known to show real talent in the arts," I smile. When he wraps two very large hands around the sore ankle, the heat radiating from him to me is … delicious. And unnerving. And exquisite. And freaky.

And …

Remarkable.

I don't know what to do. I don't think he does, either. Maybe I should move. But I don't want to. His hands are big and surprisingly soft and very, very warm. Like having a hot water bottle or heating pad wrapped around it.

"This is really weird, but I don't know what else to say because that feels amazing."

"Why is it weird? It's just one friend helping another friend so hypothermia doesn't take over."

I smile because I think we both know that threat has passed. The internal temperature of the boat's cabin is plenty toasty, so much so that I'm sure that the slight sheen on Ryan's forehead hints that he's overheating. But he doesn't complain—he's keeping it warm, for me.

Now this is a first.

"Friends. I like that. I can go with that."

"Friends do nice things for each other, Hollie Porter. And saving your ass from whatever is lurking in those woods, I'd say, makes us friends."

I nod. "Yeah … thank you. For finding me. I'm sorry I caused trouble. Again."

"Like I said, I do what I can to keep my guests happy."

For a singular moment, electricity sparks between us, like a Fourth of July sparkler that has been left in the rain and only ignites for a second. There exists the hint of fire, the suggestion that the sparkler will burn if enough heat is applied, but then it's gone.

I sit up straight and, though I don't want to, I pull my ankle from his grasp. "So, uh, where are we sleeping?"

"You can sleep in the forward cabin. I've got more blankets in the cupboard." He offers a hand so I don't have to use the still-dripping crutches. Because the curtain was drawn, the front sleeping compartment is chilly.

"Where are you going to sleep?" I say, eyeing the cushiony, V-shaped space. The forward "cabin" is a swath of carpet, flanked by the pretend-shower on the left and the closet holding the Porta Pottie on the right. Two small steps, and then a low ceiling and wall-to-wall mattress, the fabric green and blue plaid, though I'm not sure if it's retro on purpose or if it's just that old.

Looking at the built-in couch behind me, I know there's no way Ryan's monster body is going to fit there. "You're way too big for that. I'll sleep out here—you take the forward cabin. It's warmer out here anyway, and you know, hypothermia ..."

"This folds out. Into a bed."

"Still. You're a Sasquatch. That can't be comfortable."

"I'll have you know I bathe more often than Sasquatch." His eyes sparkle when he smiles. I hate myself for noticing that.

"That remains to be seen."

He relents and shows me how the wall heater works. I knock into him when yet another aggressive gust bullies into the boat. He steadies me, his hand lingering on my low back as he adjusts the dial to low-warm. "This will heat the cabin enough without turning it into a sweat lodge."

He unfolds the built-in's hide-a-bed. I was right. It barely qualifies as a twin. He was willing to sleep on this, and let me have all that space up front? Awww. That's almost ... sweet.

Keith never would've done that. No, he and his Yorkies would've staked their claim the second we climbed aboard.

And here I go again, comparing. This is a terrible game.

Ryan throws on a set of sheets, layers the blankets, fluffs a pillow in a fresh case. It's obvious he's spent time cleaning rooms and making beds. Maybe he started as a housemaid before he was a concierge. I giggle to myself, the idea of Ryan in a little black French-maid outfit.

"What's funny?"

"Did they teach you to make beds in the NHL?"

"That, my orca-loving friend, is a story for another day." He pulls the blankets back. "In you go."

"Wait. I really need a toothbrush."

"Lucky for you, I have one of those." He opens a kitchen drawer and inside is a bevy of Revelation Cove toiletries. So glad we won't run out of shower caps! Phew!

"I don't think I've ever been so happy to see a tube of toothpaste," I say.

"Once you're settled, just click off this lamp. The boat's rocking should subside soon enough. These storms don't go on forever." He ducks in behind the curtain, now just his head poking out.

"Thanks, Ryan … for everything."

"Don't mention it. Get some sleep."

I brush, longer than necessary with the rough, fold-out toothbrush, so grateful that the tiny kitchenette sink has running *warm* water. Upon crawling under the heaped blankets, my sore ankle resting atop the heavy pile, I snuggle in, the steady rocking of the boat under me a sedative. It is then that I realize how bloody exhausted I am, but not before noticing, through the space between curtain and wall, that Ryan, his shirt off, has muscles in place I didn't know muscles existed.

I should feel naughty—lecherous, even—for looking. But I don't. And I keep looking until he clicks off the small wall lamp and his Adonis form is swallowed by the dark.

Chapter Seventeen
Pregame Conference

B acon.
    The world's best alarm clock.

If the whole pig were on this boat with us, his life would be forfeit under the tines of my fork.

"Morning, Hollie Porter," Ryan says, his shadow blocking out the brilliant sunlight streaming in through the cabin's many windows, a steaming coffee cup in his hand. "Hungry?"

I can't even think of a snappy comeback. Too early. But he offers coffee. I mumble unintelligibly and throw my face into the creamy, sugary cup. The tired is still heavy in my bones.

"What time is it?"

"Nine thirty. Figured we'd have some food and then head back."

"Do we have to?"

"Have to what?"

"Head back."

"Uh, that's the reason I'm out here, yes? To save your scrawny ass from being kibble for predatory mammals?"

"It's just that ... when I talked to you on the phone, you promised there's all kinds of wildlife here. I want to see some."

"Orcas aren't enough for you?"

"I saw raccoons again too. They came to check me out right before the storm hit. But I want to see otters."

"Otters ... right. You did tell me that." He turns the bacon and scrambles a bowl of eggs. "I might know just the spot. Food first. Oh, and there are clothes—Miss Betty grabbed jeans and a few shirts from your room. I hope that's okay."

"Thanks. As much as I appreciate these gorgeous duds," I say, gesturing to my ensemble, "pink isn't really my color."

"But they kept you warm, yeah?"

"Definitely warm."

Concierge Ryan plates food and squeezes past the end of my bed to exit onto the boat's outer deck. The storm now a memory, a table is set with orange juice, glasses, and fresh flowers. How did I sleep through this?

Blissfully. Best sleep ever. Near-death experiences will do that to a girl.

Feet over the side, I can put more pressure on the ankle today. This is excellent news. Still hurts, but I can tolerate the toes touching the floor as long as it's a skip-hop. Like a one-legged seagull. Named Peg.

I tuck into the closet bathroom and splash cold water on my face, shocked at the icy smack against my cheeks. Canada, your water—it's so numbing! A quick glance in the mirror does not do the self-esteem any favors, so I tidy what can be tidied and reenter the main cabin to see that Ryan has already unmade and stashed my sleeping quarters.

"You were done sleeping, right? Just makes it easier to move around." He reaches for the crutches, the formerly pert bows now dirty and wilted.

"No crutches. I can move around. Just slower than usual."

"I have some hiking boots that might fit you. We can cinch them tight. That'll help with stability. The biggest issue with this kind of injury is not reinjuring it."

I follow my nose onto the deck and am accosted by the grand beauty of this place. It looks a million ways different in the sunlight, the blue tarp of sky cloudless and proud, as if the storm was just what she needed to wash away the muck. Calling these trees green is a shameful understatement, and the water is so clear, rocks, fish, and starfish—purple starfish!—are visible along the bottom.

My mouth must be agape.

"The starfish! They're purple!"

"Something else, eh? Now you know why I live up here."

"I couldn't see all this last night. Too dark and scary."

"Well, good thing you were on the boat. Something else came down onto the beach. Those footprints are way bigger than a raccoon's," he says, pointing toward the narrow strip of sand.

"Holy shit, what could it have been?"

"A bear. Maybe a cougar. I'd have to look closer. And their poops look different, so if they've left that behind—"

"Mmm. Poop. Let's eat," I tease.

"Obviously you didn't grow up with brothers."

"Nope, just me and my dad. You have brothers?"

"Two. And a poor tortured sister. We talked about all the bodily functions at mealtime."

I think about my dad, telling me about hospital stuff. Strange things found in orifices, oozings and scrapings and secretions. I've heard it all, from him, from Keith, from work. If I wanted to really up the ante here, I could take Ryan's poop comment and raise him a compound fracture and avulsed fingernail.

But I won't. Because there is bacon at stake.

Ryan pulls out a chair for me. I don't wait for him to sit before thrusting a strip into my mouth. "Where'd you grow up?"

"Lansing, Michigan."

"How did you end up on our beautiful Wet Coast?"

"Circuitously. My last NHL team was the Canucks, and I fell in love with Vancouver. Couldn't see myself leaving this place."

"I hear that. Portland's great."

"Yeah, some of my college buddies ended up playing for the Winterhawks for a few seasons. I visited when I could. Great beer in Portland."

I laugh with a mouthful of bacon and eggs. "We're also known for our roses and impeccable hospitality."

"Beer helps with hospitality," he says, topping up my coffee. "What about you? Where'd you grow up?"

"Same city all my life. Same house, really, until my dad met my stepmother. After high school, I moved into the dorms and then in with some friends in a shitty apartment in southeast. My dad sold our awesome house to buy a boat."

"He likes boats?"

"He knows nothing about boats. They sank it."

He chokes on his OJ. "No, they didn't."

"They did. My stepmother was a total nutbar. The two of them together were a disaster waiting to happen. That first winter, the boat sank to the bottom of the Columbia River."

"That's terrible."

"And hilarious. Serves 'em right. Dad smartened up and left her. They're still friends—she comes around to use my dad's house for her primal-scream therapy Thursdays and to visit her terrible goat. House is on the outskirts, so there's lots of room and lots of grass."

"Sounds … fascinating."

"Fascinating is the cosmos or learning how killer whales don't freeze to death in these waters," I say. "Aurora and her demon goat are not fascinating. They should be euthanized, for the good of the planet." I slather blackberry jam on the toast. The second it hits my tongue, fireworks explode in my brain. "Oh my God, this is Miss Betty's jam, isn't it."

"The very one."

"Shit's orgasmic. She should sell this."

"Wow. That's a little weird, associating jam with sex, but I'll go with it."

"What, no belly nachos for you, Concierge Ryan? Don't you have any weird food fantasies involving this fantastic jam?"

He laughs and shakes his head. "Uhhh, whipped cream and chocolate sauce, maybe. Not jam. A little too close to home for me."

"Yeah, I suppose picturing sweet Miss Betty when you're about to get naughty with your best girl doesn't exactly fill the mind with lusty, erotic thoughts."

"Stop. Please."

"Damn good jam, though. For serious."

"Speaking of nachos, have you heard from Stethoscope Man since you've been here?"

"He texted. Got his massive TV out of the apartment. I'm hoping he hasn't let the Yorkies pee on my bed while I'm gone."

"Is that a concern?"

"I dunno … he was a little shell-shocked when I told him to leave. He thought I was just sad. Which I was. But this is definitely more than that …" I can't take another bite unless I hide it in my cheeks, so I change tactics. "Tell me more about you."

"What's there to know?"

"You keep harping on me about learning hockey. Tell me how you know so much about it."

"Lansing—all of Michigan, really—is one giant hockey town. I started playing when I was little. My dad had all of us on skates the second we learned to walk. I got a scholarship to play at Michigan State University and was drafted my sophomore year by the Philadelphia Flyers. I played six seasons in the NHL, for the Flyers, St. Louis Blues, and finally the Canucks, as well as for all their farm teams. That's called the minor leagues, the lesser teams that feed the big teams."

"Farm teams. So they have nothing to do with carrots and potatoes, then." He laughs. I point to his T-shirt. "That team is …?"

"Detroit Red Wings. My favorite."

"You ever play for them?"

"Nope. I wanted to, you know, Detroit being in Michigan, hometown team, all that. Never quite worked out."

"Why'd you stop playing?"

"As Roger Dodger so kindly explained, I took a bad hit into the boards and destroyed my knee. After surgery, I didn't want to keep jumping from farm team to farm team, so I used the money I'd saved and the inheritance from my dad to start a new life."

"Your dad … died?"

"When I was sixteen. Massive heart attack. He smoked for years but quit when he had his first heart attack at thirty. It finally caught up with him, though, in 1998. Worst year of my life."

"I'm so sorry. I don't know what I'd do if my dad died."

"My mom was a rock. She kept us all in hockey and our activities. Worked her ass off to make sure we had what we needed and that life would carry on. We all made it through college. My sister's still in Lansing with her husband and two kids. She's a baby nurse, works in the intensive care with newborns. She's amazing."

"My dad's a nurse!"

"Your dad?"

"Yeah! He works with old people now, but he's done tons of different specialties."

"That's cool. He and my sister would have lots to talk about," Ryan smiles.

"Sorry. I interrupted. Continue ..."

"Oh, I, uh ... "

"Your other siblings?"

"Right. Yeah, my brother Brody played minor league hockey for a while but then decided to go to law school instead, especially after he saw me getting bounced all over the place."

"Do you miss 'em? Being so far away and all?"

"We get together on big holidays. Sometimes they come here, sometimes I go there. Plus my other brother, Tanner, he's a charter pilot. Works with me here at the Cove. You'll meet him when it's time for you to fly home—oh, and I gotta stop by his place and water the plants. He and his wife are trying to get pregnant, so they're dealing with fertility docs in Seattle."

"And what about you? No kids? No Mrs. Concierge Ryan?"

He doesn't answer verbally but instead shakes his head, sipping from his orange juice like he wants to crawl into the glass. Sensitive subject, clearly.

Before the glass is pulled from his lips, a very large seagull lands on our table. I flinch away from the surprise guest, knocking over my juice. Ryan plucks one of two remaining bacon slices from the plate and holds it out for the white and gray bird.

"Is bacon bad for seagulls?"

"They eat dead stuff. I don't think a little bacon is going to stop his heart."

"I have a terrible confession," I say, watching as the bird swallows the bacon in one long, jerky gulp. "One time some friends and I soaked a bag of Wonder Bread with vodka and got the seagulls at the beach drunk."

"You are a terrible person."

I smile at him. "I really am." I think about confessing to Mangala and the codeine. Nah.

"You ever try it with the Yorkies?"

"No! I didn't! But, God, that's brilliant. Except then I'd have to clean up their puke."

"Gross."

"You should've seen what they did after they ate the belly nachos. Yorkshire terriers plus guacamole equals no bueno." He laughs at me, and it's loud, echoing off the rock wall that vanishes into the water.

With nothing left to offer the shithawk, Ryan shoos him away before his hovering feathered friends take notice of our generosity. "Let's clean up. I want to show you something."

He is surprisingly efficient in the kitchen, something I'm very much not used to. As soon as I was old enough to not catch my ponytails on fire, I did all the cooking and cleaning, thanks to my dad's inconsistent hours. Which is why I hate cooking now. A person can only be expected to get creative with pork-and-beans and hot dogs for so long before the interest in culinary creativity dies a painful, cholesterol-laden death.

Ryan won't let me help—says I'm "still a Revelation Cove guest, despite my bad choices in midnight watercraft activities"—and I take the few unoccupied moments to pee and brush my teeth again. God, I love having clean teeth. And I must admit, not having access to my makeup bag is sort of nice.

"You get what you get," I say to my reflection in the small, warped mirror. A final check to make sure there are no green onions smooshed in between teeth, and I'm ready to tackle whatever new adventures this day will bring.

Because lately, every day has been adventure day.

"I have more tape," Ryan says, unrolling a first-aid kit. "We should keep that wrapped. And then try these boots on. What size shoe are you?"

I can't lie. He'll know. "Ten. Depends on the shoe."

"How does someone your size have such big feet?"

I point at my nose. "Really, Snuffleupagus?"

He snorts at me. "These are nine in men's. We can stuff extra socks in the toe."

Because I have—had—only one shoe on last night when I decided to go boating, and that shoe is now likely in the bottom of this very clear, very cold waterway, I don't have a lot of room to argue. Even if the boots are hideous and mannish and might have athlete's foot hiding in the leather crevices.

Ryan's expert hands, again warm and soft from the recent dish-washing, quickly tape up the ankle for maximum stability. He slides on another wool sock from what must be the world's biggest stash of wool socks and shoves its mate into the boot's toe, followed by my foot. "Try standing." I do. It works.

"Thank you. That feels … good. More stable." The pain twinges when I bend my toes to take a step, but it's manageable.

"Excellent. Now let's go find us some otters."

As I've proven my lack of marine skills, I stay out of the way, chastising myself for watching his biceps and triceps ripple against the short-sleeve T-shirt as he hoists the anchor. He's already tied my oar-free rowboat onto the ledge on the back, so once he's in front of the main wheel, we're off.

I missed so much last night. Certainly the prestorm night sky was an awe-inspiring tapestry all its own, but today, with the sun so bright and the water so clear and glistening, it's … wow. The island where I washed ashore is huge, much bigger than I expected, but an island it is. The southernmost end is a sheer rock face, robust fir trees growing out of cracks in its side, their trunks curved at perfect angles so their branches can reach skyward for luscious sunlight. Nature doesn't stop for anything, not even granite.

We're traveling south, away from the Cove, but I don't ask why. I like the idea of not having to go back yet, to face Roger and his perfect family or the knowing looks of Miss Betty and other staff who will shake their heads and click their tongues because I'm the stupid girl who thought running away via rowboat just before a storm was smart.

Ryan does radio in to the resort that he's found me—alive—and that we'll be out for the day. Pretty sure it's Miss Betty on the other side. She sounds relieved that Ryan isn't bringing back my corpse. That wouldn't have been good for business.

We travel south for about an hour, past the occasional cottage and moored boats and empty docks and even a few campsites with waving kayakers, before Ryan slows and lets the engine idle. The sun is so warm, unusual for a mid-May day, but you won't hear me complaining, especially after last night's performance wherein I pretended to be an iceberg. Ryan pulls the heavy wool blanket from the back of the couch, opens the middle front window, and climbs through to the front deck atop the sleeping cabin.

"Hollie ... you need sun. You look pale," he says, spreading the blanket and helping me outside. I shed the fleece sweatshirt and attempt to roll up my pant legs, but I don't want to mess with Ryan's boot-cast. Shoes stay on.

"Wonder if we'll see your orcas today." He smiles, returning behind the wheel. The boat is at a slow crawl, the engine a low hum.

"Don't you believe me?"

"Of course. People swim with the orcas around here all the time, especially at night. In a thunderstorm."

"It was before the thunder, smart-ass. And it was terrifying and fantastic and *real.* You think you know an orca from seeing the wildlife shows or at Sea World, but this ... these babies were the real thing. They're so big. Oh, and their baby ..."

"They travel up and down through here, having their babies in the summer, chasing the salmon runs a little later. And where there are salmon, there are seals and sea lions, so it's a smorgasbord, depending on the time of year."

"Do you know how many pods are in these waters?"

"I'm not very good with that, but I do know the southern whales are considered part of J, K, and L pods—the northern orcas are usually A, G, and Rs, but again, I don't know enough about them to know who's who. My brother, Tanner—he's spent a lot of time studying their fins and flukes. He probably would've known who your whales were last night."

"That's nuts."

"Tan will love to hear about your experiences. You be sure to tell him when he's flying you back into town."

Town. City. Home. I don't want to think about that right now. It's Friday, the sun's out, I lived through the night, and at last check, I am still on vacation.

"Be right back," Ryan says, disappearing onto the back deck. When he returns, he has two round baskets in hand.

"Crab pots?"

"You a crabber?" He turns off the engine.

"You kidding? I'm a champion pot puller. My dad and I used to crab off the docks in Charleston and Coos Bay, Oregon."

"Oregon's coast is gorgeous."

"I love it so much. I'm going to retire there someday, I swear."

"I can see it now—Hollie sitting on the dock in her motorized old-lady scooter, hair gray, face wrinkled from too much time in the sun and saltwater, arms huge from crab-pot pulling, selling her fresh Dungeness right off the dock."

"Uncanny, Nostradamus. You forgot my anchor tattoo along my bulging forearm," I say. "And how'd you know I want an old-lady scooter?"

"Well, you're going to have to prove that you can pull these pots," he says, unfastening the wires to expand the baskets. "Unless you're too injured to play." He curves his lips downward, his exaggerated sad face patronizing.

"I'll show you and your broken nose and maimed knee how bad-ass I am." I flex my biceps and hope they don't look as puny as they feel.

"Always with the nose, Ms. Porter?"

I pinch it between my fingers as I climb off the deck. He doesn't let me get away with it, though, and scoops me around the middle like a bag of flour, just as he did last night when plunging through the icy water to save my pathetic ass.

When he sets me down on the back deck, he smiles. Pauses. Looks down at me for a beat.

Wow. Those eyes are really green today. Like he ate algae and now they're all green and … green.

He musses the top of my head like you would an eight-year-old wanting an autograph.

We're flirting, aren't we. That's what this is?

It's fun.

From a steel freezer box, he pulls a chunk of dead, frozen fish. Flirty moment over.

"Eww, don't make me bait 'em. I hate fish guts."

"And you call yourself a crabber."

"It's just that I feel so bad shoving a wire through a dead fish's eyeball."

"Fish is dead. He can't feel it."

I raise an eyebrow at him. "No shit. But I feel bad … poor fish."

"Poor fish, until he's filleted under your broiler, slathered in lemon."

"Or baked on cedar. Ever done that? My dad makes a mean cedar-shake salmon. Uses a honey-mustard glaze."

"He and Miss Betty should exchange recipes. She uses a home-made maple glaze—" Ryan smacks his lips together. "Like candy."

Ryan does the dirty work of baiting the pots. I stand by to tie on the orange number buoys to mark our spot. He maneuvers the boat to where he says is a prime crab hangout and we drop the first pot. Across the inlet, we drop the second.

Thing with crabbing? You gotta wait. The hobbyist doesn't have endless amounts of time to let pots soak like the pros do, so we agree that a couple hours will do the trick. "Whatever we don't want, we can stop at a general store a few miles down and leave some with Smitty. He'll either eat it or sell it."

"You have a friend named Smitty? Who runs a general store?"

"His real name is Gerald—he's a retired investment banker—I think he just wanted to sound like a pirate."

"That's what I want to do. Retire and become a pirate."

"Spend your days drinking rum and chasing women?" Ryan says.

"Yes, Concierge Ryan, exactly that." I throw a small chunk of ice at him from the fish box.

"No need for violence, ma'am," he smiles. I like it when he smiles. It's easy and warm and this foreign feeling of happy bubbles in organs that have more mundane functions. Like digestion and circulation and respiration.

Keith never made those organs tingle. My stomach and heart and lungs never paid attention when Keith smiled. When Keith did anything, for that matter.

Stop. No more comparisons.

"Hey, you wanna go over to that beach?" He opens one of the deck benches and pulls out two small shovels. "We could clam."

"Chewing clams is like chewing bubble gum. Without the fruity goodness."

"You've not had them cooked right, then."

"And geoducks. Giant penises."

Ryan laughs loudly, slapping his forehead. "How can you have lived in Oregon your whole life and not know that it's not the clam's penis?"

"It's a foot. But it looks like a penis. A big, scary one."

"Oh, man," he says, wiping a tear from the corner of his eye, "I think you just like saying the word *penis.*"

"It's such a weird word. And such a weird organ. And you male types, you like it way too much."

"I beg to differ," he says, leaning atop the boat's side. "And judging by your antics these past few days, I'm guessing that it's one of your favorite playthings too."

"I did not sleep with him!"

"Hey," he says, hands aloft, "none of my business."

"How did we get back to talking about Hollie's bad choices? I thought we were talking about clamming."

"You mentioned penises."

"Oh. Right."

"So do you wanna?"

I stare at him for a second, my breathing a little shallow. Did he just ask me if I want …

"Go clamming, Porter. Sheesh. Get your mind out of the gutter."

"We could, but I don't really wanna eat 'em."

"If it makes you feel any better, they're not the penis clams. They're butter clams. No penises involved."

"I still don't know if I wanna eat 'em."

"How 'bout this? We dig up a few clams, and then I can take you to a spot where we could give them to someone I know would eat them."

"Smitty again?"

"You'll see." Ryan stands and offers his hand for a high five before ducking back into the main cabin to drive us to shore.

Chapter Eighteen
It's Pronounced "Gooey-duck"

If you're fussy about dirt, especially under your fingernails, clamming isn't for you. The trick is to wait for the tide to ebb, watch for bubbles in the sand, and then dig as fast as you can before the little buggers get too deep. It's hard work, burns the arm muscles, and covers you in muck.

But watching Ryan sweat and laugh as he digs like a maniac after a burrowing clam? Totally worth it. Especially when he sheds his sweatshirt and I get to watch the muscles in his arms flex and contract.

I've never been with a muscled guy. Unless you count table muscle.

I have to resist the urge to find a reason to reach out and touch him, to put my hand on his muscly muscles, to know what that feels like to touch ridged and solid rather than squishy and a little like failure.

We don't make too much sport of the clamming. A small bucketful and we're done. I'm facing the opposite direction, washing my hands in the lapping waves, digging grit from under my thumbnails, when a shadow appears over me. A quick glance over my shoulder, and I lose my already impaired one-legged balance, falling up to my elbows into the water.

"What? What are you staring at?" Ryan is standing over me. With a geoduck, its thick, fibrous, powerful neck protruding from … Ryan's fly. "Should we go?"

And I lose it. "You … are … so … mature!"

"But you're laughing, aren't you? And now you're wet again." He reaches in and pulls the massive clam from inside his Levi's. I can't stop laughing, and yes, the subtle waves have now soaked my right side, but it's so worth it. My breath comes in fits and starts and I start with that ugly laugh-squeal thing when I can't catch my breath.

Goddamn, that feels good.

Ryan, his fly rebuttoned, geoduck in our bucket, helps me from the sand and on board our vessel. "I may be immature, but you're laughing. You dirty girl. Laughing at my geoduck. Sit in the sun for a few minutes. You'll dry off," Ryan says, disappearing inside only to come back with two sort-of cold beers. "Shall we pull some pots?"

"Has it been long enough?"

"Yeah, probably. We only need a few keepers."

"How are we going to cook these?"

"Well, we can take them back to the Cove …"

I start to shake my head. "I don't wanna. I like it out here."

"Roger's probably leaving today, if you're worried about running into him again. His wife came in on their yacht. With staff."

I take a healthy swig of the beer. "That makes me feel so much better."

"Sorry."

"Ya know, it's not just Roger … I feel stupid. Tabby in the spa told me that everyone saw my naked sprint through the lodge the other night, and then the sprained ankle, and then Miss Betty bringing the crutches and seeing Roger shirtless in my room. She probably thinks I'm a total slut."

"Miss Betty thinks no such thing," Ryan says, smiling.

"How do you know?"

"She's not like that."

"All women are like that. We look at each other with the harshest eyes." I drink again. "Hell, I'd think I was a slut if I'd come across the same scene."

"Then you have some serious issues about what a slut is."

"I suppose you're an expert on this topic?"

"No, I just think it's harsh to call a woman a slut if she's simply doing what men have done without judgment for centuries."

"So progressive of you, Concierge Ryan."

"Nah, I just don't think that a woman expressing herself sexually makes her a slut."

"But I didn't *sleep* with him—I mean, I *did* sleep with him, but all we did was sleep. We didn't—"

"Hollie, it's none of my business."

"I know ... but I just want you to know ... I don't want you to think I'm a hussy."

"You don't strike me as the type." He secures our bucket of clams in the fish box. "And even if you did get naked with Roger Dodger, you wouldn't be a hussy."

"But I didn't. I stayed clothed the whole night."

"This is really bugging you, isn't it ..."

I don't know how to answer. Because it is bothering me. I should've known better that a man of Roger's wealth and importance would want to spend time with me. His wife is exquisite, and then there's me. Yeah, I'm all right, but I'm too unpracticed, too unpolished to be anything other than a ... fling.

"Your face looks like a storm's moving in. Come on. Let's keep the party going. You can drive the boat," Ryan says, grabbing my hand and leading my limping self into the main cabin.

He stands behind me and demonstrates how to throttle the engine, points out the depth finder and GPS that shows where we are and where we're going. He's so close to me, I can smell the hint of faded aftershave or cologne on his skin. I purposely take an almost imperceptible step backward so I can feel the warmth of his body radiating toward mine. I'm slightly cold from my second impromptu dip in the inlet, my clothes still damp, and his body heat shimmers like a hot desert highway.

He drapes his hand over mine where it rests on the throttle, nudging the stick upward ever so slightly and increasing the boat's speed. His long fingers and broad palm dwarfs my hand underneath, which says much about his overall size—I have big hands for a girl.

He doesn't move for a whole minute.

It is a delicious minute.

So delicious, I almost drive us into some rocks when I realize my eyes are closed.

When he reaches down to take the wheel, he brushes my boob. Crimson travels from the bottom of his T-shirt collar to his ears and he clears his throat.

I made him blush!

"I ... why don't you go out and get the hook. I'll pull along-side the first pot and idle, and we'll see just how fast Champion Pot Puller Porter can do this."

"Say that five times fast."

Ryan laughs as I hobble out back to position myself for the big show. I haven't pulled a pot since I was fifteen and Dad and I spent one of our last solo weekends at the Oregon Coast. Just before he met Aurora. Before she moved into our house and rearranged our lives with her outlandish ideas and weird pet collection.

I can do this. I'm strong. I'm mighty. I have to show Concierge Ryan that I'm a real Oregonian, a real West Coast girl, and we don't muck around with being wimpy. I've done enough wimpy stuff in the last few days.

Time to shine.

Except I miss the pot on the first go-round.

"You missed it?" he laughs from inside.

"Shut up and go around again."

He does, and SNAG! I grab the pot on the second try. "Got it!" The boat slows to a near stop, and the race is on. Pull, pull, *pull.* Hand over hand, gripping tight on the freezing nylon rope, not paying mind to the slimy strips of sea plants clinging to the length.

Goddamn, when did this get so hard?

My arms have weakened in the years spent sitting on my dis-patcher's ass.

Feel the burn, Hol. Feel the burn!

I'm panting, not because it's tiring, but because the searing pain running through my upper half will not defeat me! I will have these crabs.

"Faster! Faster! Faster! Go, Porter, go!" Ryan cheers me on, curling my exhumed line into a circle, the glistening numbered buoy at its center. "You're doing awesome!"

I cannot control the grunts coming from my throat, and then that final "ahhhhhhh" as the burn threatens to take over and loosen my grip.

"Damn! Look at that!" Ryan says excitedly, reaching for the top rope on the pot and hoisting it along the boat's side edge. "Well done! Lotsa keepers in there!"

I plop back onto the bench, proud of myself but breathing deeply to suffuse my screaming muscles with fresh oxygen.

"Hey, grab the gloves and the crab ruler, would you?" he says. My fingers are stiff but I manage to get him the thick, plasticized gloves and watch as he drops the pot to the boat's deck, opens the wire trap door, and reaches in to start checking sex and size of our haul. "Woo! These are beauts!"

Remembering protocol, I grab an empty bucket, fill it with seawater, and limp it next to Ryan so he can drop our keepers inside.

"Damn, girl, I'm impressed," he says, plunking a giant male into the bucket. A few babies go back into the inlet, along with any females, quickly distinguishable by the shape of their abdomens. "We'll keep these three big healthy males. There's a limit on these waters, but we'll get 'em over to Smitty so we don't get caught with too many on board."

I feel invigorated. "That was awesome. I still got it. My dad would be so proud."

"You got your phone? I can snap a photo so you can send it to him."

"It died. In the boat last night. Too much water."

Ryan hands me his gloves and sneaks back inside, returning with his phone in hand. "Glove up and grab a crab. I'll email this to you."

I do exactly that, not caring that I have no makeup and crazy hair and still-wet clothes and ugly boots. I have a huge Dungeness crab in my hand, the sun on my face, and a day that is turning out way better than I could've dreamed.

"Cheese!"

"Perfect." He shows me the photo. I look ... radiant. "You clean the remaining bait off the hook and I'll move us to the other pot. You ready to go again?"

The muscles of my arms and torso cringe, but my mind's ready. "Bring it, cowboy!"

We repeat the process for the second pot, though I catch its line on the first pass. By the time Ryan's pulling crabs from the wire basket, I'm feeling like I could bench press an orca. Well, if I had ten minutes to drink another beer and let my arms settle their quaking.

We end up with six keepers—we could've kept ten, but Ryan didn't want to push it, in case the fisheries guys are lurking around.

"Nice work, Porter. You surprised me," Ryan says, winking.

He winked at me.

And then ducked back inside to move the boat to our next destination.

Which can be wherever he wants to take us, as long as he's behind the wheel and I can sit here in this glorious sunshine and watch his taut, muscled backside as he stands at the helm of this mighty craft.

Uh-oh.

Chapter Nineteen

Enhydra lutris

The quick stop at Smitty's is fun. Cute store the owner and his wife have decorated in the spirit of a Blackbeard-era ship, complete with gas for Ryan to refuel. When I see him buying a basketful of groceries—butter, onions, garlic, fresh peppers, a bottle of wine, nutcrackers to break open the crab legs, rice, trail mix and lunch makings, fresh bread and a package of cinnamon rolls baked by Smitty's wife—I get excited. Nervous. Twitterpated, as my father would say.

Maybe we don't have to go back today. Maybe we get to stay out here in our own little world.

I have exactly zero problems with that.

I'm scanning their surprisingly well-stocked book aisle, looking through guidebooks about local wildlife. "Pick one. You can bird-watch while we're out today," Ryan says into my ear. I shiver at his closeness and pick a small Audubon field guide specifically for the Pacific Northwest.

Smitty is grateful for the crab and barters some groceries with Ryan, asking about the resort, family, when Tanner's back in the inlet, how the baby chase goes. Despite their geographic distance— we've got to be at least two hours away from the resort at this point— it's obvious this is a close-knit group of folks. I like watching Ryan in his element—relaxed, smiling, warm. He's good with people. Not that he wasn't relaxed and warm at the resort, but in his concierge uniform, he's different. More professional.

I think what I'm looking at is Ryan in off mode.

I like it. A lot.

In fact, watching him causes some weird new emotion to surge in my chest. Pride? Is that pride? Am I proud of this man? I hardly know him! Or am I just excited that he's here, with me, that he didn't berate and scold me after I did such a stupid thing and risked both our lives but instead has swept me into this spontaneous adventure with crabs and clams and smiling and flirting and …

When he looks over his shoulder and catches me ogling him, his smile is like a hug. I want to wrap in it, feel its warmth ensconce me, explore its soft edges until the moon tells me I have to go home.

"This is my friend Hollie," Ryan says, arm outstretched. "She's from Portland. We're out exploring today."

"Hey, take her up around Rock Bay," Smitty says, pointing. "The auklets and cormorants and pigeon guillemots are nesting. Oyster catchers too. Neat-looking bird. Gorgeous this time of year."

"A private tour of our fair land with this gallant gentleman?" Smitty's wife says. "You must be a *special* guest."

Ryan blushes again and grabs the paper bags from the counter. "I'll see you next time, Audrey," he says. "Come on, Hollie Porter. I have some more friends for you to meet."

I wave goodbye to Smitty and his wife and follow Ryan back to the boat, nearly forgetting about my bum ankle until a misplaced rock reminds me. I stumble.

"No more injuries," he teases. "You okay?"

"I got this." It hurts, but I won't let on. Just walk slower on tiptoes and lap up Ryan's "special guest" attention.

Ryan moves us northward again but banks east around the backside of one of the countless islands. I'm glad he knows where we are because it's all starting to look the same to me. It's after three o'clock, but the sun is still beating down, warming the breeze. Few things feel as freeing as wind in your hair, body stretched on the back of a boat under the bright sun. No expectation, no worries, and best of all, no Yorkies.

A quick tweak of my T-shirt sleeve reveals that I'm even getting a bit of a sunburn. In May! Unheard of. My dad won't recognize me when I get home without my vampiric, hooded eyes and translucent skin.

The boat slows as we round a rocky outcropping, and then it shuts off completely. I sit up, waiting for Ryan to come tell me we've run out of gas and we'll have to swim for it.

Instead, he drops the anchor. *Plop.*

Opens the fish box and pulls out our bucket of clams.

"What are we doing?"

He doesn't answer but proceeds to untie my small rowboat, leash it to the cruiser's backend, and toss a life jacket into my lap. From the bench box across from me he pulls two new oars, wiggling his eyebrows as he hands them over. "Don't lose this set, co-captain," he says, saluting.

He then lowers the clam bucket into the rowboat and signals for me to hand over the oars.

"Where are we going?"

"Do you trust me?" he says, arm outstretched, hand beckoning for me to come aboard. I need go no further than his eyes before I know that I trust him. Implicitly. With my life.

The one he saved last night.

I accept his chivalry wordlessly, balancing my weight into the rowboat so I don't tip us over or add too much weight on my sore foot.

He rows us away from the bigger boat, a finger pressed to his lips as we round yet another island edge near a small beach, no wider than a sidewalk. With the oars pulled in, we drift in the shallower water. Waiting for something.

We sit in silence for about five minutes before he drops the oars again and pulls us along the island's incongruous edge. I'm watching him row, searching his face for a clue about where we're going, just as he pulls the oars in and a smile spreads wide across his face, again revealing that spectacular dental masterpiece.

He says nothing. Only points.

Near the shore, I see them.

Otters.

A momma and baby. The momma's pulling the baby around in her mouth, dropping her in the water, dragging her back on shore, repeating the process. The gloriously fluffy fluff of a baby is squeaking.

She's squeaking! The baby doesn't want to swim!

I know that baby otters are born unable to swim, that their fur is so dense and fluffed out that it assures their buoyancy, but this momma … we are witnessing swimming lessons.

I don't even know the tears are falling until Ryan's hand stretches over my shoulder clutching a red cloth handkerchief.

We bob in our wee boat watching this real-life nature documentary unfold before us. Eventually the momma tires of the lessons and pulls the baby onto her belly and back into the water. They float, watching us cautiously, these huge intruders to their beautiful little lives. Within a few moments of momma reentering the inlet, three more otters join her. Three!

My hands are at my cheeks. "Are you seeing this?" I whisper. Ryan chuckles at me. He pulls a knife out of his pants pocket and pries open a clam, scooping its meat onto one half of the shell and gently placing the shell into the water so it floats. He prepares a handful of clams this way—but the otters disappear under the water.

"Where … where'd they go?"

I yelp when one pops up right next to us, floating on her back, a careful eye on us as she takes an hors d'oeuvre. Mere seconds later, the half-shells have disappeared, so Ryan keeps shucking clams. He hands one to me, drippy and slimy, and motions for me to reach over the edge of the boat.

"Be careful. They're cute, but they bite hard. Just hold it out and she'll come get it," he says quietly.

"When they're in big groups, they clutch onto one another— like this," I demonstrate by lacing one of my arms into Ryan's. "The males and females will float in separate groups called rafts. If they're alone or with just a few other otters, they'll wrap themselves in kelp so they can eat or sleep."

Ryan bobs his head and smiles. "Ya learn something new every day."

"And when they mate? The males bite the noses of their female partners. I've seen some gruesome pictures ..."

"Glad I'm not an otter."

"Me too." And then I blush, thinking about mating and Ryan and biting and *stop right now Hollie.*

I'm shaking with excitement and nerves and fear and pure, unadulterated glee. My dad is going to die when he hears about this. I wish I had a picture.

"Another misconception about otters—they don't eat starfish. Unless there's nothing else to eat," I say. "They love shellfish, obviously, and crab. Snails too." I hold out my scant offering. An otter breaks the surface of the water, grabs it from my fingers, and disappears again, only to come up about five feet away chomping on the fresh clam meat, chewing and scraping at the shell to lick clean the remaining delicacy.

We feed the otters our clams until the bucket is empty and our hands are sticky from guts. The geoduck is too big and strong for us to shuck with just a pocketknife, and when Ryan plucks it from the bucket, it squirts him right in the face. I have to cover my laugh so I don't scare the otters away. It's one of those moments you wish you could've caught on video to burn up YouTube.

Ryan holds out the ginormous penis clam and waits for the biggest otter of the group to come for it. He's a lot bigger than his comrades, but I'm still surprised to see a male with these other three and the baby. Usually the males and females don't hang out together ... unless they're mating.

"You want to know why the otters?" I ask. Ryan nods. "I saw my first otter the only time I ever met my mother. Only I didn't know she was my mother then. She was just my dad's 'friend.' We were in Monterey. At the aquarium there. This pretty lady with my eyes had clam chowder with us and gave me a stuffed momma-and-baby otter. I still have it," I pause, watching as the otters duck back under and float far enough away that we can still see them but where we're not a threat. "I didn't know she was my mother until a few years later when Dad told me. I didn't know then, at ten, if I should cry or scream or smile." Another tear splashes onto my wrist, bathing Oliver Otter. "I still don't know."

Ryan is quiet, his face sympathetic. Looking at him, it dawns on me that I've spent over an hour in this boat with him, sharing nothing more than a few nerdy facts about the *Enhydra lutris*, and yet, the fulfillment is like that felt after a huge meal.

Sated. Whole.

Happy.

The contentment on his face says what his mouth doesn't. I dare say he concurs.

Ryan dips the oars back into the water and gently eases us away from my new friends. I watch until we've rounded the corner and they've faded from sight.

"Thank you," I whisper. I can't say anything else, but the smile stretched across Ryan's five o'clock-shadowed face tells me I don't have to.

Chapter Twenty

Watersport

Even with the tiny kitchen, Ryan knows his way around the food. He uncorks wine and gives me a knife to slice garlic for the melting butter. Our crabs are boiling—I swear I hear them scream when they go into the pot, but Ryan says I'm delusional. He's got a little barbecue on the deck with charcoals smoldering for our foil-wrapped French bread. I set the outer table with a very fancy plastic tablecloth, a roll of paper towels each, and of course, the vino.

It is a feast unseen by mine eyes before this hallowed date.

Ryan plates a crab for me and shows me where to extract the best meat. It's been a while since I've done this—and last time, my dad shelled the crab for me—so it's a fun lesson. Especially because it means he sits close enough that I can see the tiny mole just below his left ear. And he has detached earlobes. And little smile lines at the creases of his eyes. And eyelashes that almost look fake, they're so long. He's enough taller than me that if I were to rest my head against him, it would find its place against his upper arm, just at his shoulder.

Cozy.

When he catches me looking at him, he stops talking and glances at my lips.

I want to kiss him.

Kiss me.

"Would you like garlic butter … or regular?" he says. But he speaks slowly, as if he's considering my lips as carefully as I'm considering his. His Adam's apple bobs as he swallows hard, a sly smirk tugging at the corner of his lips.

Rather than kissing me, he offers a crab fork with a piece of very delectable, butter-soaked meat. I close my mouth around it without taking my eyes off his, even when he looks away and leans back in his chair.

"Who are you, Hollie Porter?"

A quiet laugh escapes my throat. "Me? I'm no one. I'm just a girl who loves otters."

"Where do you see yourself in five years?"

"Are we going to do this? You're going to play Dr. Phil with me?"

"I'm just trying to figure you out. Clearly you're confident, smart, fun loving, but you show up at the Cove and it seems to me that something's missing. Like ... you're looking for something but you don't quite know what it is."

"That sounds about right."

"Tell me about you. I want to know more."

"What's there to know? I work for 911. I hate it. I hate listening to people die or hear how they pay my salary so I owe them some part of my soul. My coworkers are creepy assholes. I dumped my boyfriend and came up here ..."

"Okay, tell me three things about you that I wouldn't be able to figure out by reading your Facebook wall."

"Seriously?"

"Why not?"

"I'm going to need more wine, Concierge Ryan," I say. He tops up my glass. I again notice how nice his ass looks in jeans. "Let's see—umm, my best friend broke up with me and I miss her terribly, even though I shouldn't because she was a jerkface."

"Ah, you're better off without her, then. Number two?"

"Mmmm, I am physically incapable of saying no to anyone."

"That could come in handy," he says. I kick my foot at him playfully. "So give me an example of when Hollie can't say no."

"Like, I have this obnoxious old lady who lives downstairs—Mrs. Hubert. I swear to God she's stalking me—every time I walk by, day or night, she shouts at me about getting her cat's food or how she needs milk for her coffee."

"Doesn't she have family?"

"Yeah! She does! But her kids never come around because she's such a crotchety witch, so she picks on me instead."

"And you never say no to her."

"No."

"Why not?"

"I dunno … I guess I feel bad for her. Her hands are all gnarled and knobby and her cat, Mr. Boots, he's blind and has to wear a diaper."

Ryan busts up. I can't help but chuckle in agreement. "I have to see this cat wearing a diaper."

"He looks like Gollum. All his hair fell out so he doesn't look like Mr. Boots anymore."

"Stop! You're making this up!"

Two fingers presented, I salute. "Scout's honor."

"When you get home, you're going to have to send me pictures of this cat."

"I could do that. Only that means I'll have to buy Mrs. Hubert's cat food and coffee creamer."

"I'll give you the money," he laughs, reaching into his rear pocket for his wallet. "A tin of Friskies: one dollar. A pint of half-and-half: three dollars. Seeing Mr. Boots the Hairless Cat in his diaper: priceless."

I lean too far back in my fold-up chair and almost kiss the deck. This is the best kind of laughter.

"Okay, okay … back on track here, Porter." He wipes the corner of his eye. "Who else have you not said no to?"

"Are we really going to have this conversation?"

"We don't have to. But you owe me one more Porter-ism."

"Nuh-uh."

"One more super-secret secret about Hollie Porter. Give it up. No cheating."

"Gah, this is hard. I dunno …" I sip. "Oh! I spent my tuition money on a private investigator only to learn that my mother is a criminal."

"Oooh. Dude. Buzzkill."

"Yeah, little bit. Oh, and don't tell my dad. If you ever talk to him. Or whatever. He thinks that I didn't get approved for the student loan and that's why I dropped out."

"Earlier, with the otters … you said you only met her once."

"Yeah. She left when I was a baby."

"I'm sorry … I didn't mean to …"

"No, no, God, Ryan, don't worry. It's not like we bonded and she broke my heart. I just had this dumb fantasy that I'd find her and we'd have this crazy reunion and she'd feel terrible for abandoning her newborn and we'd ride off on our sparkly unicorns into the rainbow sunset."

"I think that's normal."

"Which part?"

"The part about the sparkly unicorns … What? You don't have one?"

"Of course I do. My dad got one for me. Brat." I drain my wine glass. "He'd sell his soul to the devil for me, and that's enough."

"Sounds like a good guy."

"He is … He sent me here."

Ryan reaches out and places a long finger on the arm of my fold-up chair. "I'm glad he did that."

"Me too …"

Flame flares out of the corner of my eye. "Shit! The bread!"

Ryan jumps up and douses the barbecue with a glass of water. "All good! We're safe." With tongs, he pulls the bread off the rack and drags it onto the boat's floor. Gingerly, he pries apart the foil. "And some of the bread survived!"

"Victory!" I say, raising my empty glass. Some equals three pieces survived. The rest is going into the water.

"Fishes like burnt French bread, right?" he teases.

After the barbecue has been quieted and Ryan's sure we're not going to catch on fire, he sits again, cracking more crab to share with me. "Tell me about the best and worst calls you ever had at 911."

"Really?"

"Yeah. I've always been curious what goes on behind the scenes in a place like that."

"It's not nearly as exciting as you might think."

"You guys are the hub of the excitement! Police chases, big fires, rescues of damsels-in-distress ..."

"I wish. More like a lot of snarky mean people in polyester pants who look way too forward to staff potlucks and make fun of the people who call in for our help."

"Really?"

"Well, not all of them. Some of the dispatchers are cool. I just happen to be in a section with some real winners." An image of Troll Lady and Les pops into my head, them sneaking out of the handicapped bathroom, wrongfully thinking none of us know what's going on. Eww.

"But what about the calls? Give me some insider info."

"The worst call I ever had? Hmmm ... there have been a few. I don't like it when people die on me. Right before my little impromptu holiday up here, I had a guy dressed as Batman who had a heart attack after he took Viagra and drank too much whisky. That was pretty sucky because his wife was really upset—she couldn't do the chest compressions properly because she was afraid he'd be pissed at her for cutting through his costume."

"And he bit it?"

"Mm-hmm," I say, lifting my wine in a toast. "Rest in peace, Batman Jerry."

Ryan clinks my glass and we drink to the masked crusader.

"I think the very worst calls I get, other than the rude people who scream at me when I tell them their neighbor's barking dog is not an emergency, are the kids. When the kids are sick or hurt or even dead. I had a little girl die once."

"Oh my God ..."

"Yeah ... she'd gotten into some medicine while her parents were asleep, and when they found her, she was already gone. That was a really shitty night."

"Damn. That sucks. I don't think I could handle it if a kid died."

"I had to do some aftercare counseling for that one. A few of us did."

"So what about the best calls?"

I smile, thinking about Mona and Herb. "The best ones end up happy—no one dies and the patient ends up being okay. The ambulance will arrive and take care of everything. Sometimes I get lucky and the caller will tell me a story while we wait for EMS."

"Really? Like what?"

"Just the other day, ironically, a sweet old woman, Mona, called—her husband was having a diabetic reaction. The whole time as I talked her through the call, she was worried but calm. When we got Herb some insulin and he started to come around, Mona told me how they met, how long they'd been together, which is like sixty years or something. She tried to set me up with one of her sons ..."

Ryan laughs. "Seriously? That is awesome!"

"Yeah. She was a hoot. And the thing is? I wanted to stay on the phone with her all day. Even when I could hear that our guys had arrived and the call was almost finished, I didn't want her to hang up. I wanted to hear more about her life with Herb, about their ducks at this great big park in Portland—they got married there— and about how they still go there every day and feed the birds and sit on their special bench and talk about their grandbabies and great grandbabies. That call ... that was the best."

"And Herb was okay?"

I pause for a moment, thinking about that day, how everything spiraled after that phone call. "Yeah. I think so. I don't usually follow up with callers because there are so many, but I think he was going to be fine."

"You seem really touched by her story."

I nod yes. "I was. I am. Thing is ... her parting words to me were, *you only get to live this life once, Hollie.* She told me to not waste a second."

"Are you still wasting seconds?"

"Well, that night, I called your fabulous resort ..."

"Drunk."

"Yes, drunk. But I'd just kicked out my lame boyfriend, so I earned that drunk."

"Touché," he says, refilling our glasses. "It appears that maybe Mona's advice sunk in."

"Maybe. A little."

"Next question—"

"More questions?"

"I told you—I want to know Hollie Porter."

"Beyond my mad skills in watersports?"

"When we get back, I'm calling the Olympic rowing team to see if they need a new bowman. Only you can't lose the oars."

"Shut up! Geeze!" I throw a crab claw at him. "*Their* boats will have anchor locks."

"Next question."

"Right, okay, fine. But if that bottle is starting to feel light, we may have to raid that whisky in there."

Ryan throws his head back. "You're a lush, Porter."

"Get on with it, Concierge Ryan, before these mosquitoes start to take blood I can't get back."

"Okay. If you could do any job in the whole wide world—considering you hate being a dispatcher—what would it be?" he asks.

"Anything?"

"Yup."

"Work with sea life. Without a doubt."

"Like at Sea World or ..."

"No, like, at an aquarium. Or at the beach. Maybe with Greenpeace or something. I'd love to be an educator. You know, teach people about the critters and where they live, how they eat, all that stuff. I'd love to work in animal rehab, but I faint when I see blood, so that's always held me back from getting into veterinary medicine."

"Why not study to become a biologist?"

"Because I didn't really think that was a possibility when I started college. My dad is all about the medical field. He's a nurse, our extended family is dotted with doctors and nurses dating back a million generations, so it's kind of expected. Plus my dad wanted me to get a good union job. When the 911 thing came up, I figured I could make my dad happy and keep him from nagging too much until I figured out what to do with my life."

"Did he want you to go into nursing?"

"Probably. But the whole blood thing ... My dad wanted to be a doctor, actually."

"Why isn't he one? Although it's not as unusual nowadays for men to be nurses, I suppose."

"It's definitely more accepted now than when he started twenty-odd years ago, but he was a year from finishing medical school when I came along. Then my mother left abruptly when I was a month old and he had to drop out of med school because he knew he'd never be able to do a residency with a new baby and he didn't want me raised by strangers, you know, in daycare or whatever."

"Wow."

"Yeah. My dad's an incredible man."

"Well, if it means anything, I think he did a great job with his daughter," Ryan says, wiping his hands on a damp towel.

"You don't have to say that."

He leans forward and brushes a finger across my cheek. Shivers erupt. Everywhere. "I wouldn't if I didn't mean it."

"I'll be sure to tell him ..." I don't finish the sentence because Ryan's lips brush across mine. He tastes buttery, and the recent sip of wine lingers on his tongue. He kisses me, his fingers soft against my face, on my neck. The kiss deepens, and he rubs a hand down the side of my head, atop my hair, before pulling back. Smiling.

We're both smiling. Like cats with canaries. Big, fat canaries with bellies full of crab and wine and lust.

Our foreheads touch, and a subtle laugh passes between us before he sits back in his chair. I don't give him time to catch his breath. I'm up and on his lap, straddling him, my fingers buried in his thick hair, my thumbs trailing along his bristled jawline, his hands on my ass, pulling me toward him. My ankle screams in protest, but I couldn't give a flying shit at this point. Let it break and fall off because right now, I have this man's face to mark as my own.

I've been kissed a few times in my life.

But never like this.

Not where my nerve endings are electric, where the ends of my hair threaten to ignite, where I want nothing more than to see Ryan, all of him, every glorious inch. Every scar, every reminder of his struggles and triumphs and former glories, every line and curve and dip.

He pulls back, one hand on my lower back, edging around my waistline and moving upward on my ribs, the second hand cupped around the back of my head like he's saving me from drowning in him. Because I might be doing just that.

The air has chilled, the tired sun tiptoeing behind the surrounding mountains, as if she's giving us privacy, but it's hot enough between us that there is no attention paid to temperature.

We are our own ecosystem.

He parts his lips, as if to speak, but I cut him off. "I want you."

That's all he needs. We're up and out of that chair, his hands holding me, my weight balanced on his arms like he's carrying nothing more than a feather, the bulk of his biceps and shoulders and back mine for the taking.

Cognizant of my sore ankle, he lowers me onto the plush duvet of the forward cabin's triangular bunk, kneeling before me, almost worshipful, on the narrow step at the end of the bed. I don't let him get far, instead pulling off his T-shirt so I can see him, so I can run my hands over the abdomen that makes every man before him look like a poser, so I can watch as goosebumps form on the surface of his farmer-tanned skin and watch as his breathing shortens while my fingertips explore the perfect amount of chest hair, up toward his collarbones, trace the muscle along the top of his shoulders, brush against the stubble on his neck and bury each digit to the hilt in his loose, dark curls.

In return, he gently removes my boots, so careful to not hurt me but not so careful that he forgets why we're here or what we're doing.

He runs his fingers over my wrist, over Oliver Otter. "What does it say?"

"*Enhydra lutris.* Latin name for sea otter."

"I love it when you talk dirty, Miss Porter." He kisses my tattoo and proceeds to remove my shirt. He freezes, stops to behold me, his hands gently cupping the sides of my bra. I am instantly grateful that I had the forethought to throw on a nice black-lace number before running away last night.

He buries his face in my chest and kisses the space between, moving up my sternum to my neck, under my chin, and finally to my lips, gently nudging me onto my back. He stops kissing me long enough to pull back and rest a huge hand on my tummy.

The light spill from the main cabin highlights the tips of his eyelashes, the swell in his wine-reddened lips, deepening the shadow along his unshaved face.

"Are you okay? Does your ankle hurt?"

"Now's the part where I tell you I've never been more okay in my entire life, and if you don't do unholy things to my body on this boat, I will write a tersely worded letter to your managers. Post haste."

Ryan laughs and leans down to kiss me again, to bury me with his form.

"Wait," I say, hand on his pec.

"What?" He leans back on an elbow.

"I … I want to look at you."

"Why?"

"Because … you're beautiful."

"Even with my crooked nose?"

I push forward and pull his head into me so I can kiss the bridge. "Especially … with your crooked nose." He angles back, one long finger tucking itself under the edge of my bra. I suck in and a quiver rockets through me. He smiles.

"And as long as I live, I never, ever want to forget this moment," I say. An unexpected tear sneaks out of the corner of my right eye. I hope he doesn't see it.

His thumb brushing it away confirms he does.

His lips leave their mark on the tip of my nose, on each cheekbone, my eyebrows. "Hollie Porter, as your concierge, I'll do everything I can to make it unforgettable."

CHAPTER TWENTY-ONE
FUN WHILE IT LASTED

"Hollie ... wake up," says the voice next to me. The dreamy voice attached to the dreamy lips that kiss my cheek, my lips. Like Prince Charming kissing Snow White.

Except I'm pretty sure Snow White's mouth didn't taste like this, that she didn't fall asleep exhausted after a *very* vigorous work-out, teeth still coated in red wine and shellfish and ... other things.

"Hol, you have to see this." Mmm, he's already shortening my name. This is a good sign.

I open my eyes. Ryan is at the end of the bed, already clothed on his lower half—to my disappointment—his outstretched hand signaling for me to get up.

I, on the contrary, am not dressed. "Wrap in a blanket. You have to see this. Hurry!"

I tuck the sheet around me like a bath towel and crawl to the end of the bed. My ankle throbs, reminding me that I wasn't very careful with my movements in the overnight hours (so worth it), but before I can protest, Ryan scoops me into his arms and moves to the back door.

On the deck, the seabirds have made a righteous mess of the leftover crab. But something brown and furry is moving around the rowboat, still tied to the cruiser's stern.

"They must've smelled the clams from the boat."

"Were there some left?"

"No, but I'm sure we spilled plenty of guts inside. And they know the boat."

"You've done this before?" He nods. "That's why they trust you," I say. My heart sinks a little in my chest. Does he bring all his boat girls out here and show them the otter trick?

"I usually bring my nieces out when my sister is in town. They're like you. They love the sea critters." Heart reinflates. Nieces. Not boat girls.

"Can we tiptoe out and see them?"

"Just remember they're wild animals," he says, setting me down. "They might scare when they see you. And don't pet them. Just in case you get close enough."

"Yes, sir."

Ryan pinches my ass as I step through the narrow door and out onto the deck. It's a mess. Whatever food we left out is a distant memory and paper towels, shredded by beaks and claws, litter the table and the side benches. I move as carefully as I can with the unstable ankle—I didn't realize until now how supportive that boot was—and freeze when a large, blond-headed otter in the rowboat sees me. We stare at one another for a millisecond before she slithers off the boat's middle bench and into the water. Her friend follows suit. I perch on the bigger boat's lounging bench, the chilled morning air tickling my bare shoulders, and watch as three otters dive and reemerge not ten feet from the side of the cruiser.

The second of the threesome dives and disappears. Bubbles break the water's surface and just as the other two go under, their missing comrade pops up—with an urchin on her belly!

Ryan ducks through the door with two steaming cups in hand. The otters dive when they see him, but they don't go far. Curious little buggers, they come back around, one even touching the side of the big boat, sniffing toward us like a cat might beg for scraps at the table.

"Look at her! I think she wants more clams!"

Ryan smiles. "We're out. And I can't give her any crab because the damn gulls already made short work of whatever we left out here."

"I guess we didn't really clean up much, did we?"

"I'd say we had more pressing matters to tend to."

"And to that, Concierge Ryan, I concur. Your establishment will definitely be getting a five-star rating from this satisfied customer."

"Why, thank you, Miss Porter. I do aim to please," he says.

And again, that hint of doubt pops into my head that maybe he aims to please more often than not. Maybe I'm not the first girl to have seen the naughtier side of this pleasure craft.

"Why the frown?" Ryan asks.

"Just thinkin' … I guess we're going to have to go back at some point."

"Sadly, yes. Miss Betty will be needing help today. Weekends are busy."

"Right …"

"But first, let's enjoy this coffee and this glorious sunrise, dig into Audrey's sumptuous cinnamon rolls. And I should make a quick stop at Tanner's cabin. I was supposed to water the plants while they're gone and I've failed."

"You're a bad brother. They'll come home to dead plants?"

"I just megadose the sad ones with my secret stash of Miracle-Gro. They'll be perfect by the time Tanner gets the plane parked."

My stomach seizes. God, the plane. I have to take that back to reality soon. Like, tomorrow. I've already stayed a day longer than I was supposed to.

"I don't want to ever leave this place," I say.

"This part of the world has that impact on folks. That's why I'm still here." Ryan tucks me into him and wraps his free arm around my front, cuddling me tight, so close that it's as if he never wants to let me go.

But one night spent with someone in the throes of passion is not enough for him—or me—to beg the other one to stay. I have to accept this for what it is … a gift. A sexy, fantastic, toe-curling, mind-numbing, palpitation-inducing gift. And when I get home, I will spend the next few weeks in a terrible depression because he is here and I am there and I am a foolish girl who gives her heart too easily but this time it feels different and I've never experienced this fireworks-display of awesomeness in such a short time and he's so remarkable and unlike anyone I've ever met …

I have a serious problem.

I turn my head and kiss the side of his jaw, his divine, scruffy, brilliantly manly jaw. He meets my lips with his own, and the game begins anew. Yet this time, the opening ceremonies are shorter because we're mostly already naked. A delightful side effect.

Two hours later, we're in desperate need of hydration and sustenance.

Ryan answers the radio when it crackles to life—Miss Betty wondering if everything's okay—and I think I hear a hint of embarrassment in his voice when he answers. I giggle as he tries to tell her that we've been fishing and exploring all that nature has to offer.

I'll say …

I help by tidying up the deck, gathering garbage and empty wine bottles. He tries to protest when I fill the small sink with suds, but I insist. I've moved beyond a mere guest. Now I'm in that gray area that says washing dishes and making beds is acceptable.

Once the boat has been returned to its regular glory, Ryan moves to pull the anchor. I hop along behind.

"Oh, I got this. You don't need to help," he says.

"I know. I just like watching."

"You like watching me pull the anchor?"

"Have you ever watched you pull the anchor?"

He laughs at me. "Uh, can't say that I have."

"Well, the muscles … they ripple in all the right places. It's hot." I fan myself and pucker my lips. "Now, pull, boy. Don't keep me waiting."

Ryan smirks and starts the hand-over-hand of the heavy anchor's rope. It's just as fun to watch the second time around. "I have a winch for this, but it died and I'm not the mechanic in the family. I'm waiting for Tanner to work his magic."

"Sounds like he's a handy guy to know."

"Tan's great. You'll love him."

Does this imply that I'll meet him someday?

Oh, right. Of course—the floatplane—he's the regular pilot. The one who will ferry me back to that reality known as Hollie's Hellish Holocaust of Hellishness.

Ryan moves back into the main cabin and we're off, heading to Tanner's place to water the dead plants. I scan the rock faces of the passing islands, drink in every detail, as if I will never see it again.

Because I may not. And I want this etched into my forever memory, like a tattoo on flesh. The verdant colors, the lick of the water against the alternately sandy and rocky beaches, the white froth of our boat's wake, the gulls flying alongside as if racing, the stately cranes perched on forgotten pilings, the eagles in their massive nests, the colony of raucous sea lions on a long rocky perch in the middle of the inlet.

Every single detail.

"Hey, while we're there, we can shower and clean up. You know, before going back to the civilized world."

"Yeah … that would be nice," I say quietly, not feeling enthused about going back anywhere. These last thirty-six hours have been … maybe the best of my life. When a tear drizzles down my cheek, I spin on the couch and look out the window so Ryan doesn't see me being a needy wimp.

It is what it is, Hol. Like Dr. Seuss says, from Dad's lips to your ears: *Don't cry because it's over, smile because it happened.*

I am. Smiling. At least I'm trying to.

Ryan is too busy piloting the boat to notice that I'm having a hard time corralling the tears. Which is good. It gives me time to duck into the bathroom and splash cold water on my face. But a simple glance into the mirror shows me a face I haven't seen in a while.

Hey, Relaxed Hollie. How are you, babe?

Yesterday's sun is evident in my cheeks, along my nose. I look … happy.

Until I remember that my happiness is transient, and then the ugly cry threatens to reclaim my face.

I splash more glacial water, enough to keep the tears frozen in my eyelids. "Suck it up, Princess," I whisper to the mirror.

I brush my teeth long enough to remove yet another layer of enamel, just to give my eyes time to lose their puffy, yes-I've-been-crying-a-little-because-this-has-been-perfect-don't-mind-me appearance. The waning engine is my signal that we must be getting closer.

"You okay in there?"

"Yeah … just freshening up. I'm a compulsive brusher." I flash my pearly whites.

"And they are a thing of beauty," he says, pulling me into him. He kisses the side of my head and I wrap my arms around his waist, tucking under his arm. He drives one-handed and nods ahead. "Tanner's place. We're here."

He kisses my head again and slows the boat way down, until we're coasting toward the finger-like dock stretching from the beach. "Just keep the wheel straight. The engine's off. I'm going to jump out and tie off."

He slips through the back door, jumps out, and in under a minute, the boat is halted, bobbing against the wooden dock, the buoy squeaking under the pressure of fiberglass against wood. Ryan boards the boat again, grabs the keys and his phone, and helps me out.

"After we get cleaned up, I'm going to wrap that again for you."

"Yeah, the boot was amazing."

"Let me grab 'em." He sneaks back inside and grabs the boots, discarded so gently last night before our—*ahem*—dessert tray arrived. "Tanner has a first-aid kit inside, so I'm sure there's tape. We'll fix you up, Miss Porter. In the meantime, though," he kneels in front of me, "climb on."

"Now this is what I call first-rate concierge service."

"Anything for the lady." He kisses my arm looped around his neck.

He piggybacks me all the way up to what is a gorgeous house—this is no mere cabin. Windows stretch across the entire front of the dark-wood structure topped with a cerulean metal roof. I count eight floor-to-ceiling, thick, white-paned windows, each easily three or more feet across. An orca weathervane squeaks in the mild breeze, and hanging planters in an explosion of spring colors line the long, railed porch. Flowerbeds hug the house's front, flanked by rich green grass that ends at a border of rock and railroad ties.

"So glad to see these aren't dead," Ryan says, twirling one of the planters. Inside, the décor and layout looks very similar to that of Revelation Cove. Natural woods, brick, wide stone fireplace, shimmering hardwood floors, stainless appliances. It's breathtaking.

"Something else, eh?" he says, settling me onto the couch.

"I want to stay here forever," I say. "Think your brother would mind?"

"He might not, but his wife might be a little worried. Hot young thing like you running around in her bikini?"

"I don't have a bikini, remember? Just that chaste nunsuit you picked out for me in the gift shop."

"Hey, it did the job, didn't it? Kept Roger Dodger out of the deep end of your pool."

"Ryan!" I feign shock.

"All the more for me, my princess," he says, leaning over me on the couch. I squish back into the cushions, his weight against me welcome as he eases his body over mine. "How about a shower?" he whispers against my lips. I don't have time to answer before he throws me over his shoulder, spanking my ass as we move into the bathroom.

We undress each other in feverish strips and pulls, and inside the tile-and-glass enclosure, I'm awestruck at the multitude of showerheads. This is a bathroom you'd see at a home and garden show—real people don't have bathrooms like this.

Ryan takes his time lathering my shoulders, my back, around to the front, cupping his hands under breasts and tweaking nipples accordingly, kissing the places he rinses first, kneeling before me as he washes my legs, knees, good ankle followed by bum ankle, back up, hands stopping when his fingers bury themselves in the wee jungle.

(So glad the panty tarantula had a good trimming, especially now that we're in such bright light.)

It doesn't take long for me to pull him into me, only how will I ever look his brother in the eye knowing what we've done in this resplendent shower? "Hi, Tanner, nice to meet you. Thank you for building such a nice shower so I could defile your brother in style."

Ryan hoists me onto his hips, leaning me against the wall as we sprint for the finish line.

A girl could get used to this. Really. Fucking. Fast.

Given that we're not on the boat, and no one's around for miles, neither of us is quiet when we break through the ribbon, when the victory horn is blown. He leans his head back into the water stream, both of us shaking and panting, before leaning down and kissing me hard on the mouth.

"You should stay," he whispers.

"What?" I have to hear him say it again.

"Stay. Don't go home. Just for a few more days," he says, his green eyes boring into mine. I'm so glad the water's running so he can't see the water my own eyes are producing.

I so want to say yes.

I never want to leave.

Maybe I can stay another day, another two days, but after that …

He sets me down and folds his body around me, my nakedness pressed against his, my hands unsure of where his body ends and mine begins. I ignore the heartbeat in my ankle because I don't want to move from this perfect moment.

We take turns washing one another's hair, which is just as hot and sexy and romantic as it is in the movies. I knew it could be. I *knew* it. I feel like I'm going to burst out of this fancy shower and hear someone yell, "Cut!"

Yeah. It's that hot.

When all the parts have been titillated and scrubbed, Ryan opts to stay in long enough to shave. I dry off and dress in my less-than-clean clothes and find a comb to detangle my hair, quickly plaiting the damp strands so they will dry wavy. "Ryan, can I find some juice in the fridge? I'm parched from all that exercise," I say into the shower. His face is coated in white foam.

"Help yourself. There might be beer in there too if you want."

Beer. That sounds mighty nice.

I skip-hop into the kitchen, my ankle mad at me for being so rough with it these last few hours. I can walk on the toes but that heel has no interest in being on the floor unless it is swaddled in tape and my makeshift cast.

Fickle foot.

I indeed find beer, some fine quality microbrews in sweating bottles in the back of the side-by-side stainless fridge. While leaning against the counter, I notice a stack of photos and pick up the top one.

That has to be Tanner. The carbon copy of Ryan, save a few gray hairs instead of Ryan's dark, thick locks. He's not as big, easy to see where he stands next to little brother in the subsequent photos. That must be Tanner's wife. She's lovely. Blond, not drop-dead gorgeous but certainly someone you'd look at a second time if she walked by. Her Revelation Cove tank top shows she takes care of her body. I'd kill for arms like that.

The next photo in the stack squeezes the beer in my throat. Pushes it against the roof of my mouth, the carbonation stinging my nose.

It's Ryan. With a woman.

A beautiful woman. In the first photo, she's standing next to him, her arms wrapped around his waist, her floral-print dress rippling in a breeze, her sun-kissed hair evidence of a nice day.

Don't panic, Hol. Maybe it's his sister, the one visiting from Lansing.

The next photo undoes that theory. She's in Ryan's arms, the same way he's carried me on numerous occasions over the very recent past.

I should stop looking through these.

This is not right.

The beer is souring in my stomach.

Especially with the very next shot where her arms are wrapped around Ryan's neck, his hand at her back, their lips … touching.

They're kissing.

This is his girlfriend. Fuck, for all I know, it's his wife. She's out of town, maybe with Tanner and *his* wife, and they're all coming back today and that's why we have to go back.

I feel like I'm going to throw up. My heart is pounding in my chest, and the room is off-kilter.

I flip the photograph over to see if there's a print date on it. No, no, *no*.

These were taken a month ago.

You've got to be kidding me. I knew this was too fucking good to be real.

When I hear the shower turn off, I know it's now or never. I have to make a choice.

I limp over to the boots, pull on one of the wool socks stuffed in the innards, and force my feet inside. I have to get out of here.

When Ryan asks if I found the beer, his dripping, towel-wrapped, rippled body is met with the slamming of the door as I hobble across the yard and into the woods behind the house.

CHAPTER TWENTY-TWO
CHLOE THE COUGAR DOES NOT WEAR RIBBONS

"**H**ollie! Hollie! Where the hell are you?"

I hear him, but I don't turn back. I don't call out to him, even though I've tripped and may have just gone all the way with the ankle because it is screaming profanities at my brain and the boot is tightening to the point that it might have to be cut from my body. Oh, and I did in fact throw up the beer.

First sign of a broken bone.

"Goddammit, Hollie, you're not safe out here. Please … come back. It's not what you think."

"If it's not what I think, then what the hell is it, Ryan?"

"Say something else—I'll follow your voice. Are you okay?"

"Don't come any closer. I want to go back. I want to go home," I say, no longer able to keep the tears from cascading down my face and strangling my voice.

"Hollie, please … let's go back into the cabin and we can talk about this. I swear to you …"

I hear something in the woods to my left. Frozen, I listen, waiting for the forest sounds to give me some clue as to what's waiting, watching. When a crow launches itself off the branch and hops onto the ground across from me, I almost wet my pants.

Even though we're in broad daylight, these are unfamiliar woods. I have to admit that I'm a little scared.

I pull myself up using the help of a downed tree, yelping when the ankle gives way underneath my weight.

"Are you hurt? Where the hell *are* you?" Ryan yells. His voice is off to my right, but I can't yet see him. When the trees aren't close enough for me to use as support between hops, I crawl across the ground, dirtying my formerly pristine, shower-scrubbed hands, the undergrowth thick with discarded pine needles and dropped foliage from the massive Douglas firs. I don't necessarily have to worry about snakes in this part of the world—at least I hope I don't— but the bugs are plentiful. Chunky black beetles scurry about like crazed patrons of a burning pancake house when I dislodge their barky hideout.

"Hollie, please!" Ryan shouts again. He's getting closer. Another branch snaps and I am motionless, listening for what might be tracking me. When Ryan emerges from behind a heavily draped tree, I'm glad it's him and not a bear, and then pissed off that it's him and not a bear.

"Leave me alone."

"I'm not going to leave you alone. I need you to let me help you. I don't have any bear spray or anything on me, and these woods are very much not empty of wildlife at this time of year."

"You lied to me."

"I did not lie to you."

"Are you—are you married?" My yell dissolves into a choked whisper.

"No, Hollie, I swear to you. I am not married." He holds up his left hand to show me a bare wedding finger. Which means nothing. He could've taken his ring off. Roger Dodger did that. I had zero idea his swimsuit-model wife would be waltzing in on her yacht.

"Proves nothing."

"My word should be proof enough," he says. "Please, it's important for us to go back to the house at least. Let's talk. I can explain."

"Who is she, Ryan? Those photos were from a month ago. A month!" I launch a handful of dirt at him.

"If you don't give me your hand, I'm going to hoist you over my shoulder again."

"Don't. Please."

"Why not?" He kneels in front of me. "Did you ... did you throw up?"

"I think I broke it for real this time."

"Ah, shit, Hollie. Okay, up you go."

"Ryan ..." I'm not even trying to hide the ugly crying at this point. "Who is she?"

He picks me up under my armpits and sets me down on a mossy log.

"Her name is Alyssa. We were together ... for a while."

"How long is a while?"

"Hollie, please—isn't it enough for me to guarantee to you that it's over?" His face darkens. "I ... we were engaged. But we couldn't decide on a wedding date that would make everyone happy, so it kept getting pushed back. We'd break up, get back together, then break up again. When I got hurt and left the league, I decided to come up to Revelation Cove. She wasn't happy."

"She didn't like it?"

"Remember the other day when you made a joke about the coach's daughter?"

"Oh."

"Daddy made sure she never wanted for anything, so the idea of moving to a remote island with no shopping malls or fancy parties was not her idea of bliss. I couldn't give her the hockey-wife lifestyle that she wanted."

"Because you're not a hockey player anymore."

"Exactly. When my career ended, my identity had to change. She couldn't deal with that," Ryan says.

"But those photos ... they were taken recently."

"They weren't, though. That's just when they were printed. Those were taken four or five years ago."

"But why are they there? Why are they on the counter, now, four or five years later? Were you walking down Memory Lane or something? Sad about your lost love?" I sniff. I need a Kleenex.

Ryan sighs heavily. "Why does this even matter?"

"Because I need to know you're not lying to me. My track record on this trip so far—not so great."

"Alyssa got in touch with us a few months back—she had a flood in her storage unit and her scrapbooks all got trashed. She loves scrapbooking, so she wanted us to send whatever photos we have so she can rebuild the books."

"Sounds like someone's not over you."

He slides his hand up to my elbow. "Hollie, I didn't talk to her. She talked to Tanner and Sarah and my mom. If she wants to spend her time gluing pictures of her old life …"

"But you look the same," I say.

"Good genes?" he smiles. "If you look closer, you'll see I don't look the same. I'm a little heavier now, thanks to my magical knee."

Now I feel stupid.

"Hey, if you want, we can go back to the cabin, call Alyssa, and you can talk to her new husband. If he's not at the rink. His team is still in the playoffs."

"He's a hockey player …"

"If he's not available, you can probably talk to her nanny. I'm sure Alyssa's not the one walking the baby around at night."

"You're telling me the truth?" I say, searching his face for evidence of falsehood.

"I have no reason to lie to you." The moisture in his eyes tells me he's either a skilled actor or that I've just forced him to rehash some really gross shit.

Once again, Hollie Porter rises to the occasion.

Another branch snaps. Ryan's eyes widen to the point where I fear they will pop out of his head.

"Fuuuuuck," he whispers. "Hollie. Don't. Move." He stands, making himself as big and menacing as he can.

To no avail.

The golden cat springs out of the bush and throws himself at Ryan before I even know what the fuck has happened.

"Hollie, RUN!" he screams at me, fighting and wrestling this huge, powerful cat that is screeching and growling and snapping at his forearm. I scramble over the log and hit the ground running, slamming into trees as I go from the excruciating pain exploding up the side of my ankle. I hear Ryan scream my name again, and it's in that moment that I realize …

I have to go back.

If I don't, he's going to die. That cougar is going to kill him.

I pivot and haul myself as fast as I can back into the small clearing, and before rational thought crosses my mind, I swing the biggest stick I can carry at the tawny cat's back. It releases Ryan's arm from its mouth, hisses and screeches at me, swiping a massive paw at my stick.

My chest seizes—those fangs … just like with the orca, there is something about seeing this cat. Her teeth. Her outstretched claws. In real life.

I don't have a moment to taste the fear, thick like blood against the roof of my mouth. I swing and hit and scream and stab and do everything I can to get this beautiful, deadly beast off Ryan's body.

"Hol …" His voice is strained but he throws something at me. It bounces across the cushioned forest floor. A pocketknife!

I scramble for it just as the cat returns her attention to Ryan's arm, biting, scratching, tearing. The fabric of his T-shirt is no protection—thank God he's wearing jeans—but if I don't stab this cat, she's going to clamp onto Ryan's neck and drag him off into these woods.

I unfold the blade and lunge, making contact with the cougar's shoulder. She snarls and slaps at me, claws snagging the flesh on and just above my wrist, but I stab again. She spins off Ryan's torso, back onto the dirt. I thrust again, missing the cat's now bleeding shoulder, but she seems to relent, turning and bolting off into the woods, leaving nothing behind but clumps of fur and a final glance of her long, golden-tipped tail.

Holy hell, that is a lot of blood.

The lightheaded, woozy, gonna-pass-out feeling shimmers over me like a gauzy curtain falling from its rod. A train speeding at the station with no brakes, my pulse plunders my chest, vessels, into my temple. In slow motion, I hear nothing but my own staccato breathing. See nothing but more blood than should ever be outside a living human being.

Someone's groaning. "Hollie …" I stare at him, at the blood, at the flesh that is no longer solid and perfect but mangled and striped.

"Hollie … we gotta … we gotta get out of here." He's trying to sit up.

And just like that, in the presence of so much carnage, my senses snap back, a huge rubber band popped against my forehead.

"Ryan, Ryan, oh *God* …" Touching him means I pull away drenched in him. Red, sticky, hot.

The side of my left arm is deeply scratched, mixing my blood into his.

His face is coated in crimson. I can't tell where the wounds are for all the blood. One look at his shredded arm, the bone exposed in the upper portion, the bicep filleted like nothing more than a slab of steak, and I realize we are in very deep trouble.

"Come on. You gotta stand. We can't stay here. She'll come back for you …"

Ryan's eyes are wide. Scared. He needs my help.

I've trained for this. I've lived around this.

I know this.

Using the pocketknife, I shred the lengths of his jeans and tear the denim into strips. I need to push that flayed skin back together, to close it over the bone until we can get help.

"It's so shredded …" A moment's panic flashes behind my eyes. No time. Go. Move. Act.

I fold the bigger flaps along the front of his left upper arm and wrap the denim under and around, using a smaller strip to tie it in place. Ryan shrieks against the tightening fabric.

"Stay with me, Ryan. Ryan, look at me. Can you breathe?"

I hover over his mouth to listen for airway. He sounds clear but coughs, spitting the blood spilling into his mouth from a slice in his lip. He's breathing. His airway is intact.

"I'm going to sit you up. Can you walk?"

"Yeah ... I think so."

"I need you to put all your weight on me. As much as you can. Throw your right arm over my shoulders ..." I push him into a sitting position—he yowls louder than the cougar—but he's able to get himself to his knees. My ankle is going to make this a thousand times harder than it should be, but I have to bite down and get through this.

I have to get him help.

If I don't, he's going to bleed to death.

"I don't know ... why she was out here ...," Ryan says.

"Come on, my sweet, sweet boy, hang on to me. Let's do this. One step at a time. She's gone. We're going to get you on that boat and back to the lodge and Miss Betty will fix everything."

Ryan chuckles, but it is not happy. Not funny. It sounds sad.

God, he's so heavy. This is going to take too long. He's going to die out here. And it's all my fucking fault.

Now is not the time. Save him. You can do this.

Ryan seems to perk up slightly as we reach the edge of the forest. We stop only for a second when I have to turn to the side and throw up again. That's what happens to me when I'm in severe pain. The time I broke my finger in gym class playing volleyball? I barfed on the gym teacher four times before my dad arrived.

Five more steps, and the cabin is ahead. So close. We're going to be okay.

We can do this.

I ease Ryan onto a huge rock just near the edge of the cabin's yard. He's started trembling and his eyes are like marbles in his head. He's blinking slowly, too slowly. I cup my hands on his cheeks.

"Ryan, honey, look at me. Look at me." He does, the shuddering of his body and fear in his face giving me a proper glimpse of what he looked like as a child. "Where are the keys to the boat?"

"Inside ... on the counter. With my phone."

"Don't move."

I throw myself into motion, three hops to every toe touch that surges bile into my throat. The keys are on the counter, just as he said, next to the photos.

The photos that started this whole fucking thing.

No time for this. Grab the phone. Grab the keys.

I slam the front door behind me. Ryan has fallen over and is now sideways on the ground, on his uninjured right side.

"Ryan! Don't you leave me! Don't you fucking die out here!" I say, pulling his head into my lap. I have to get him off the ground.

He opens his eyes. A slow smile crawls across his pallid face. "I was sleepy."

"No! No sleeping. Come on, we gotta get on the boat."

"I'm in good hands, aren't I, Hollie Porter ..." He tries to lift his ribboned arm but it is not responding. Pain. Only the pain registers across his forehead.

"You're in the best hands. I'm going to get you home and we're going to get you fixed up, and then you're going to do all those naughty things to me that you did in that shower in there. Okay? Does that sound like a good plan?"

He smiles again, his eyes closing.

"No! Wake up. Come on. Up we go," I say, pushing and groaning with every last ounce of energy I can find hiding in the recesses of my body. I manage to get him back on his feet but the blood streams off his left arm in rivulets, splatting on the rocky path that leads to the dock like some morbid *Hansel and Gretel* breadcrumb trail.

A horrifying thought settles on me when his shoe catches on the first board of the wooden dock: if he falls in that water, we're fucked.

"Ryan, lean on me. You cannot fall asleep yet. I need you to get on the boat, okay? We're almost there. Let's get on the boat. We can do this."

The progress is slow, so slow, but he stays conscious enough to drag his feet to the boat's side. I hang onto the side railing with the tightest fist I can make, pulling the boat toward me so Ryan can sit his ass on the side and swing his legs around.

"One leg over ... good, good ... now the other." I hop on and shove the small plastic table and fold-up chairs out of way to give him space. He collapses on the back deck, and I know that this is the end of the line. He's not going any farther.

"Ryan, *Ryan!*" His eyes open. "I'm going to get us help. Please, promise me you're not going to fall asleep. *Don't fall asleep.*"

The blood from his arm is now puddling underneath, gathering in a taunting red pool atop the textured white fiberglass.

I have to untie the boat.

I throw the line off and slam through into the main cabin. Crank the engine over.

"Fuck ... I don't know where I am."

Pick up the radio. "Hello? Hello? Is anyone there?" It crackles. Nothing but static. "Hello! Hello! Help us! This is Ryan and Hollie—we need help!"

More crackles. I click on the GPS screen, hoping it can tell me where to go from here, how to get us back to Revelation Cove to people who can save Ryan.

It's not fair that he leaves me so soon.

"Revelation Cove here. Who is this?" the radio sputters. A female voice.

"Oh, thank GOD. It's Hollie Porter. I'm out on the boat with Ryan Fielding. We need help. A cougar—Ryan was attacked by a cougar. I—he's bleeding. So much. We need help!"

"Hollie, this is Betty. Listen to me. Where are you?"

"At Tanner's cabin. We stopped to water the plants ..." The tears sting my eyes, clench at my throat.

"Hollie, Tanner's cabin is not far. Are you listening to me? The GPS will have the coordinates in it to get you home." She walks me through turning the device on, but when I hit the satellite button, the screen says *low signal.*

"Move the boat out into open water. Can you do that?"

"Yeah … yes, I can." I can drive a boat. I've driven with my dad a few times on rented boats and Ryan showed me the other night. I can do this. Engine's on. Anchor's up. Line's free. Throttle forward.

The boat lurches, water spewing behind us as I slam it into drive.

A quick glance over my head reveals that Ryan hasn't moved, but the once-white floor is tainted by the one thing that will keep Ryan's heart beating.

I move into wider water, out of the cabin's quaint alcove. "Try again with the GPS, Hollie."

I do. The screen lights up!

"It's working!"

"Okay, hit the little blue button on the side. It's the go-to button. Revelation Cove is preprogrammed into it. The GPS will tell you where to go."

But this isn't like GPS in a car—there are no street signs here!

"How will I know if I'm going the right way?" I yelp.

"Use the compass and listen to the GPS. Go north. We're north and west of your current location. You can be here in twenty minutes if you push it."

"He's in bad shape, Betty. We have to get him to a hospital—" I leave off the part about so much blood.

"I'm on the line with the air ambulance. The Coast Guard will be here when you arrive." Her voice breaks at the end. When she comes back on, she's not as strong as a second ago. "Please hurry, Hollie. Please …"

Hearing the fear in her voice, I open the throttle on the boat and chant to the higher beings I've never paid much attention to, begging and pleading that they let him live, that if they don't take this wonderful, warm, loving man away from us, I will follow through on all the lame promises I've ever made and I will never ask for another thing as long as I live.

Please. I will be good.

Save him.

CHAPTER TWENTY-THREE
PUTTING HUMPTY
TOGETHER AGAIN

I need to work on my landings.

No one says a word when I slide the boat sideways into Revelation Cove's outer dock. The damage is minimal, and I didn't hit Miss Lily or the other plane parked down the way, but still.

The Coast Guard is indeed there—two vessels with a helicopter hovering overhead, waiting for us so they can scoop Ryan's limp, unconscious form off the boat's deck, now slippery with his blood.

So much blood.

I don't have time to say goodbye or even kiss his forehead before he's on a stretcher, medics surrounding him like lions on a bloodied, weak prey, starting IVs and cutting away the makeshift denim bandaging on his upper arm, strapping oxygen around his face, injecting, listening, palpating, checking pupils.

Huge tears spill down Miss Betty's face as she watches the medics do their work, her arms wrapped tight around Tabby and a few other staff members, all of them sobbing, their faces drawn with shock and sadness. Miss Betty is the heart of this operation, the mother duck, and her ducklings are surrounding her, wrapping her in loyalty and strength.

When I am escorted off the boat, it only takes a moment for the catastrophe of this day to overwhelm me. In true form, I vomit into the water, spitting nothing but the remnants of terror and adrenaline into its clear depths. Another medic kneels beside me and takes one look at my left wrist and hand.

I hadn't noticed how much of my own blood was dripping all over the world.

And then the lightheaded spinnies return. It's loud, so loud, the noise in my head underscored by the hovering helicopter moving overhead, lowering a line to pick up Ryan and take him somewhere they can save him.

Please save him.

I suddenly want to go with him. "I have to go with him!" I holler. No one hears me.

I try to stand, but my ankle has had enough, and I stumble forward, screaming when the cougar's handiwork on my left wrist reasserts itself.

"Chris, over here!" another medic shouts. He lays me back on the dock and examines my arm. Above me, down at the end of the dock, Ryan's body is hoisted skyward in the air ambulance's rescue basket, up, up, up, and away.

Before they can splash warm saline onto my arm, I'm crying so hard, I can't catch my breath. An oxygen mask is shoved onto my face, and it helps, not because I'm so injured but because I am freaking the fuck out and hyperventilating and yes my ankle hurts and shit my wrist stings from that mean mean cat but *God please don't let Ryan die.*

Miss Betty kneels next to me and places a cool hand on my cheek. Calm flows from her, into my face, and I feel … settled. Not alone.

I pull the mask off, chest heaving from sobs. "I'm so sorry … I tried … the cougar came out of nowhere."

"You were perfect. You did everything right, Hollie. Thank you so much for saving my little boy." She pulls me into her chest, into a hug so tight, I don't ever want to let go. So I don't. We cry and cry, and the medics wrap up my wrist that will likely need stitches. We don't stop hugging until the medics put me on a stretcher and carry me into the resort to administer the care they can provide on site.

But because I'm medically stable, I refuse to leave. I can't leave here yet. I have to wait with Miss Betty, to hear what happens with Ryan.

Her little boy.

I should've known.

Miss Betty is Ryan's mom.

I argue with the Coast Guard guys because I refuse to leave until Ryan's brother arrives at the Cove. He can fly me home tomorrow. I'll need to call my dad and have him come get me in Seattle. There's no way I can take the train home with whatever's going on with the ankle.

And then I start crying again. I really, really want my daddy right now.

It's a long night. Once the resort is quiet and the guests have gone back inside and the staff members have taken care of everything so Miss Betty and I can sit by the phone, I realize how very, very tired I am.

I sleep sitting up, leg elevated and ankle packed in ice, in a plush wingback chair in Miss Betty's suite, jumping every time the phone rings as news spreads about the attack. About three o'clock in the morning, Tanner arrives with his wife Sarah. Tired hellos are exchanged as we wait for the hospital to call.

"Tanner, this is Hollie. She saved our Ryan."

Foregoing the customary how-do-you-do handshake, Tanner hugs me, just as tight as his mother did, and kisses my cheek, kneeling beside my chair, thanking me profusely but then asking a million questions about exactly what happened. Says something about needing to know every detail about the cougar—conservation officers will need to hunt her down. If she's out during the day and attacks a human, she's probably sick.

Which could be very dangerous for Ryan. Infection and all that.

Considering the circumstances, Miss Betty is holding herself together remarkably well, even when the Department of Fish and Wildlife officers show up. Even when the hospital calls and says Ryan is in surgery to reattach the tendons and muscles ripped apart by the cougar's claws. He's lost a lot of blood. Required transfusions.

Otherwise, he should be fine.

"He should be fine," she says, over and over again, tears aplenty all around.

As the sun rises over Revelation Cove, the sky hums with news helicopters looking for space to land on the golf course so they can get the scoop.

Tanner agrees to fly out imminently—to Vancouver first where he will drop his mother and wife off to go be with Ryan, and then down to Seattle's Lake Union. He tries to offer to take me to Portland, but I won't hear of it. He needs to be with his brother.

I need to be with his brother.

Alas, my vacation is over. In the wilds of British Columbia, I lost some blood, I lost some fear, and I found my heart.

And now he's in a hospital room in another country hundreds of miles away.

My dad is waiting for me at the Kenmore terminal on Lake Union. His eyes about drop out of his skull when he sees Tanner carrying my bruised, bandaged body down the dock and into the terminal. The men exchange quick hellos, and my dad controls himself, adopting his stoic *I'm a medical professional I got this* face. As Tanner hands me over, Dad thanks and wishes him the best of luck for his brother's speedy recovery.

I'm surprised Dad knows this part already—on the phone, I told him that I'd been in an accident involving wildlife and that I needed him to come to Seattle to get me. I didn't tell him about Ryan or the cougar or how injured I am, or that we need to go directly to an emergency room when we get home. I knew I'd have a three-hour car ride to spill all that. The details had to be kept to a minimum so I wouldn't bawl into the phone like a scared four-year-old.

Because that's exactly how I've felt since that cougar growled over my shoulder.

And like the loving, truehearted soldier of parenting he is, Dad jumped in the car to come get me. No questions asked.

Seems he didn't have to go far to get those questions answered, though. On the front seat of his Prius, a newspaper headline shouts, "Former NHLer Nearly Killed in Cougar Attack."

Dad slides me into the front seat, his movements gentle as he buckles my seat belt. I'm already whimpering.

He crouches on the wet pavement alongside my open door. "So … you were the guest who saved him …"

I nod. Dad wipes my tears away. That only makes me cry harder. I can't speak, so I lift my left arm and cringe as I pull back the sleeve of the Revelation Cove hoodie. "I need stitches. And I think my ankle might be broken."

"Let's get you home, then. The crew at the hospital will be thrilled to treat my little Hollie, Daddy's little superhero."

As I pull my otters from my hastily packed bag, I don't feel very much like a superhero.

CHAPTER TWENTY-FOUR
OBLIQUE IS MY BEST ANGLE

Seventeen stitches. Antibiotics. Tetanus booster that hurt worse than the stitches. Oblique fracture of the distal fibula.

The doctor didn't believe me when I said I'd walked on it. Ran, even. He just shook his head and told my dad maybe the cougar hit me in the head.

And then he used that word again, nodding to the newspaper my dad won't stop carrying around, shoving into everyone's face who will listen, that I'm the girl who saved the NHL star. I'm the "hero."

Not a hero. Just Hollie.

And I'm dying to know how Ryan's doing. My dad tried to call Vancouver General, but the press is all over it, so the hospital isn't releasing any details. I could call Revelation Cove, but Miss Betty won't be there. She and Tanner will be at the hospital. With Ryan.

Which is where I should be.

I'm reading the newspaper article and a detail jumps out at me that I hadn't noticed earlier. "'Former NHL defenseman and enforcer Ryan Fielding, while in the British Columbian wilderness south of his resort at Revelation Cove, was mauled by a wayward cougar …'"

His resort?

I scan farther. "'Fielding played for six seasons in the NHL, retiring from the Canucks after a career-ending knee injury. In a business move some called risky, Fielding and his older pilot brother Tanner Fielding helm the now five-year-old Revelation Cove, one of British Columbia's finest resort destinations. Fielding has proven himself a savvy entrepreneur and the resort regularly earns high marks on travel editors' top-choice lists ...'"

He owns it.

He's not the concierge. He's the damn *owner.*

Why didn't he tell me?

A spark of hurt flames in my chest—this is not something to keep secret, not when you're showing each other the most private parts of your body and soul.

Why wouldn't he tell me that he was the owner and not just the guy behind the desk who arranged whale-watching and fishing excursions?

More importantly, would it have mattered?

Maybe. Look how I behaved with Roger Dodger. Why was I so willing to give up the prize to that skeezball? Because he was rich? Powerful? Successful?

I should be ashamed of myself.

As the cast tech wraps my ankle, the teasing starts. "How'd you ever manage to deal with all that blood, Hols?" Dad says.

"I just did, Dad." I just ... did.

"I told you you'd get over it. Maybe you can rethink nursing school now."

"Dad, I'm not going to nursing school. Or medical school. Not now, not ever."

"I'm just sayin' ..."

"Can we not talk about this right now?"

He pats my hand. "I'm going to go downstairs and get these prescriptions filled," he says, kissing the side of my dirty hair. "Hey, Mark, make that a waterproof cast. This girl needs a bath."

I slap at him as he walks away. Always the kidder.

The crutches are harder to navigate with the stitched left arm, so one of Dad's orderly buddies gives me the limousine treatment and wheels me out to the car. The argument about where I'd be staying was easily resolved when I started crying again—Dad insists that I come out to his house but I told him I just want to be in my own bed, that I don't have the strength to fight off Mangala or see

Dr. Aurora if she shows up or hear about how wonderful Moonstar is and I don't want any goddamned cupcakes. He relents but only on the condition that I let him come stay with me for a few days. He offers to call Keith, and I think the abruptness of my answer cements in his head that indeed, Keith is a thing of my past.

Because he so is.

And the fact that I haven't thought about him for the past few days, not in any meaningful capacity, reaffirms to me that, despite my earlier self-doubt, I absolutely made the right decision.

As we're driving home, I notice for the first time the billboard rallying support for the Portland Winterhawks hockey team. "Winterhawks are in the playoffs?" I say.

Dad smiles at me. "Since when do you follow hockey?"

"Since now."

"Mm-hmm."

A guy walking across the crosswalk is wearing the Detroit Red Wings jersey—and he has a beard. I laugh to myself. *Someone didn't get the memo. Red Wings are eliminated. Time to shave, buddy.*

Heading along Burnside, a half-smile accompanies a snort as a Monday Merchant comes into view. I start to tell my dad how I met the guy who owns the Merchant empire, but then I think better of it. Too many questions, not enough energy to answer them all. And what an embarrassing misstep on my part.

Guess I'll be spending more of my time at Trader Joe's. Take *that*, Roger Dodger.

When we turn into the apartment complex, I'm flooded with relief that Keith's truck isn't in the lot. I don't have the energy to talk to him about why we should maybe get back together. I'm so glad my dad didn't call him. Another check in the Win Column for Daddy-O.

Mrs. Hubert is waiting at her kitchen window, as per usual. The springs on the back door whine as she opens to shuffle out onto the concrete stoop. "Hollie, what have you gone and done to yourself?" she says.

My dad runs interference. "Hollie's a hero, Mrs. Hubert. She saved a famous hockey player from a cougar attack."

"I don't believe that."

"Well, you don't have to. She did it, though. She fought a cougar, and won."

"A cougar? As in a cat? She can't even handle those damn rat dogs. How could she handle a cougar?"

"Goodbye, Mrs. Hubert."

"You let me know when she's back moving around. I need groceries!"

I tuck my head into my dad's shoulder as he carries me up the stairs. He grunts with every step—he's not as big or strong as Ryan, or even Tanner. I should've walked up.

But I don't want to. I want to be taken care of right now. My physical injuries are painful, yes, but it's my heart that's hemorrhaging.

How did that happen so fast?

Dad settles me on the couch and opens all the windows to air the place out. It's muggy, and the fresh air wafting through the kitchen and bedroom feels nice. A large shadow dusts the main wall in the living room from Keith's now-removed TV. Without even asking, Dad hefts my trusty Magnavox in from the bedroom and sets it on the vacant cabinet.

"You thirsty? Hungry?"

"I'm sleepy."

He brings water and the pills—antibiotics and a pain reliever. "I'm going out to get you some groceries. Any special requests?"

"Chocolate. Lots and lots of chocolate," I say. He ruffles my hair. "Oh, and go down to the other stairs so Mrs. Hubert doesn't see you walk by. She'll make you buy her food too."

"Hollie, you have to stop helping that woman. She has children, you know."

"Dad … later …"

He kisses my forehead again. "When I get back, if you're up for it, we can wash your hair."

When the door clicks closed, I'm already drifting off, away from the throb in my ankle, away from Mrs. Hubert's whining or my dirty hair or my empty apartment, sinking into the thoughts about if Ryan made it through surgery and if he's thinking of me as much as I'm thinking about him.

CHAPTER TWENTY-FIVE
CAUSE CÉLÈBRE

When I wake, I'm assailed by the aroma of simmering garlic and meat and ... is that basil? Dad's making his famous spaghetti sauce.

My stomach growls an applause.

I try to sit forward, but ohhhh my God. Every. Thing. Hurts. Gonna need another one of those Delightfully Luscious Orange Unicorn Pills of Tantalizing Deliverance from Pain.

Dad's talking to someone. "Oh, that's excellent news. Sure, sure. And they've got drains in place? ... What's the prognosis? ... Yeah, for sure. Good thing he's not playing second line anymore, right? [Laughter.] ... You bet, I'll tell her. Give Mr. Fielding our best ..."

Mr. Fielding?

Ryan!

"You are absolutely welcome. My Hollie is a great girl ... yes, so brave ... We'd love to come up to the resort ... [More chuckling] Yes, this time without the cougars, thanks ... Thanks again, Mrs. Fielding. You take care now."

"Dad!"

He comes into the living room, the phone no longer at his ear. "Who was that?"

"Betty Fielding. Seems your hockey friend is going to be okay."

"Did she say anything else?"

"Just some medical stuff that will gross you out—he has an infection in the bone of his upper arm, but—"

"Dad, did she ... did she say anything about me? Does Ryan ... does he want to talk to me?"

Realization dawns in my father's eyes. Ryan isn't just some guy at the resort who I saved on a nature hike. Following this recognition, though, my father's face falls.

For me. He feels bad for me.

"No, honey, that was all. She just wanted to check on you, see what the doctor said, see how you were holding up."

"Oh … okay."

"How're you feeling?"

"Like I got in a fight with a cougar."

"You hungry?"

"Starved."

He plates up food and brings me a TV tray. He was clearly busy while I slept. Sitting next to the TV is a DVD player and a stack of movies.

"I thought you could use some quiet time," he says, handing me the boxes. I slurp the spaghetti sauce off the noodles, the rich tomato sauce steeped in flavor. Party in my mouth.

The movies … chick flicks. Stuff Keith hated so I'd take myself to the theatre to see. Alone. At least I didn't have to share my popcorn or Red Vines as I watched ninety minutes of romance, love lost and found, happy endings unfold on the big screen.

But my fork freezes midlift. The third movie in the stack—it's a documentary. About otters. And then another one. I look up at Dad.

"I went to the gift shop over at OMSI. They had all sorts of videos about your otters. The gal sent me to the University of Portland bookstore, and they had even more." In total, Dad's brought nine nature videos, not all of them about otters. I pick up the one with two breaching orcas on the front and chuckle.

"This," I wag in front of him, "remind me to tell you about the orcas."

"Do I want to hear this story?" He smiles and sets a glass of chocolate milk on my tray, festooned with whipped cream and sprinkles. My dad rocks.

"Oh, you so do."

We eat, and then he helps me into the bathroom so he can wash my hair. I tell him all about my spontaneous swimming date with three of the largest members of the dolphin family, how I was so dumb out in a rowboat, oarless and alone in a cocktail dress, mad because some stupid guy stood me up. My dad has to sit back on bent legs to control his laughter as I tell him about falling into the water with the giant seafaring, predatory mammals, how they didn't eat me, but then of course, the sky erupted with thunder and lightning and more rain than I've ever seen.

On the story goes, every wild, hilarious detail that didn't seem very hilarious at the time but in hindsight ...

"I don't believe it. You? My Hollie swimming with orcas? My afraid-of-her-own-shadow Hollie?"

"I'm not afraid of my own shadow," I say, pulling my soaked, soapy head away from the tub.

"You've been afraid of your own shadow since you were four and first noticed you had one."

The water and soap oozes down the side of my head, down my neck, soaking my T-shirt and the stained bathmat under me. Suds seep into my ears and amplify the sound of my voice. "Why do you say that?"

"Because it's true. You do everything everyone tells you to do because you're afraid that if you say no, they won't like you. You deal with Mrs. Hubert's bullying because you're too chicken to tell that old hag to get stuffed. And what about Keith? You haven't been happy with him from the second he moved those ratty little mutts into your apartment, and yet, two years—was it two years?—gone."

"I don't want to have this conversation with you," I say, shoving my head back under the tap.

"Hollie, that look in your eye when I mentioned Mr. Fielding— that's a new look for you. Maybe it was the cougar, maybe it was him, I don't know, but you've shown that when life kicks you in the balls, you know how to kick back."

"I did what anyone else would've done in that situation."

"That's a convenient thing to tell yourself. You reacted the way you did because you saw someone you cared about in trouble. Not everyone would've done the same thing."

"Dad, your point?"

"My point is, if you like him, go after him. Don't wait. The tired cliché about opportunity knocking? She only knocks for so long before her knuckles bloody and she gives up."

"What if—"

"Nope. No time for what-ifs, Hollie Cat. You faced down your shadow. Time to put her away for good. If this young man means something to you …"

I don't want to admit that in a very short time, Ryan Fielding has come to mean something to me. I don't tell my dad how Ryan found me soaked to the bone, risking hypothermia, or how we had two perfect days on that boat. How he cooked me breakfast and took me crabbing and clamming and we hand-fed the otters or how we fed each other crab and drank wine and kissed and laughed … I don't need to tell my dad how Ryan and I got busy in that amazing shower or how the cougar attack was really my fault, because I saw some photos I didn't understand and ran into the woods, again acting like an immature fool.

I can't tell him that. Because if I do, I might start crying, and I may not be able to stop.

The doorbell rings. Dad turns off the water, hands me a towel, and tells me to stay put until he gets back. I'm not an invalid, so once my hair is wrapped up, I hop out into the living room just as he's bumping the door closed with his butt.

In his arms is a huge bouquet. So big, I'm not even sure where we're going to put it.

I'm nervous to read the card. He sets down the wide-mouthed vase and plucks the small square from the card fork. "All our thanks and all our love, your family at Revelation Cove," Dad reads.

"Wow … that's … wonderful."

I don't have time to feel crestfallen about the card's lack of mention of Ryan—the doorbell rings again.

"Can I help you?"

"Hi, I'm Jake Stephens with *The Oregonian*. Does Hollie Porter live here?"

"Dad, no!"

"Why, yes, she sure does."

"I was wondering if I could come in and talk to Hollie for a few minutes about what happened up north, with the cougar and the hockey player."

My dad swings the door wide and invites Jake Stephens in before I can scamper back into the bathroom. "I'm—uh—not really ready for company."

"Are you Hollie?" the reporter says.

"Yeah ..."

"It's so nice to meet you. You're a real hometown hero, you know that?"

"I'm not. Anyone would've done the same thing."

"Hol, why don't you ..." Dad points to the towel on my head.

"Right. Hang on a second." I use the hallway walls for support and amble back into the bathroom to comb out my hair. A little lip gloss. Some powder on my sunburned cheeks. I'm not exactly ready for my close-up in stretched-out yoga pants and Beavers sweatshirt, but it'll have to do.

"Ahhh, here she is," Dad says, helping me from the hall over to the couch. "Can't quite use the crutches yet due to the stitches on her arm. Cougar got her there."

"Wow, you must've been terrified."

The conversation continues with him asking me questions and me trying to provide simple answers—I don't want to reveal anything about Ryan or his life, now that I know he's a business owner and well-loved hockey guy.

"Did you hear what the Winterhawks are doing for you?"

"For me?"

"They called my editor just before I came over—it's meant to be a surprise, so pretend I didn't tell you—Ryan Fielding has done quite a lot for the charity they're affiliated with, so the

'Hawks front office is giving you and your dad box seats for the playoffs."

"Wow! Really? Hot dog!" My dad gets very excited about tickets to sporting events—especially *free* tickets.

"Like I said, when they call you, act surprised," Stephens says, winking at me.

Don't wink at me. Only Ryan's allowed to do that.

Ahhh, that ache in my chest again.

During the course of our chat, the doorbell rings two more times with more flowers, one from the Vancouver Canucks head office—"Thanks for being a part of our team! We Are All Canucks, even if you're in Portland! Best wishes"—and another from the folks at dispatch with a far less sentimental "Get well soon." Wonder how the party-planning committee came up with that all on its own.

The whole news-travels-fast adage is proven yet again when a smaller bouquet arrives from none other than Keith and the Yorkies. He even draws three paw prints, as if the dogs signed the card.

Seriously.

When Jake Stephens has gotten everything and then some for his story (my dad talked his ear off and even offered to show him wallet-sized photos of me in grade school), he leaves his card behind and asks when would be a good time for their staff photographer to pop by in the next day or two. I let my dad deal with this stuff and hop down the hall to my bedroom, away from the flowers and the phone calls and the newspapers and TV reports that talk about how I'm a hero.

I'm not heroic.

I'm just a girl who's fallen in love with a boy six hours and a whole world away.

Chapter Twenty-Six
The Raft

The house phone is ringing. I dive at it, hoping it will be the number I most want to see in the world. It's not.

Six days later, my fifteen minutes of fame are over, and I'm back to a quiet apartment with wilting flowers and no news on how Ryan is doing other than the occasional online report from the Canucks and Revelation Cove websites that say "he is recovering well in hospital and thanks all the fans and resort guests, past, present, and future, for their outpouring of love and support."

I've Googled *Ryan Fielding* and learned more about him than maybe he wanted me to know—about his tumultuous hockey career, his very public broken engagement, the two arrests he's got under his belt for beating the living hell out of a couple guys at different bars when he was young and pumped full of testosterone, how he turned things around when he and two other retired NHL players, along with brother Tanner Fielding, opened the resort.

These revelations don't change the way I feel when I think about him—this is from a life before now, a Ryan I wouldn't have had access to.

I've pulled up the phone number Miss Betty called from at least a hundred times.

I just can't bring myself to hit the *call* button. Maybe my shadow hasn't retreated after all.

When I finally do answer the ringing phone, it's not a voice I'm excited to hear again.

"Hollie? It's Patty." Polyester Patty. "I know you've been recovering from your ordeal and we wanted to give you time to heal, but there are some issues left unresolved with your little ... disappearing act."

"Mm-hmm."

"I think we'll need to schedule a sit-down to discuss how you were basically a no-show for work. I know this isn't fun to talk about these things, especially right now given everything you've just been through, but we're a team, and we have to work together to build a community that we can all rely on, like a big family ..."

She drones on about how I called in sick under false pretenses and then left the country, how they had to scramble to cover my shifts and how Keith came in and talked to her about how "worried" he was about me, that I might be having a nervous breakdown because I broke up with him and that I wasn't really sick but rather skipped town and didn't tell anyone where I was going.

So, basically, a perfect summary of all the stupid shit I did last week before I landed at Revelation Cove.

Before my life changed in immeasurable, unbelievable ways.

I'm no longer the Hollie Polyester Patty is talking about. I left her in those woods, left her behind when I was tying up shredded flesh and dragging a failing body out of the trees, away from a mortal threat that could've ended us, if she wanted to.

"And then there's the issue of the outstanding review memo ..."

An unfamiliar something or other burns in my chest, accelerates my heart. "No."

"Pardon me?"

"No."

Patty is silent for a moment. I sit straighter on the couch. "I'm not coming in. Not for a disciplinary hearing, not for a sit-down, not for a review memo meeting, not for the party-planning committee. Just ... no."

"So, are you saying—"

"I quit. You can mail my last check."

"Hollie, you've sustained a pretty big trauma, and we have counselors who would be happy to help you through whatever you're dealing with. We can get you back into the training modules until you feel solid enough to rejoin the floor team."

"No."

"I don't think you mean that. Tell you what, come in tomorrow, let's just have a casual chat. You and me. No one else. No pressure, no other managers, no memos."

"Patty, you can clean up my console and my dad will come get my stuff. I need my otter figurine back—everything else, you can keep."

"Hollie—"

"It's time for my next pain pill. Take care of yourself," I say, hanging up.

My dad's pissed. I call and ask him if he'll stop by dispatch after his shift so he can pick up my stuff.

"It's a good job, Hollie! You can't just throw it away."

"Dad, remember all your talk about opportunity and her bloody knuckles and my shadow?"

"Hollie, don't twist my words. Be reasonable, kiddo. In a few weeks, you'll regret this. You'll wish you hadn't walked away."

"Dad, if I don't do this, in a few weeks I guarantee I will regret *not* walking away."

He sighs into the phone. "I'll stop by dispatch and then get you some dinner. Any requests?"

I fall asleep on the couch. Watching a nature documentary, this one ironically about cougars. The one who attacked us was probably sick or starving. Apparently it's not at all unusual for cougars to swim amongst the islands up there. YouTube has a handful of videos of Canadian cougars swimming alongside fishing boats, unsuspecting anglers going about their business when they come upon a giant, dog-paddling feline. Hilarious, if not otherwise terrifying.

My pain has diminished considerably throughout—Percocet, the wonder of modern medicine! I've checked and rechecked for new text messages, hoping against hope to find one from Revelation Cove. Dad lovingly replaced my fried cell phone and they were able to bring it back to life long enough to transfer all my numbers, but the only thing that is waiting for me is a voice mail from Moonstar about "you are so brave fighting off that big kitty and I'm sending over cupcakes and I will pop by as soon as I get back into town but Mr. Amazing Perfect Husband and I are jetting off to Some Third World Country to save rainforests with plumes of frosting and unbleached organic flour because starving people who don't have access to clean drinking water love cupcakes!"

When the cupcakes arrived, I gave them to the dumpster. Okay, yes, fine, I ate two. Maybe three. Please don't tell Moonstar how good they are. I will never hear the end of it.

But it's Ryan who consumes my thoughts, like I'm some weird teenager with an unstable crush on the lead singer of a boy band. He's the first thing I think of when I wake and the last thought that crosses my mind before drifting off. I have replayed our first night on the boat, our second night, the shower at the cabin … and the attack.

It's on a loop, a delicious, breathtaking, heart-pounding loop, the memories laden with both pleasure and pain, though, lucky for me, no matter how many stitches or broken bones, I will always remember those three days as my Best Ever.

The doorbell rings. My heart spazzes like it does every single time, that tiny voice in my head whispering *it might be him it might be him.* Only it never is.

And it isn't this time, either.

"Hi," FedEx guy checks the envelope, "this is for Hollie Porter."

"I'm Hollie Porter." I sign his little digital scanner thingie. "Any idea what this is?"

"Nope. It's from California overnight. That's all I know."

California?

I click the door closed quietly, afraid if Mrs. Hubert hears my voice, she'll start hollering up the stairs about groceries or the weather or why she hasn't seen Keith's truck around lately.

I hop back to the couch and read the shipping label on the cardboard envelope. It's from the Monterey Bay Aquarium, Monterey, California.

I don't remember sending away for anything. And I don't think such an important-looking envelope is in thanks for my annual fifty-dollar donation. They'd be bankrupt FedEx'ing thanks to donors.

Inside is an itinerary—dates for next month for otter watch at a variety of tracking stations in the Monterey area run by the Friends of the Sea Otter—as well as a bumper sticker, T-shirt, and a glossy brochure from the Monterey Bay Aquarium's Sea Otter Research and Conservation Program. A separate page on Aquarium letterhead details my scheduled two-week unpaid internship to get hands-on experience "with local flora and fauna, both within the otter conservancy community and within the greater Aquarium environment."

What the hell …?

This has to be my dad's doing. Where did he—*how* did he …? Does not compute.

A letter is enclosed with my name handwritten on its envelope. The letter inside thanks me for the "significant donation" to their program that will enable the organization to further their conservation and otter counting efforts for the coming year.

There has to be a mistake. While I would love to give all my money away to my favorite charity, there's the need for me to pay rent and eat solid food. Since when did fifty bucks qualify as significant?

I read and reread the letter again. It goes on to explain how donor monies are used to count and track sea otter populations, to aid in recovery and rehabilitation during marine crises such as oil spills, and to support protective legislation concerning not only California's Southern sea otter population of 3,000 animals but the 65,000 to 78,000 members of the Northern sea otter community found in Washington, Canada, and Alaska.

Otters in Canada. Like the ones Ryan showed me. The ones we fed.

My dad didn't arrange this.

My eyes sting. I try calling him but it goes to voice mail. He must be driving.

I need some air. I gotta look at something beyond these four walls. Ryan can arrange for me to go to California to watch otters but he can't call me? Did he even do this? Is Miss Betty somehow behind this?

Oh my God, is Ryan dead? Is this her way of telling me?

No. If he were dead, it would've been all over the news.

Right?

I pull on the T-shirt included in the package, knot my hair into a bun, and throw on clean yoga pants. It's a walk, not a beauty pageant. We're a few days away from June, and it seems Portland is already wearing her summer dress, the light breeze warm, the scent of fresh-cut grass perfuming the air.

I've mastered the crutches, though I haven't quite figured out how to get Mrs. Hubert to stop stalking me out her kitchen window.

"Hollie, is that you?"

I stop three stairs from the bottom.

"Hollie Porter, I know that's you. Don't you try to sneak by here without talking to me."

Sigh. "Hello, Mrs. Hubert."

"How are you feeling, dear? Because let me tell you, my arthritis is flaring up terrible and I just can't get my kids to come by. I need your help. I need you to get me some half-and-half and a fresh bag of frozen peas, and Mr. Boots needs more wet food." She reaches behind for her wallet and digs out cash. "Here's ten dollars. That should cover it." It never covers it. This woman owes many pennies to the Bank of Hollie.

"Mrs. Hubert, I can't drive yet. I'm not going to the store. I'm just going for a walk. To see the ducks."

"Well, when you get back then, you can run to the market for me. I'll wait—"

I hear Ryan's voice in my head. *You gotta start telling people no, Hollie. It's okay to do that.*

"I can't get you your half-and-half or peas or cat food. You're going to have to get it yourself."

"But—"

"No, Mrs. Hubert."

Her hands drop to her sides and she looks away. For a second, I think the quivering lip is going to give way to her crying. And then I will feel like a righteous asshole for telling this housebound old woman with deformed hands and a naked cat that I can't go to the grocery store for her.

I am a terrible person.

"Well … I was wondering how long it would be before you grew some cojones."

"Excuse me?"

Her quivering lip thins into what might be her version of a smile. Her eyes sparkle a little, not with tears but with something alive—Mrs. Hubert is being … funny?

"I've been bossing you around for as long as you've lived in this building, and you're just now standing up to me? You're a slow learner, child."

I'm not sure if I should bitch-slap her or laugh.

"Wow … okay."

She holds out the ten-dollar bill. "Take this. Go buy yourself a drink. Or some coffee. Or whatever the kids are doing these days."

"I don't need your money, Mrs. Hubert."

She releases the bill and it floats to the ground in front of me. If I don't put the crutch's rubber foot on it, it will fly away.

"Buy some duck food, then. The stall is open until five. Don't feed them any processed bread. It's bad for 'em." She closes the screen door and shuffles away. I don't move until I hear Bob Barker's voice ring through her tiny 900 sq. ft. box.

Just as I reach the edge of the lot, my dad pulls in. Rolls down his window. "Look at you, up and around. Where you going?"

"Gonna go feed the ducks."

"I've got dinner for you, and your stuff from dispatch." He holds up my otters. I'm so happy to see them, I snatch them from his hands and kiss them before stuffing them into my pants pocket. Dad snorts at me.

I give him my keys. "A letter arrived for me. Go up and read it."

He kisses the back of my still-bandaged hand, and I'm off, feeling lighter than I have in a week, even though I've just told off the neighbor and Ryan is fading into nothing more than a collection of memories I'll box up and store in that room in my head that I reserve for my most cherished secrets. If I close my eyes, I can still feel his giant hand resting atop mine, see that smile that could melt glaciers …

The crosswalk chirps at me. The park paths are relatively quiet, rightfully so as it is near dinnertime on a Sunday afternoon. A pink-cheeked toddler runs past me, her yellow sweater buttoned under her chin, the vibrant flowers of her billowy dress bouncing with every wobbly pound her chubby sandaled feet make on the path. "Guck! Guck! Guck!" she yells, trying in vain to chase down a drake and his mate. The baby squeals with glee when the ducks launch themselves across the water and into the air. When she notices me watching her, she points and claps her hands. "Guck!"

The parents scoop her up and head away from the pond, much to her audible dismay. I continue along the path in search of my destination. The green benches near Firwood Lake.

Where Mona and Herb go, every single day.

Or where they went. I don't know how they are. I wonder if I could get Polyester Patty to check on them for me … Not likely. Not after I told her off. Patty's like an elephant—she eats her weight every day at lunch, makes huge, stinky shits, and she never forgets. (No offense to elephants.)

Mona and Herb and their perfect little life will have to forever remain one of those mysteries I think of when I'm feeling melancholy, when I'm remembering that every day is a day to be lived, that shadows are meant to be chased, that I have to not just listen to what Mona said but install her wisdom in my life, as if I were installing new cupboards.

I stretch on the bench, foregoing the duck food because I don't feel like walking to the other end of the park where the duck-food guy is only to find that he's closed up shop so he can go smoke weed with his cronies in the woods. The sun filters through the tall cedars and even taller firs and the branches of the willowy willows in the middle of the pond, and for a moment, I'm a little kid again, listening to my dad tell me his story about Drake the Duck who raised his clutch of eggs when Molly Mallard took a vacation, and how Drake and his babies played and swam and ate bugs and every night before bed, when it was time to brush their little duck teeth, Drake would tell his ducklings about a little girl named Hollie and how she had magical powers and could fly around the world and make rainbows come out of her fingertips.

Of course, I could never fly or make rainbows. But when I was five, I was confident that every baby duck I'd see at this pond knew I was that magical Hollie their dad had told them about.

I swipe a hand across my face when the first tear makes landfall on my shirt.

Why am I crying?

You just quit a job you hated. You felt something people go their whole lives without ever experiencing. You felt the sun on your face for three whole days and fed otters by hand and fought off a cougar. Someone is sending you to California to play with otters for two whole weeks.

You're brave and you saved the man who saved you first.

I should be dancing, hopping one-footed around this park like a rum-soaked pirate on shore leave, hugging babies and pinching cheeks and clapping for lovers sharing their first kisses over near the dog park where they've brought their poochies for some play-time …

"Excuse me …" A quiet male voice attached to a pair of sports sandals asks.

God, not now. I don't want to explain to a stranger why I'm sitting here crying.

I don't look up. I have to wipe away the tears streaming down my face. Sniff hard so I don't have snot running down my lip.

"Is this seat taken?" The voice is louder this time.

Familiar.

I'm terrified to look.

When I do, the sun is in the way and my hand shielding my eyes doesn't do a good job and there's no way that could be him and how the hell could it be he is so far away and I'm here and we're apart and blocking his face is a bouquet of wildflowers but it has to be him and and and …

He doesn't wait for me to respond. He sits, the bench squeaking under his weight.

"Hi," Ryan says, presenting the paper-wrapped cluster of daisies. "You're a hard woman to find."

"Not if you know where to look." I'm crying for real now. I bury my nose in the flowers' sunny faces.

"Good thing your dad knew that."

"What … what are you … how *are* you?"

"Alive, thanks to you."

His whole left upper half is bandaged, his arm bundled in white and held tight against his chest. The scratches on his face are deep but stitched, the blue threads just barely visible under the surface. More scars for him to brag about. His left eye is blackened but the healing is active, the skin fading to a rainbow of colors—purples, pinks, yellow, green.

"You left without saying goodbye," he says.

"You were sort of out of it." He nods. "How was the helicopter ride?"

"Loud. And painful."

"No doubt." He lifts my left hand to his lips and kisses my fingertips.

"I needed to find you … to say thanks."

"I did what anyone else would've done."

"Your dad said you'd say that."

"I'm glad you're okay. I … I wanted to call. We *did* call. The hospital wouldn't tell us anything. I wanted to call Miss Betty—your mom," I laugh, "about a million times."

I look down at the flowers. A ripple of laughter escapes my throat when I see the price tag attached to the wrapping. "Really?" I hold it up for him. "Monday Merchant? You bought flowers for me from Roger Dodger?"

Ryan smiles. "Hey, just supporting the local economy."

"I'd punch you if you weren't already held together with duct tape." I gently pinch his chin and twist his face slightly left, then right. "I see they didn't do anything with that nose." I get a real laugh this time. "Nah, I'm glad they didn't touch it. It's hot."

"You think my nose is hot?"

"Maybe."

He scoots closer, if that's possible. "I would've called first, but I had to see you. They released me this morning because I wouldn't stop harassing the nurses."

"Why doesn't that surprise me?"

"Tanner flew me down."

"You came here first? Before going home?"

Ryan laughs. "I think this is the part you're missing, Hollie Porter." He rubs his lips against the back of my bandaged hand. A little hint of moisture teases the corner of his very green eyes. "You are home. Wherever you are, that's where I'll be."

"You can't say that. You haven't seen my apartment yet."

"Smart-ass ... I'm trying to be serious here."

"You can't know that yet, Ryan. It's been—what—two weeks? Not even two weeks."

"And here's the part where I tell you that fairy tales and unicorns are real, and sometimes ... sometimes you just know."

Mona pops into my head. *I knew Herby was the one when he spent the whole night talking to me in the stinky coatroom instead of dancing the night away with his friends.*

"We hardly know each other." Highlights of his life story have only been brought to my attention secondary to the stalker-friendly magic of the Internet.

"I think we know the important stuff. Do you have a weird past as a serial killer or Tupperware hoarder that I should know about?"

I look around us, as if to confess something dire. "You got me: I am a serial killer of Tupperware." He laughs again, deep and throaty. "But what about the resort?"

"What about it?"

"You're not saying that you'll move to Portland …"

"Well … that depends on you. The resort is where I live, but Miss Betty and Tanner and I were talking, and once you get back from your time in Monterey—"

"That was you."

He nods, his smile wide and proud.

"Thank you."

"We figured that would be a good start for you to get your hands dirty, you know, before we offer you the new position on staff."

"What new position is that?"

"Well, we think that there is definitely an opening at Revelation Cove for a wildlife education specialist."

"I can't …" And I stop talking, halting that ridiculous thought like a drunk clown at a children's party, before the untrue words cross my lips.

Yes, I can.

I cup my hands around his stubbled cheeks, a light finger tracing his stitches.

"Damn cat got you good," I say. "And you need a shave. Didn't you hear? Detroit was eliminated."

"Are you going to kiss me, or do I have to take a page out of your book and force myself on you?"

"Ha! I don't recall you putting up much of a fight."

"You got me drunk! How could I resist in that state?"

With his good hand, he brushes that stupid river of tears leaking out of my left eye and closes the distance between us, his lips on mine. He pushes his face into mine until he moves the wrong way and grimaces.

"Don't overdo it, stud," I tease.

His back against the bench, he scoots as close to me as he can without pulling me onto his lap. The lump in my pocket from the figurine digs into his thigh.

"Is that a gun in your pocket, or are you just happy to see me?"

"Sorry." I dig out the otters. "My dad picked up my stuff from work."

Ryan traces the white of the tiny clamshell clutched against the baby otter's belly.

"You and your otters … *Enhydra lutris.*"

"You remembered!"

"How could I forget? You've tattooed it on my heart."

I groan. "Do they teach you this cheese in the NHL?"

He gingerly lifts my left arm, his fingertips gripping so lightly, I can hardly feel it, and slides his undamaged arm under mine. His fingers weave through and he closes his huge hand around my trembling, electric fingers.

I could get lost in those eyes, the rims now moist with what I hope are happy man tears.

"This, Hollie Porter, this is our raft. *We* are a raft."

"Like the otters …"

"And that means we have to float together so we don't drift apart."

"Otters don't usually float in mixed-gender rafts."

"Our raft, our rules," he says. "Just don't bite my nose when we mate."

"You're awfully presumptuous about the future, aren't you, Mr. Fielding?"

"I shoot to score, baby."

"Not according to your NHL record."

Ryan laughs through a kiss hardly decent given current environs, but I don't care. About anything. Everything I need is right here, sucking on my face.

And when the old couple shuffles onto the bench next to us and the wife helps her husband move his walker so he can sit, I know … this raft is exactly where I'm meant to be.

Acknowledging Our Raftmates

Thanks to these folks who, while not otters, were wildly helpful in the creation of this work:

Always first and foremost, my fantastic agent, Dan Lazar, who puts up with way more than his share from me, and his dynamic, shiny assistant Torie Doherty-Munro. Your editorial feedback and therapeutic support is unrivaled and very much appreciated. Thanks too to Julie Trelstad, the Writers House digital rights manager, for helping us make this happen. What a grand experiment!

To my cousin Ann Moffitt Whitson for the medical advice and jargon and for introducing me to Jacob Mayhew—his help with the fine details about the city of my birth is so appreciated! Any errors and fantastical exaggerations within are mine alone. (It should be noted that the 911 stuff was pulled from my terrifying three-month stint as an operator-in-training in a tiny Oregon county back in the '90s. I worked with some real characters. I'm sure Portland's Bureau of Emergency Communications is devoid of folks like Les and Troll Lady and Polyester Patty.) Thanks to Melanie Guptill Ainsworth for the helpful clamming advice. It's been a long time since I got that dirty.

To my better-than-sisters, Angeline Kace and Heather Hildenbrand; to Kendall Grey for being the mirror to my madness; to Shana Benedict for being a fabulous prereader and everyone's favorite blogger (http://bookvacations.wordpress.com/); to Evelyn Lafont for support and that eagle eye; to Adrienne Crezo for her mad skills in All the Things; and to London Sarah (McDonald), my birthday twin, for being my First and Best Fan and for excellent feedback to tie up those loose strings. Your friendship is to me what the Ring is to that scant-haired, loin-cloth-wearing, cave-dwelling fellow who helps Frodo.

For inspiration? Thank you, Marian Keyes, who showed me how writing things that make you smile is absolutely acceptable, and required. I interviewed her in 2006 and while she probably doesn't remember me, the mark left behind by her books and spirit is indelible; to Ryan Kesler, the Vancouver Canucks' #17, thanks for being my favorite hockey player and providing inspiration without even knowing it; and to Canadian actor Peter Mooney (*Rookie Blue*, *Camelot*)—you don't know me, but you are my Ryan Fielding. Thank you for a fun few months.

To Portland, city of my birth and childhood, and Oregon's gorgeous coast; to Beautiful British Columbia for being such a significant part of my life for the last twelve years. Otters, orca, and cougars (and raccoons and bears and coyotes), I love you all.

And best for last: to the miniature humans who share this house and who aren't so miniature anymore. Thanks for letting Mom and Dad talk make-believe at mealtimes so we could breathe life into Hollie and Ryan. And guys, the kitten is hanging from the light fixture again.

About the Author(s)

Eliza Gordon is actually two people: the Wyfey, Jennifer Sommersby ("Eliza"), writer and editor, and Husband, Gary Young ("Gordon"), screenwriter and visual FX artist extraordinaire. Gordon helps build the skeleton; Eliza packs on the meat and rearranges the limbs. Combs the hair. Fixes the teeth. You understand. After meeting and marrying in Los Angeles, this American-Canadian duo moved to the Great White Rainy North where they live with their collection of children and one very spoiled, high-flying kitten.

The name Eliza Gordon was chosen to honor two amazing people, Martha Elizabeth (Porter) Young and Kenneth Gordon Young, who sadly left us in 2005, just four months apart. Not a day goes by that we don't love and miss you. Your love for one another continues to inspire.

Made in the USA
Charleston, SC
23 February 2014